Mary Spring Walker

The Rev. Dr. Willoughby and His Wine

Mary Spring Walker

The Rev. Dr. Willoughby and His Wine

ISBN/EAN: 9783337322045

Printed in Europe, USA, Canada, Australia, Japan

Cover: Foto ©Andreas Hilbeck / pixelio.de

More available books at **www.hansebooks.com**

THE

REV. DR. WILLOUGHBY,

AND

HIS WINE.

BY

MARY SPRING WALKER,

AUTHOR OF "THE FAMILY DOCTOR; OR, MRS. BARRY AND HER BOURBON,"
ETC.

GLASGOW:

SCOTTISH TEMPERANCE LEAGUE.

LONDON: HOULSTON & SONS; AND NATIONAL
TEMPERANCE LEAGUE.

EDINBURGH: JOHN MENZIES & CO.

1895.

NOTE.

"DR. WILLOUGHBY" is a reprint of one of the most recent publications of the American National Temperance Society. It presents the question in an aspect somewhat novel, and has enjoyed a wide popularity on the other side of the Atlantic. It has been deemed worthy of republication by the Directors of the Scottish Temperance League; and they indulge the hope that it may prove not less suitable to the circumstances of British society at the present time, nor less acceptable in this country, than it has been in America.

SCOTTISH TEMPERANCE LEAGUE,
108 HOPE STREET,
GLASGOW, *1st March, 1870.*

CONTENTS.

THE

REV. DR. WILLOUGHBY,

AND

HIS WINE.

CHAPTER I.

PARSON WILLOUGHBY IS IN HIS STUDY.

"There are foolish shepherds (Zech. xi. 15). There are shepherds that feed themselves and not their flocks (Ezek. xxxiv. 2). There are hard-hearted and pitiless shepherds (Zech. xi. 3). There are shepherds that, instead of healing, smite, push, and wound the diseased (Ezek. xxxiv. 4, 21). There are shepherds that cause their flocks to go astray (Jer. i. 6). And there are shepherds that feed their flocks (Acts xx. 28)."—JOHN BUNYAN.

"THE fact is, brethren," said Dr. Willoughby, "I have for the most part stood aloof from all these works of moral reform. I have no taste for them. In my view, they interfere with the simple preaching of the Gospel. I have made it my business to preach 'Christ and Him crucified;' and

I believe that in showing men the sinfulness of their own hearts, and their need of a Saviour, the whole ground is covered. Cleanse the fountain, and the stream will be pure. Let a man's soul be renewed, and his outward life will take care of itself. I believe all works of moral reform are superseded by the preaching of the Gospel."

The speaker was a man past middle life, of a dignified presence, with a lofty, impending forehead, and a keen, black eye under shaggy brows. He spoke in a clear voice, with great deliberation, and as one having authority. Grouped about him, in the arm-chairs and comfortable lounging-places with which the room was abundantly furnished, sat a dozen clergymen, in the easy attitude of men whose day's work was done, and whom a good dinner had left comfortable in body and mind.

"You express my views exactly, Doctor," said an elderly man with a double chin, and an immense white neck-tie. "In my judgment, the mistake modern reformists make just lies here : to accomplish any special work, they substitute a human instrumentality for the Gospel. Yes, sir ; the force of man's weak resolution is put in place of the power of divine grace. I have no patience with the mistaken zeal of these fellows, in the ministry or out, who go bellowing through the world, ' Reform ! Reform !' throwing open the door of fanaticism ; and, with a lighted fagot in one hand, and a drawn sword in the other, cut and slash in the name of philanthropy and charity. We ought, as ministers of Jesus Christ, to oppose fanaticism in every form; and for my part, I glory in the name of a Conservative, taking the ground of Conservatism enlightened by the Gospel."

"I believe it to be the only safe course to pursue," said Dr. Willoughby; "and in regard to this temperance movement, to which some allusion has been made, it has so remote a bearing upon the great object for which the ministry was instituted—is so delicate and impracticable—and, in the hands of wire-pulling demagogues, has become so mixed up, and befogged, and interwoven with politics—that I have no disposition to meddle with it."

A young man sitting on the outside of the circle manifested great uneasiness during this conversation; and now, bending forward, seemed about to speak, but was prevented by a brisk, little, black-eyed man, a professor in the neighbouring theological seminary, who eagerly responded to Dr. Willoughby's remarks.

"You are right, Brother Willoughby, quite right," he said. "We must let these outsiders alone. In all our works of philanthropy and charity, we are, in my opinion, safe just so long as we keep to God's appointed way. The church is that way. All these outside workings—this joining hands in a work of moral reform, as a 'hail fellow, well met,' with the worldlings and the sinners—are a daubing ourselves with untempered mortar. Brethren, it's like forsaking the fellowship of God's chosen people—leaving the road that carried the patriarchs and prophets to the celestial city, with the Holy Spirit to fire our engine, and the Lord Jesus for our conductor, and jumping aboard a fast train on another track, with strange fire in the engine, and the ruff-scuff of the streets, the ring-streaked and the speckled, in the cars. My Bible gives me no direction to join a teetotal society. Let us keep within the pale of the church, Brother Willoughby, and we shall, in all our endeavours to benefit our fellow-men, have the Master's approval, and what measure of success He sees fit to give us."

"Father," said a pale young man at Dr. Willoughby's right hand, "have you trained your people so well, that they suffer you to hold this position in peace?"

The tones of his voice were peculiarly soft and musical, and Dr. Willoughby's face assumed its most benignant expression as he turned to reply.

"Why, as to that, Louis," he said, "there are uneasy spirits in every community—men who have their pet schemes, and whose zeal for the time being is narrowed down to a single issue; who ride their hobby and dwell on their one idea, till they come to think *their* way is the only right way. I have such in my church—good Christian men, whose hearts are better than their heads. I have a high respect for them. I believe they are actuated by the best of motives. They come to me every now and then, clamouring for some new measure. They want the pledge circulated, or a popular temperance lecturer procured, or some new organization started, and I treat them with great courtesy, and gratify them when I can. I do this conscientiously, for I agree with them in the main. I acknowledge the force of all they say concerning the great and growing evil of intemperance in our midst. I lament it as they do; and we only differ as to the ways and means of eradicating it. As Brother Nash has very justly remarked, they put too much confidence in human instrumentality."

"They try to improve on the Gospel, sir," said the gentleman alluded to. "They propose to do for the poor victim of sin what only the almighty grace of God can do. And they are tools, sir, in the hands of wire-pulling politicians—miserable demagogues, who, under the specious name of temperance, have raised themselves to power by pandering to the passions of zealots and fanatics. They break up the peace of churches, sir; they sow dissension, and set brethren at variance. They march in the ranks of political strife, and light the fires of fanaticism on our very hearthstones, and in our Christian assemblies."

The young man who had before manifested a disposition to speak, now addressed Dr. Willoughby. He was of manly proportions, with a fair, open, and rather florid face, a clear gray eye, and a profusion of light-brown curly hair. He was a stranger to most present, having been lately installed as pastor of the

Congregational Church in Grantley, a manufacturing village some thirty miles distant.

"Dr. Willoughby," he said, very respectfully, "will you tell me what you understand, sir, by a work of moral reform?"

The Doctor gave the questioner a searching look from under his shaggy brows.

"A work of moral reform, Brother Richmond," he said, "I understand to be a united action, by a body of men, to correct some wrong-doing in the community —the endeavour to suppress personal or public vice."

"Yes; and if successful, that which is decidedly immoral and vicious *is* suppressed, and the community becomes conformed externally, at least, to the known commands and will of God. Am I right there, Dr. Willoughby?"

"Undoubtedly."

"Then, does not moral reform tend directly to man's salvation? It is not, of course, a work of salvation itself; but, by removing the greatest obstacles to the success of the Gospel, does it not 'prepare the way of the Lord?' If this is not a minister's business, whose is it? If we can justify ourselves in standing aloof from works of moral reform under the plea that our business is to preach the Gospel, who will do this work? If Christianity, which has the promise of the life that now is, as well as that which is to come, does not take the lead in every enterprise of philanthropy, where is suffering humanity to look for aid? The Gospel! what is it? 'The grace of God bringeth salvation, teaching us that, denying ungodliness and worldly lusts, we should live soberly, righteously, and godly, in this present world.' My dear brethren, we cannot separate moral reform from religion. The two go hand in hand. And most strikingly is this true of the temperance work. . To succeed, we must have the weight and authority of God's law, and all the energizing love of the Gospel. If the church stand back, if ministers keep silent, the temperance reform will in a great measure fail;—it will be a mere dietetic. or sanitary movement, evanescent, and without binding force. It is God's battle, and *we* must fight it."

He spoke rapidly, his handsome face flushing with excitement and enthusiasm.

"The cross once seen is death to every vice," said the Professor. "Brother Richmond, it has occurred to me many times, that if you ultra-temperance men would spend a quarter of the time in earnest conversation with men, about the salvation of their souls, that you devote to urging them to sign the total abstinence pledge, you would accomplish more for the glory of God."

"Did you ever attempt," he replied, "to persuade a man, thoroughly under the influence of this vice, to become a Christian? Is there any such opponent to the conviction and conversion of sinners as intemperance? 'The sin of intemperance,' said good old Dr. Nettleton, in 1829, 'has caused more trouble, and done more dishonour to the cause of Christ, than any other vice that can be named.' 'I dread,' said the martyr Williams, a little before his death,—'I dread to see the American flag come into the Pacific. She may bring missionaries in her cabin, but in her hold are the fire-waters of damnation.' And Archdeacon Jeffreys, after a residence of nineteen years in Bombay, declared that, 'without the introduction of the total abstinence principle, Christianity would be a curse to India rather than a blessing; for the Hindoo, on renouncing caste, by which he is forbidden to drink, would rush at once to the bottle, and the Christian church become the most drunken part in India.' 'Plead with men to come to Christ?' So I will, and I will tell the poor inebriate that the first step to be taken is to forsake his cups, for 'no drunkard can inherit the kingdom of God.' Brethren, God helping me, I will say to my people wherever I labour, 'I take you to record this day, that I am pure from the blood of all men.'"

"My young brother," said Dr. Willoughby, with great dignity, "I deplore with you the evils of intemperance. I, too, would plead with the inebriate to forsake his cups, because his only chance of safety lies in abstinence. I have no disposition to meddle with your belief. Be a teetotaler if you like, and persuade others to join you. This is a part of your Christian liberty; and though I hold that there is a better way, that temperance is a higher virtue than abstinence, that my liberty consists in using the world, I shall not quarrel with you if you take the extreme ground—struck by the prevalence of intemperance in our midst—that to partake of the wine-cup ever so soberly is a luxury you are called upon to relinquish. But when you talk about bringing the weight and authority of God's law to bear on your side, and maintain that the battle for teetotalism is God's battle, you make a great and fundamental mistake. A divine permission, my dear brother, is not a divine requirement; and you will allow me to say that the attempt you ultra-temperance men are making, to force the Bible to inculcate teetotalism, must necessarily fail, and the failure damages the cause. Let me ask you one question, Brother Richmond. Was the greatest reformist and philanthropist the world ever saw,—He who, knowing the end from the beginning, must have foreseen all the evil that would grow out of the abuse of intoxicating drink,—was the Lord Jesus Christ, 'God manifest in the flesh,' a total abstainer? Did He inculcate, either by example or precept, this belief of yours? Did He not come eating and drinking? Did He not make wine on a festive occasion, and use it at the institution of the Lord's supper,—wine, too, that would make men drunk? These facts have got to be met by temperance men. Be careful, Brother Richmond, lest you teach for doctrine the commandments of men. You cannot condemn God, that you yourself may be righteous,"

At this moment there was a confused noise in the hall, the door of the study was thrown wide open, and the Irish girl who had waited upon the minister at dinner appeared.

"And, shure, Dr. Willoughby," she said, half-crying, and making strange backward gestures with her arms, "I niver opened a crack o' the door to him, till he thrittened to take the life o' me the next time I wint to mass, and his old shanty is between here an' St. Patrick's church. Holy Mother, protect me! In wid ye thin, ye ill-mannered baste, disturbin' their riverences wid yer nonsense!"

"Clear the track, Katie," said a bold ringing voice behind her, "and I'll make it all right with the parson;" and Katie withdrawing her substantial person from the doorway, there appeared in her stead a short, gray-headed man, who stood holding his hat in both hands, and bowing all round to the company. Whether he was old or young, it was impossible from his appearance to decide. The short hair that curled tight to his head was gray, but his large blue eyes, though wandering and troubled in their expression, were as clear as an infant's. His forehead was un-wrinkled, and, where protected from the weather, remarkably white. His features were regular, and he would have been good-looking but for a scar, which, extending the whole length of one cheek, and across the mouth, dreadfully disfigured that side of his face, and entirely changed its expression.

"What do you want, Martin?" said Dr. Willoughby, impatiently, as the visitor, with strange grimaces and contortions, continued his bows to the company.

He advanced toward Dr. Willoughby's chair, and, with a face full of earnestness and solemnity, began to speak.

"I sought for one," said he, "and, behold, there are ten gathered together in the name of the Lord. Welcome, heralds of salvation! Hail, ye watchmen on the heights of Zion!—ye candlesticks of the Lord!—ye lights of the world!—ye cities set upon a hill!—ye captains of salvation, arrayed in the panoply of Jehovah, and ready to do battle valiantly against the strongholds of Satan! 'How beautiful upon the mountains are the feet of him that bringeth good tidings!'

'How blessed are our eyes,
That see this heavenly sight!'"

Then, looking earnestly in Dr. Willoughby's face, "Parson," he said, "I bear a message to you. You are wanted in the front ranks. The soldiers have arrayed themselves for the battle, and they are but waiting for their leader to advance to victory. The serried hosts of the destroyer are encamped—."

"Come, come, Joe, that will do," said Dr. Willoughby; "leave your message till another time. I am busy, as you see, with these gentlemen. We are discussing very important matters, and cannot be interrupted." Then, as the visitor raised his arm with a preparatory gesture, the minister added sternly, "Not a word, Joe, not another word. You must go this moment."

He dropped his head instantly, both face and attitude expressing disappointment and dejection.

"And what shall I tell them, parson?" he said, very sadly.

"Tell whom?"

"Them that sent me with my message."

"Tell them," said Dr. Willoughby, "that I am in my study, and cannot be disturbed."

"Parson Willoughby is in his study," said Joe Martin, with his eyes fastened on the floor. Then, looking round upon the company, he repeated in a louder voice, "Parson Willoughby is in his study. Ruin and destruction are in our midst. Iniquity runs down our streets like a river. Foul cesspools of corruption are in every corner. The soul-destroying minions of Satan, from their antechambers of hell, are revelling in wealth wrung from widows' tears, and hoarding up gold coined from orphans' groans; and the anguished cry for help comes up from wretched victims, writhing victims,—writhing in the grasp of that fell destroyer, whose touch is pollution, and whose sting is death. But Parson Willoughby is in his study.

"And our young men are falling, and 'the mourners go about the streets,' and the gray hairs of the father are brought down in sorrow to the grave, and lovely woman mourns her blighted hopes, and wives are widows, and fathers are fiends, and parents are paupers, and homes are hells, and the incendiary lights his lurid torch, and the midnight assassin sharpens his parricidal axe, and still the honour-destroying, sense-consuming, contagion-breathing, woe-creating, soul-damning work goes on, and the groans, and prayers, and shrieks of the victims, ascending to high heaven, might bring tears of pity from the haggard eyes of a demon damned,—but Parson Willoughby is in his study!"

At the conclusion of this strange speech, which he delivered with great rapidity, and accompanied with the most extravagant gestures, Joe Martin bowed gravely to the company, and left the room.

The ministers looked doubtfully in each other's faces, and then, their host setting the example, they indulged in a hearty laugh.

"Cracked. decidedly," said the elderly man with the neck-tie; "and what a curious face he has!"

"You have seen him before, Brother Nash," Dr. Willoughby said.

"Impossible!"

"Yes, in this very room frequently, though it was many years ago. Don't you remember a curly-headed, handsome boy you used to meet here sometimes, when you were settled over in Barton, who came to my study to recite Latin. Poor fellow! I heard him twice a week for over two years. You remember that boy, Nash? Why, you have seen him time and time again."

"And do you mean to tell me, Brother Willoughby, that this crazy, gray-headed man, who has given us such a flaming temperance address, is that boy?"

"The very same.   Remind me to tell you his story some time—that is, what I know of it—for there is a great mystery hanging over part of his life."

The discussion interrupted by Joe's visit was not renewed, the meeting breaking up directly.   Mr. Richmond was the first to take his departure; but after walking a few steps, he remembered that he had left his gloves on Dr. Willoughby's study table, and accordingly retraced his steps.   When he opened the door, the ministers were standing in groups of twos and threes, talking familiarly together. There was a pause when he made his appearance. Then the pale young man, who had called Dr. Willoughby father, said :—

" Well, brethren, *I* drink wine, and by the grace of God I mean to."

" Amen! thank God for that," said Dr. Willoughby; "and, brethren, I take great credit to myself for his conversion. He was a radical teetotaler when I first knew him."

An expression of pain crossed Mr. Richmond's face, as he silently took his gloves from the table.

" Wait a moment, Richmond," said the young man, who was Dr. Willoughby's son-in-law. " I am going your way, and will walk to the depôt with you."

CHAPTER II.

GOOD FATHER PAUL.

"If wine had been among the number of things forbidden, Paul would not have permitted it, nor would have said it was to be used. This passage is against the *simple ones* of our brethren, who, when they see any persons disgracing themselves by drunkenness, instead of reproving such, blame the fruit given them by God, and say, 'Let there be no wine.' We would say, in answer to such, 'Let there be no drunkenness, for wine is the work of God, but drunkenness is the work of the devil. Wine maketh not drunkenness, but intemperance produceth it. Do not accuse that which is the workmanship of God, but accuse the madness of a fellowmortal.'"—St. Chrysostom's *Homilies*.

HE young men walked arm in arm down the street of the country town, leading from Dr. Willoughby's residence to the depôt. Mr. Thayer was the first to speak.

"I am ready for my lecture, Allan," he said. "I saw the pent-up fire in your face, and came out with you that you might give it vent. Come, fancy we are in 'No. 37, corner room, three flights front,' in old Union, and you playing Mentor again."

He turned gaily to his companion as he spoke, but there was no answering smile on Allan Richmond's face.

"Why, what ails you, man?" said Louis Thayer; "you look as sour as a November day. Come, in the words of the hymn we used to sing together, I adjure you to

'Speak, and let the worst be known;
Speaking may relieve you.'"

"I know not what to say," he replied. "Louis, I was never so grieved and surprised in my life. I cannot understand it. Was it Louis Thayer, the staunch total abstinence man I knew in the seminary, who sat in complaisant silence while Christian philanthropists were denounced as enthusiasts and fanatics, and then boasted that he touched the unclean thing, and claimed the aid and countenance of God's grace in doing it? Louis, what has changed you so? 'Truly Ephraim hath mixed himself with the people.'"

"One would think I had forsaken the faith of the fathers, and gone clean over to idolatry," he rejoined, laughing. "Why, man alive, did you expect to find me unchanged after all these years? Age brings wisdom, you know. Have you sloughed off none of the crude notions of your college and seminary life?" Then speaking more seriously, "The fact is, Allan, I found very soon after you and I came out of our cell, talking with men older and wiser than myself, and coming to see the other side of the matter, that the ground we took on the temperance question was extreme, and could not be sustained. After my marriage, and while I was looking about for a settlement, I spent a couple of months in my father-in-law's family, and I found a Christian minister, with large experience, and eminently successful in his profession, drinking wine moderately on festive occasions, and in his family, and defending its use from the Bible. I must say I felt a little shocked at first. I could not quite understand it. I held my position against him as a teetotaler for awhile, till he made it clear to me that the Scripture doctrine is not total abstinence from intoxicating drinks; that as a rule of duty it is utterly unknown in the word of God, and, in fact, condemned by Christian ethics. He presented the subject to me in such a different light, that my views were greatly modified and enlarged; but I was never quite converted till I became a Timothy to a good Father Paul, who, by timely counsel and skilful medical advice, dissipated my over-nice scruples, and cured my bodily ailments.

"My first year in the ministry was a pull. I wrote two sermons a week, and prepared a lecture besides. There was no end to visiting, and funerals, and calls for extra duty. You know how it is, for you have had the same experience, only you are stronger physically than I am. Well, in the midst of a very precious revival, my old enemy, neuralgia, seized me. Night after night I did not close my eyes to sleep. The doctor did me no good, for you see my mental anxiety kept up the nervous excitement. Father Willoughby came out to see me in the midst of it. 'You want stimulants,' said he ; and he sent home for a dozen bottles of old port, and some Cognac brandy. He told me to drink all I could bear. O Allan, the blessed relief from pain it brought me ! In three days I was a well man, and ready for work. I know not what Paul's prescription did for Timothy, but I know *my* father in the gospel cured me. It is but common justice to speak well of a bridge that has carried you safely over, and wine has been a 'good creature of God' to me. I come home weary after the labours of the Sabbath, and my sense of fatigue is met most pleasantly by a little alcoholic stimulant."

"But you are not looking well, Louis," his friend said, gravely.

They had reached the depôt, and were pacing the platform, waiting for the train. There was good reason for the remark. The young minister's cheek was pale, and his step, in contrast to the quick, elastic tread of his companion, betokened languor or fatigue, and there was at times a tremulous motion to his mouth that expressed great nervous sensibility, if not weakness.

"I am perfectly well," he said, hastily, " only tired and overworked. The fatigue of moving and settling my books and furniture has been very great, and the excitement of preaching to a new congregation, composed of a very different class of people from my other parish, and the necessity of making new acquaintances, and accommodating myself to my position here, have worn upon me a little. When I get things arranged to my mind, and the machinery of my church in good running order, I shall be all right again. And how goes the world with *you*, Allan? Are you settled to your mind? Are you going to like Grantley? Have you a pleasant boarding-place? you poor, lonely, old

bachelor. By the way, you saw our little sister Grace at dinner. Does she look like the girl you used to talk so much about that last year in the seminary?"

Allan Richmond blushed like a schoolboy. "She is very lovely," he said, and stopped.

"You mention it as though it were a subject for mourning and lamentation," said his companion.

"So it may be to me," he said, "for it removes me and my hopes at an infinite distance from her. Louis, how could I ever dream of winning her?"

"You are too modest, Allan. Why should you not win her as well as another? She will spend the holidays with us. Shall we see you in the city then?"

These were parting words, Mr. Richmond springing on the cars, and exchanging a hurried good-bye with his friend after the train was in motion.

CHAPTER III.

THE CITY MINISTER'S WIFE.

" Wanted, a perfect lady,
   Delicate, gentle, refined,
With every beauty of person,
   And every endowment of mind;
Fitted by early culture
   To move in fashionable life,
To shine a gem in the parlour,—
   Wanted, a minister's wife!"

" AND now, mother, that this important dinner is cooked and eaten, and the responsibility of superintending and presiding is off your mind, I suppose we may claim a share of your attention," said Frances Thayer, Dr. Willoughby's eldest daughter, the afternoon of the ministers' meeting described in a preceding chapter.

" It passed off very well," said Mrs. Willoughby, with a sigh of relief.

" Of course it did, mother. Your company dinners all pass off well. It is unaccountable to me how so old a housekeeper as you are can allow yourself to become nervous over a dinner. Why, I entertained six delegates the other day when the Sunday-school Convention met in the city, and it was very little trouble."

" Frances, you know nothing about it. With your well-trained city servants, a market just round the corner, and a confectioner in the next block, you haven't the least idea what it is to get up a dinner in the country for a dozen hungry ministers, with only a green Irish girl to help you. And, then, you have the faculty of taking things easily. I believe you are not as nervous as most women."

Mrs. Willoughby looked with pardonable pride as she spoke, upon the tall, handsome young woman, who, richly dressed, sat in a negligent attitude, with one elbow resting upon her mother's work-table. Her figure was full and rounded, there was a healthy bloom upon her cheek and lip, her eyes, like her father's, were black and piercing, and her abundant hair was brushed fearlessly back from a forehead that in breadth and outline was his own. Her sister—a young girl with a slender figure, fair complexion, and blue eyes—though less striking in appearance, was not wanting in personal attractions, and the smile that dimpled her cheeks and lit up her dove-like eyes made her at times very pretty.

" But I don't suppose," continued Mrs. Willoughby, a little fretfully, " that Louis invites half the company your father does. The Doctor knows all the ministers in the county, and I often tell him he is too hospitable. I am sure our house is a perfect hotel ; and I have done little for the last twenty years but wait upon ministers,"

Mrs. Thayer laughed merrily.

"Well, mother, it is good business," she said, "and it does not appear to have worn upon you. How well I remember the travelling agents who used to 'put up' with us, as they called it, though, I am sure, we 'put up' with them, in entertaining them so long. There was good old Father Scranton, you know, who always came out in the morning to put on his boots by the kitchen fire, and watch Brother Willoughby's 'stirrin' gals,' as he called Grace and me, 'get breakfast;' and Mr. Nash, who was sure to drop in when we had a picked-up dinner, especially hash, as we children said, because it rhymed with his name; and the minister with the gruff voice, who 'ahemed' the door open; and the old bachelor minister with the hooked nose, by which, we used to say, he could hang to the cherry-tree and pick with both hands, and who served you such a mean trick, mother, when he undertook to mark his shirts, and spilled indelible ink on your best chamber carpet, and then dragged the hearth-rug over it, instead of covering the spot with a twenty-dollar bill, as he should have done. And, oh! Grace, once when you were a little bit of a thing, you ran to meet me, exclaiming, 'Fanny, Fanny, we have ministers for dinner!'"

She laughed heartily at her reminiscences, her mother and sister joining in her merriment.

"Fanny, it does me good to see you again," Mrs. Willoughby said. "You are as lively as ever,

Marrying a minister, and feeling the responsibility of your position, have not sobered you in the least. Grace and I are too quiet. We sit here all day like a couple of old ladies. But tell me about your parish, dear. I have not seen you long enough to have a good talk since the installation. Do you like the Wilmot Street people as well as you expected? Is Louis happy?"

"We are on the wave, mother, you know," she returned. "The people quite worship their new minister. I am afraid sometimes they will spoil him, they praise him so openly; and yet, perhaps, it is just the encouragement Louis needs, for he is really morbid in his self-depreciation. People tell me all ministers are low-spirited at times, but I never remember to have seen father so discouraged and disheartened as Louis frequently is."

"Your father has enjoyed perfect health all his life, my dear, and is very calm and equable in his temperament, while Louis is excitable and nervous, and not physically strong."

"I know it, mother; and just now he is dreadfully overworked. He says it will be easier by and by, when he is over this hard spot; and I hope it will, for he is labouring quite beyond his strength. He studies very hard. I beg him to use his old sermons; but when he looks them over he throws one after another aside in disgust, and says he has outgrown them. It is a fact, they were written for a very different class of people.   Mother, we have the most fashionable congregation in the city.   People from the other churches flock to Wilmot Street.   Last Sabbath evening, we had Judge Harding, and ex-Governor Binks, and the Honourable Mr. Wilder, and I don't know how many more of the first men in the city.   Not an easy congregation to preach to, was it? *But my husband was equal to the occasion, and he did himself credit; but was so nervous and excited after the effort, that he did not close his eyes to sleep till near morning; and the next day came the reaction."

" Well, I suppose it cannot be helped; but you must try to have him spare himself all he can."

" It is quite impossible, mother, at present.   The people are continually making demands upon his time that he cannot resist.   There is a great deal of social life in the Wilmot Street church; and just now we are having a round of parties.   I enjoy them exceedingly, but Louis complains that they absorb too much of his time; and the heat and glare of the crowded rooms, and the small talk in which he must join, unfit him for his work in the study.   And the early part of the week he is too languid and weary to write; and it often happens that his sermon is not commenced till Thursday or Friday, and then he must drive night and day to finish it."

" You must do the best you can for him, Frances. See that he has plenty of nourishing food, and takes exercise regularly.   If my father were living, he would say, 'String him up with plenty of good port wine, and give him three hours a day on the back of a quiet pony.' Father was one of the old-fashioned doctors."

"He has no time for horseback riding, mother. Three hours a day, indeed! He scarcely has half-an-hour he can call his own. Why, you will hardly believe it, but he declared that he could not spend time to attend this meeting at his father's house; but I insisted upon his coming. He is drinking the wine father was so kind as to send him, and it is doing him good."

That evening, when Dr. Willoughby and Mr. Thayer joined the family group, the Doctor said,—

"This college friend of yours, Louis, this Richards—."

"Richmond, father," said his youngest daughter.

"Yes, Richmond,—so it is, dear. I am getting to be an old man in my memory of names."

"Grace seems to have no difficulty in recalling the name," said her brother, a little mischievously.

"I have heard it too often from your lips," she replied.

"What were you about to say, father?" said Louis Thayer.

"That he appears to belong to the intense school. He is very ultra in his views, is he not, my son?"

"On the temperance question, yes. Richmond is a capital fellow—frank, outspoken, whole-souled, and generous to a fault. He was the best scholar in his class, and would have been very popular but for these peculiar notions that he thrusts into notice on all occasions.

"How very disagreeable!" said Frances Thayer. "I detest a man of one idea; and it seems worse in a minister than in any one else. The young man who supplied the Wilmot Street before you preached for them, Louis, did you know he was such a person? Mrs. Barstow told me that he openly insulted a friend of hers in her own parlour, by refusing a glass of wine she offered him at a social gathering, doing it in such a solemn, disagreeable way, as to draw the attention of the whole company, and cause her to feel almost as though she had committed a sin in providing wine for her guests."

"I hope your friend will not be so indiscreet as to carry his ultra views into his new pulpit," said Dr. Willoughby. "He will work mischief if he does. I know all about that Grantley church. There are two or three influential men there, engaged in the liquor trade, and the subject will not bear touching. It is the last place for a man with radical views on the temperance question."

"You may depend upon it, father, that Richmond will preach, and talk, and pray temperance, wherever he is," said Louis Thayer.

"Then he will find himself in hot water very soon," said the old gentleman, "and he will create a division of feeling that will greatly injure that church. It is a pity; for they are not strong enough to endure a storm. I was in hopes, after all their candidating, they had secured a good minister."

"And so they have, father," said Mr. Thayer, warmly. "Allan Richmond was my dearest friend in college, and my classmate in the seminary. He is a good preacher, and will make a faithful, hard-working pastor. Come, Fanny, it is after nine o'clock, and we have three miles to ride."

She rose reluctantly.

"Why not remain and drive over in the morning?" the mother asked.

"I cannot leave my babies, mother," Mrs. Thayer said.

"And I cannot leave my sermon," said her husband.

When the carriage was at the door, and the young minister was shaking hands with his father-in-law, Mrs. Willoughby said:—

"Doctor, you have not forgotten the wine, I hope!"

"All right, my dear; it's packed away in a basket under the seat. Only half-a-dozen bottles of old sherry," he replied to the young man's faint remonstrance. "I flatter myself it's a better article than you know how to find in the city; and my wife says you need it. A little 'for the stomach's sake,' you know, my son,—ha, ha!"

"Good Father Paul," said Louis Thayer to his wife, as they drove from the door; "he means I shall not lack for Timothy's medicine."

"Father is very thoughtful and generous," she

replied. "But, O Louis, I have such a piece of news to tell you. Who do you think is paying attention to Grace?"

"The new school-teacher, perhaps, or Deacon Riley's eldest son. He walked home from church with her the Sabbath I e changed with your father."

"Nonsense! you know Grace would not think of either of them. Louis, it is Mr. Landon, the lawyer."

"What! Horace Landon, who has an office in Broad Street, Fanny? You don't mean it."

"Yes. I knew you would be surprised. He is one of the first lawyers in the city, and very wealthy, you know, for he has inherited all his father's money."

"But he is too old for Grace."

"Oh, no! Mother says he is not much over forty, and I am sure he is quite young-looking. And, Louis, think of the position it will give Grace. How delightful to have her near us, living in such style! Mother is very much pleased."

"You speak as if it were a settled thing."

"Well, so it is, or at least very nearly so. He has asked father's permission to pay his addresses; and mother says Grace evidently likes him."

"Is it possible Father Willoughby approves of this?"

"Certainly, Louis,—why not? Is it not in every respect a desirable match?"

"I cannot say what Horace Landon is now," he replied, gravely; "but when I knew him in college he was an infidel. He was much older than myself.

I was not acquainted with him personally. I did not care to know him. He had the name of being a brilliant, witty fellow, fascinating in appearance and manners, flush with money, and drew around him a circle of young men who gained no good by the companionship. He gave wine-parties, and his room was full of infidel books, which he circulated. He was considered one of the most dangerous men in college. You surprise me very much, Fanny!"

"You knew him years ago, Louis," she said. "Men change their views, you know. Depend upon it, it is all right, or father would not have given his consent."

"Poor Richmond!" said Mr. Thayer.

"And why poor Richmond?" she asked in surprise. "What has he to do with it?"

"He saw Grace for the first time one commencement day, years ago, and was greatly pleased with her; indeed, I may call it love at first sight; but he was poor, and in debt, and she was very young. He confided his hopes of one day winning her, to me, and I am sure he has never abandoned them; for he displayed a great deal of feeling when I spoke of her to-day. It is awkward too; for, of course, I knew nothing of this, and rallied him about her, and I suppose gave him some encouragement."

"A poor country minister!" said Frances Thayer, rather disdainfully. "Grace can do better than that."

"My dear, her sister married a *poor country minister*," he said, mimicking her tone.

"Yes; and he would be just that to-day," she rejoined, "were it not for a wife who was ambitious to see him in a position he is in every respect qualified to fill."

"Indeed! That word *position* is a great favourite of yours, Fanny."

"And you do not give it sufficient importance," she replied. "I really believe, Louis, that you sometimes regret leaving that small parish among the hills for a fashionable church in a growing city."

He made her no reply; but touching his horse smartly with the whip, the spirited animal carried them over the ground at such a pace as to give no further opportunity for conversation.

"You will not go to your study to-night," she said, when they stopped at their own door in the city. "It is late, and you are tired."

"There is no escape, Fanny. The sermon must be written."

He drove his horse to the livery stable, and, returning, was going upstairs to his study, when his wife called him from the nursery door.

"At least you must stop long enough to say good-night to the baby," she said, when he obeyed her summons. "See, the little fellow is wide awake. Here, take your boy,"—for the child was making frantic efforts to escape from her arms,—"and look at Everett in his crib, and tell me if there are two as noble children to be found in the city to-night."

He took the infant, and, resting his pale cheek against its little rosy face, enjoyed for a moment the quiet of this domestic scene; then he went away wearily to his study.

CHAPTER IV.

DAN TAYLOR.

" A ' down-east ' Yankee, lank and long,
' Cute ' of hand, and ' glib ' of tongue."

"DOCTOR," said Mrs. Willoughby one day, "you must have another talk with Dan. He is getting into bad habits again. He leaves his work every forenoon to go down to Briggs' saloon for a dram. You really must attend to it, Doctor, immediately. Your last talk kept him steady for a long time."

Dan Taylor was Dr. Willoughby's hired man. Besides a large garden, which was his particular pride and delight, the minister owned a few acres of cultivated land, and a wood-lot a mile out of the village. Through the spring and summer months Dan was busy on the farm, and in winter there was wood to be drawn and prepared for family use, the horse, and cow, and pigs to be cared for, and various odd jobs to be done about the house. It was also one of his duties to drive the Doctor—whose eyesight was beginning to fail him in the night—to his evening meetings in the outer districts of the town; and as he had lived in the family several years, proving himself to be honest, faithful, and obliging, he had gradually become quite an important personage in the establishment. .

But Dan had one serious fault: he loved whisky, and he would drink it. Not to excess, for his Yankee prudence and Dr. Willoughby's counsels and reprimands kept him within bounds; but his stone bottle was snugly stowed away in the hay-mow, or under the corn-crib; and about eleven o'clock in the forenoon, Dan was sure to come to the well for a drink of water. His stay at the well was short, his visit to the barn or the corn-crib longer, and he generally returned to his work with a beaming face. But latterly a small restaurant and drinking-saloon at the corner of the street, a few roods from Dr. Willoughby's door, where before the middle of the day half-a-dozen loafers were sure to be lounging, offered stronger attractions to Dan than his place of secret indulgence; hence Mrs. Willoughby's request.

"You really must attend to it immediately," she repeated. "People are beginning to talk, and wonder you allow it to go on."

"Send Dan to the study when he has had his dinner," said the minister.

Now, when Mrs. Willoughby delivered the message, Dan understood perfectly what was coming, for it was by no means the first time he had been summoned to the Doctor's presence to receive a lecture upon temperance, but he answered with great alacrity:—

"Wants to see me, does he, for somethin' peticulur? Wal, I'll slick up a leetle, and go right up there."

He went to the kitchen glass, pulled up his shirt-collar, tied his cotton handkerchief, and brushed his long side-locks' till they were plastered tight to his lank cheeks, then with a bold step ushered himself into his master's presence. The minister pushed back his chair from his desk, and deliberately laid aside his glasses.

"Sit down, Daniel," said he; "I want a little conversation with you."

Dan dropped his hat on the floor, and deposited himself carefully on the edge of a chair.

"Yes, sir," said he. "Miss Willoughby, she jest told me, and sez I to Katie, 'I'll bet my old jack-knife,' sez I, 'the Doctor wants to consult with me 'bout that ccow he's so farce to buy over to Swansey's.' Wal, yesterday, you know, I was a-haulin' wood,—when you kin spare five minutes, Doctor, jest step out an' look at that are stick o' hickory. It's good timber and no mistake,—wall, I found I had an hour o' daylight to spar, an' I left my team in White's shed, an' footed it over to Swansey's, for, sez I, 'I may as well have a look at that crittur myself, or as like as not the Doctor'll git shaved,' sez I; folks lew like to cheat ministers, an' they know a sight more 'bout sermons than they do 'bout ccows. No offence, Doctor. Every man to his trade, you know. Don't you remember how you an' I worked over that stove-pipe in Miss Willoughby's best charmber, and couldn't make the jints fit nohcow, an' you blistered yer hands, an' got sut in yer eyes, an' I rammed my head agin the chimbly, trying to find the pesky hole, an' arter a spell both on us gin eout, an' I went deown ter the tin shop, an' up comes a smart little Irish feller. Crackey! if them jints didn't slip inter each other as slick as grease, an' jest as limp an' limber as an injur rubber stove-pipe! 'How did yer dew't?' sez I. He squinted at me kinder droll-like, an' sez he, 'Dan Taylor for workin' a farm, Pat Merritt for puttin' up stove-pipes, and the Riverend Dr. Willoughby for prachin' the Gospel.'

"But I was a-going ter tell yer 'bout that ccow. Don't you buy her, Doctor. 'What,' sez I to Swansey, 'yer haint got the face,' sez I, 'tew ask a hundred an' fifteen dollars for that are heifer calf?' sez I. 'Heifer calf!' sez he, bilin' mad, 'she's a three-year-old ccow, pure Alderney breed, and gives thirteen quarts o' milk a day.' 'I don't ker nothin' about yer Alderney breed,' sez I; 'I ken tell a good ccow when I see her, an' this ere stinted, half-starved beast aint wuth her keepin'. Thirteen quarts o' milk a day!' sez I; 'she aint got milk enough in her bag this minit to make gruel for a sick grasshopper. I warn't raised on a dairy farm up in Vermount for nothin',' sez I. Wal, that's the 'pinion I come to 'bout Swansey's Alderney ccow. I shant charge you nothin' for't, Doctor."

"I did not send for you about the cow, Dan, though I am glad you looked at her, but—."

"Wal, now, Doctor, I ax yer pardon for interruptin' of yer, but while I'm a-talkin' jest let me tell yer a neat thing the bay horse done t'other day."

Pride in his bay horse was Dr. Willoughby's weakness, and he could not deny himself the gratification of hearing the story.

"The day all them ministers was heie to dinner," said Dan, "there was a slim feller, with long har,—he's settled over in Barton. I don't remember his name,—you know who I mean, Doctor?"

"The Rev. Mr. Rowley?" said Dr. Willoughby.

"Yes; Rowley or Rowdy, or some sich name. Wal, that man kep' up a great fuss over his hoss all day; kep' a-hangin' round the barn, an' peekin inter the stable, an' gin me his orders as though I didn't understand my bizness. Wal, when I was hitchin' up for him to start away, I looked the crittur over, to see what thar was so toppin' 'bout him. 'There's a hoss for yer,' sez Mr. Rowdy."

"Rowley, Dan, Rowley."

"Wal, Rowley or Rowdy; it don't make no odds. 'There's a horse for yer,' sez he; 'good colour, fine eye, head up; what dew yer think of him?' 'Fair,' sez I. Then I fetched out Charley. I was only waitin' for the company to go, 'fore I went down the Barton Road to fetch up that parcel o' books the stage left for ye. 'What dew yer think o' *him?*' sez I.

'Oh, he looks like a good family hoss,' sez he; 'no fancy 'bout him.' 'No,' sez I, 'Dr. Willoughby don't believe in ministers keepin' fancy horses.' I was kinder riled, ye see; but I never said another word 'bout the hoss. Thinks I, if a man that pretends to know anything 'bout a hoss can't see that animal's good pints, I aint the chap to let on 'bout 'em. Why, sir, for depth of chest, clean head, sharp ears, and strong quarters, that feller's beast couldn't hold a candle to our Charley. But as I told yer, I never said another word about the hoss, an' he driv' off up town, an' I finished hitchin' up Charley to the light waggon, an' started down the road. I driv' along kinder leisurely, and fust I knew there come clatterin' past that Rowdy."

" Dan," said Dr. Willoughby, "if you cannot call the gentleman by his right name, you need not tell your story."

" Why, hev I got it wrong agin? Well, I allers did misremember names. I ax your pardin, Doctor; I'll call him parson arter this, then I'll be sure an' git it right, though I say for't, he didn't look much like a parson that time, with his long hair a-flyin' an' his coat-tails a-streamin' eout behind. ' That 's yer game, is it?' sez I. Charley didn't 'pear tew like it nuther, but begun to step a leetle high. I kep' him easy till we got along to that clean stretch o' road between here an' White's. ' Neow, Charley,' sez I, 'let him put his fancy article alongside o' the doctor's *family hoss.*' Doctor, I'd gin my Sunday suit if yeu'd seen that race. I allers told yer Charley was a trotter. I never see a hoss yit shaped as he is,—large behind, wide stifles, an' muscles creepin' clear down most to the hock jint,—that warn't a good roadster; but come to see him alongside of a trained runner, I'm free to own the Row—the parson's beast done well,—I believed in him more'n ever. (I'll tell ye what, Doctor, if yeou'll give me the trainin' of him for six months, I'll put him on the course next September, an' if he don't dew his mile in 2.30, my name aint Dan Taylor.)

. " Wal, they kep' alongside of each other a spell, then the bay gave his head a little toss, as much as ter say, ' Come, we've had enough o' this,' an' put out those legs o' his'n, and went by as easy as you'd outwalk a three-year-old child. I looked back (I knew it was saucy, Doctor, but I couldn't help it noways), an' put my thumb up side o' my nose."

Dr. Willoughby enjoyed the story intensely; and if Dan's object in telling it was to soften his asperity, and incline him to look favourably upon his servant's offences, he was eminently successful.

" But Miss Willoughby said yeou had somethin' peticulur to say tew me, Doctor," said Dan with a demure face.

" Yes, Dan, I want a little serious conversation with you."

" Wal, now, that's curus—ain't it, Doctor? I've

ben thinkin' for some time I'd ought ter git religion an' jine the church. 'Fore my old mother died, she was allers talkin' pious to me. Sez she, ' Danyel, yeu are a-havin' blessed privileges,' sez she, ' a-livin' rite under the drippin's of the sanctuary; yeu won't never hev sich another chance agin, mebbe,' sez she; an' I think so myself, Doctor; only yer know a feller's allers a-stavin' it off. But my mind has been oncommon solemnized lately. The last time you held a meetin' over in Brighton deestrict, it seems as though I was kinder lifted right up, an' felt good all over; but there, Doctor, there can't nobody listen ter ycour preachin' without bein' tetched—."

" Dan," said Dr. Willoughby, gravely, " you disturbed the solemnity of that meeting very much by improper conduct, which, if you had been yourself, you would not have been guilty of."

" Me disturb the meetin'!" he exclaimed. " Oh, Doctor, what did I do?"

" What did you do? In the first place, you set all the young people tittering by sitting down on a chair, which, if you had had your eyes about you, you would have seen was broken, and so saved yourself an awkward tumble; and when you were down, you lay, sprawled out on the floor like a great frog, for full a minute, before you had sense enough to pick yourself up. And you sang through your nose horribly, sir, and wheezed and sighed all the evening like a pair of cracked bellows."

" Wal, neow, Doctor, how was I to know the dumbed old cheer hadn't got but three legs? What dew they want tew leave sich a thing settin' up agin the wall for? An' I tell yeu, it hurts a man o' my heft to come down caswack in a sittin' posture on the floor. I'd like to have some o' them gals that snickered so at me try it once. An' as for singin' through my nose, Doctor, yer know I hev a tech o' the catarrh, an' I allers was phthisiky. But yer see I was so oncommon overcome that night, I didn't hardly know what I was about. I ax yer pardon humbly, Doctor, for disturbin' the meetin'."

" Don't try to put me off with any such nonsense, Dan. You were half tipsy, and you know it."

Dan lifted both hands, and screwed his face into an expression of injured innocence that was very ludicrous.

" Neow that cuts me right to the heart," he said. " There aint nothin' so hard to bear as to be accused wrongfully." Then, putting on a sanctimonious air, " Wal," said he, " it's a comfort to think I aint the fust man folks has thought had got a leetle too much aboard, when he was full of another kind o' speerit. For when those good men's tongues was a-running so glib in the day o' Pentecost, people standin' round thought they was drunk. By the way, Doctor, aint that a good pint to make agin the teetotalers?—for, sez Peter, sez he, ' these are not drunken, as ye suppose, seein 's it's but the third hour of the day,' as much as tew say, if 'twas later, like as not they would be; an' yer see that's good common sense; for unless a feller's a regelar sot, he ain't a-goin' to git high afore nine o'clock in the mornin'."

"Daniel, I am afraid it makes very little difference to you whether it's morning or evening. You had been drinking whisky, sir, that night, for I smelt your breath."

"Doctor, I don't deny I tuk a couple o' large spunfuls or so, jest afore we started, to keep cout the cold. It was an awful blusterin' night, yer know, an' arter I'd hitched up, an' was a-waitin' for yeu, Miss Willeyby, she come out with a tumbler, an' she got a leetle hot water, an' a lump o' white sugar, an' a sprinklin' o' nutmeg, an', thinks I, she's fixin' up somethin' for the Doctor, to keep his insides warm; and I coaxed Katie to get me a teacup, and some brown sugar, an' I had a leetle whisky I keep in the house for colicy spells I'm subject tew, an' I made a little warm sling, and it doue me a sight o' good. Neow, that's the livin' truth, as sure as I'm a sinner, an' I'm free to confess there couldn't be nothing surer. Wal, neow, Doctor, jest answer me one question. Don't you think speerits is a blessin'?"

"They are a blessing that is terribly abused by some people, Daniel."

"I say for't, Doctor, if you ain't up and gin the very answer Deacon Selew gin to Obadiah Biddle when he was 'pinted by the church to deal with the old man

You see, Obadiah was a good, consistent Christian, but he would get slewed 'bout every other day in the week. So they 'pinted Deacon Selew to go an' hav' a talk with him. Wal, he went over one mornin', an' found the old man dozin' afore the kitchen fire. 'Take a dram, deacon,' sez he, when he'd got roused up. 'Wal, yes,' sez the deacon, 'I don't ker if I do. I aint agin a dram when a body wants it.' 'Deacon Selew,' says Brother Biddle, while they was a-sippin', 'don't you think speerits is a blessin'?'' (An', doctor, if you didn't gin the deacon's answer jest neow cenermost word for word, my name aint Dan Taylor.) 'Speerits is a blessin',' sez the deacon, sez he, 'that some on us abuses.' 'Wal, neow, deacon,' sez Brother Biddle, 'who *dew* you think abuses the blessin'?' 'Brother,' sez Deacon Selew, as solemn as the grave, '*folks talk,*— don't *yeu* think sometimes, Brother Biddle, *yeu* drink tew much?' 'Wal, it's hard to say, deacon; sometimes I've thought I was a-drinkin' too much, an' then agin I warn't sure. What is man? A poor worrum of the dust. So I left it to the Lord to say whether I was a-goin' too far in speerits. I put the whole 'sponsibility onter Him. I prayed, ef I was a-drinkin' too much, for Him to take away my appetite for speerits. I've prayed that prayer three times, an' He hain't done it. So now, Deacon Selew, I'm much obleeged to yeu, but ye see I've cleared myself of the 'sponsibility—.'"

Here Katie rushed into the room. "Shure an'

there's a big hog in the door-yard," she cried, "rootin'
up all the scrubbery."

Dan was off like a shot, and for that time escaped
his lecture.

CHAPTER V.

TEMPERANCE *VERSUS* ABSTINENCE.

" There are moments in our lives, when such
      As will not help to lift us, strike us down!
    When the green bough just bends so near our clutch,
      When the light rope so easily was thrown,
    That they are murderers that beheld us drown."

MRS. NORTON.

" IF ye plaze, ma'am," said Katie O'Reilly, putting her head in at the door of the room one morning where Dr. Willoughby with his wife and daughter were eating breakfast,—" if ye plaze, ma'am, there's a b'y stuck in the windy. An' if ye don't believe it," she added, observing the incredulous looks of her listeners, " ye may jist hear him howlin' yerselves."

Sounds of distress, apparently proceeding from a very small voice, at this moment making their way through the open door, seemed to verify the truth of Katie's statement; and Mrs. Willoughby and Grace hastened to the kitchen, where a strange sight presented itself. A square of glass had for some days been broken from one of the small, old-fashioned windows, Katie resisting Dan's attempt to replace it with entreaties to " lave her a brathing-hole," and through this aperture pro-

truded a bullet-shaped head, covered with a shock of
fiery-red hair, standing up in all directions from a
freckled face, with a pair of wide blue eyes that were
rolling from side to side in an extremity of terror, and
an open mouth, from which issued a dismal wailing.

"Mercy on us, what is the child about?" said Mrs.
Willoughby. "Boy, stop · crying directly, and take
your head from the window."

He obeyed her first command; and, in his attempt
to further do her bidding, twisted his head frantically
from side to side, his face growing frightfully red, and
his eyes nearly starting from their sockets.

"If you plaze, ma'am," interposed Katie, "the b'y's
head is stuck, and the two feet of him standin' on me
wash-bench, outside the windy; and it's meself has
had him by the heels tryin' to pull him out from behind
'fore ivir I called to ye."

"Dear, dear," said Mrs. Willoughby, "what an
uncomfortable position! There, don't cry, boy; and
keep perfectly still, or you'll choke yourself to death.
Doctor, how are we to get him out?"

"Where a head went in," said the minister, gravely,
"it is but reasonable to conclude it can go out."

"She's made it bigger, she has, a-bumpin' of it agin
the side of the winder," said the sufferer, breaking out
into fresh wailing at the recital of his wrongs.

"An' sure, ma'am," said Katie, "I jist cuffed the
ears of him for blockin' me windy wid his sassy face,
an' me paceably bakin' me cakes by the fire; and that

is all the knockin' he's had from me, ma'am, let alone a scrape or two, mabbe, whin I had holt of the heels of him outside; an' it's not me will thry agin, if ye stay there howlin' till next Michaelmas, ye ongrateful baste!"

"Oh, stop, Katie; and, Doctor, don't stand there twirling your napkin, but contrive some way to get him out. I am sure his head grows bigger every minute. Oh, there comes Dan; he will help. See here, Dan,—this unfortunate child has put his head through the broken pane, and that cruel Katie has bumped it so, that he can't get it back again, and it is continually increasing in size; and I don't see but you will have to cut away the window, though how ever you are to do it without cutting into *him*, I don't know."

At this terrible possibility the boy's wailing recommenced.

"Shut up!" said Dan, authoritatively. "The more you yell, the bigger you swell! That's poetry, ain't it?" said Dan, amazed at his own genius. "Miss Willoughby, don't you fret. I calcilate to get that shaver cout in half a jiffy."

He put both hands in his pocket, whistled "Hail Columbia," and went outside to survey the situation.

"Dan," said Grace, who had followed him, "you can push him through easily. His head is the biggest part of him."

"Miss Grace," returned Dan, "yeu's a still one,

but yer deep. That are's a suggestion I'm a-goin' to follow."

"Yes, try it, Dan," said Mrs. Willoughby. "No, Katie," to the officious damsel, "we want none of your help. That poor child's head is black and blue, I dare say, with the bumps you have given him."

"Neow, Mrs. Willoughby," said Dan, "if yeou'll stand inside and catch him when he comes, I'll leave ahead;" and a moment after, a little limp body advanced slowly into the room, and was received with open arms by Mrs. Willoughby, who was anxiously awaiting the arrival.

Set upon his feet in the middle of the room, the cause of all this commotion proved to be a small boy, perhaps eight years old, ragged and dirty, his whole appearance indicating poverty and neglect. He rubbed his eyes with his dirty knuckles, looked ruefully round, and stood motionless.

"What is your name, little boy, and whom do you want to see?" said Grace, kindly.

"My name is Bub Davis, and I want to see the minister," said the child.

"And why didn't ye knock at the door like a Christian?" said Dan.

"'Cause," said the boy, looking timidly up in his deliverer's face, "'cause I wanted to smell the slapjacks."

"Mother, the child is hungry," said Grace. "Quick, Katie, bake some warm cakes. You poor little fellow, you shall smell them, and taste them too."

While the cakes were baking, Mrs. Willoughby examined the boy's head phrenologically.

"I really don't find any bumps," she said. "Yes, here is quite a large one on this side. Keep still, child, I am not going to hurt you. Grace, run to the medicine closet, and get the bottle of Bay rum, and some thick brown paper."

"I ain't a-goin' to take it," said Bub Davis.

The lady looked at him in astonishment.

"Dear me, child," she said, "nobody wants you to take it. I am going to rub a little on the outside of your head, to take down the swelling, and make it feel cool and good."

"I ain't a-goin' to take it," repeated the boy. "I promised ma I wouldn't. It's nasty stuff. It makes pa sick and cross. I ain't a-goin' to take it."

After this repeated expression of his determined purpose, the young teetotaler put his feet close together like an obstinate mule, and looked defiantly in his tempter's face.

"What a singular child!" said Mrs. Willoughby. "Doctor, do you hear that?" But the Doctor had disappeared. "Well, never mind about it now, dear. Eat your breakfast, and if your head swells very bad we'll put cold water on it."

He needed no second bidding, and Katie's substantial buckwheat cakes disappeared as fast as she could cook them.

"Is it 'lasses?" he inquired eagerly, peeping into the syrup-cup.

"Yes," said Grace; and she poured a bountiful supply upon his plate.

"Oh, my!" and his greedy eyes told the rest of the story.

When he had eaten till he could eat no more, Grace pursued her inquiries.

"Why do you want to see the minister?" she asked.

"Pa sends his respects, and he's sick, and wants the minister should come and see him."

"I will tell him," said Grace; and the visitor departed in a more legitimate way than he entered, Dan giving it as his private opinion that his head was no longer the biggest part of him, and that a yoke of oxen couldn't pull him through that hole in his present condition.

"They must be miserably poor, father," Grace said, when she reported the child's errand. "The boy ate like one famished, and his clothes were thin and old."

"Yes; and that family might be in as comfortable circumstances as any mechanic's in town," he replied. "Davis is a good workman, and can earn his twenty dollars a week when he is sober; but I understand he has not done a day's work for a month."

"He has been sick, the boy said."

"Yes, dear; from the effects of hard drinking. He is wearing out an iron constitution by this evil habit. I am glad he has sent for me. He has given me an opportunity to deal faithfully with him, which I shall not be slow to improve."

"Don't be too hard on him, Doctor," said Mrs. Willoughby. "I am sure he must be miserable enough, lying there so sick and poor, without being lectured. Poor fellow! perhaps he is tempted beyond his strength, and can't help drinking."

"There speaks the sickly sentimentalism of the day," said Dr. Willoughby. "Why not call things by their right names, my dear? You do not speak of the profligate or the murderer as a 'poor fellow.' He is a sinner, acknowledged to be such, and everywhere in the Bible the drunkard is classed with these. From the time when under the law of Moses he was to be 'stoned with stones till he die,' to the day when Christ declared that from within, out of the heart of man, proceed many vile habits which defile the man, drunkenness is distinctly declared to be a *sin*, and I have no patience with the mistaken pity that speaks of the drunkard as 'unfortunate,' as more sinned against than sinning. He is a sinner,—a great sinner in the sight of God,—and his only remedy is in the grace and power of the Gospel."

"Dear me, Doctor, I am sure I didn't mean to say he wasn't a sinner, only I felt sorry for him."

An hour later, Dr. Willoughby took his gold-headed cane, and walked down the street to John Davis's home. A miserable home it was, and a poor wreck of manhood who, from his bed, lifted a haggard, unshaven face, and stretched out a gaunt, shaking hand to welcome the minister.

"It's kind of you to come, sir, and I wouldn't have troubled you if I could have crawled to your door."

"I came cheerfully, Davis," said the Doctor, "but I am sorry to find you so feeble. You have been very sick."

"I came as near goin'," he replied, in his weak, hollow voice, "as ever a man did. The doctor says I'll never pull through such another spell."

"God is good to you, Davis, in giving you one more opportunity to repent," said the minister. "You feel this, I hope. These repeated warnings cannot be in vain. You have made resolutions, I trust, on this sick-bed,—which came so near being your bed of death, —that you will never dare to break."

He twisted the bed-clothes with his bony fingers.

"It makes a man feel solemn-like," he said, "to stand as I've done for a week past, lookin' death right in the eye. And I calculate to do different, Doctor, when I get round again; and you see that's why I wanted to talk with you, for I've been thinkin', and my wife's been beggin' of me to sign the pledge, and quit drinkin', and I told her this mornin', says I, 'Jennie, I'll talk it over with the minister, and get his mind on the subject.' I'm free to own, Doctor, that I haven't done as I ought to of late years. I haven't been to church with my wife, though I promised my old mother on her death-bed that I would;

but I have a great respect for you, sir, and I wanted to consult with you about takin' this important step, and so I made bold to send my boy round for you."

"You did perfectly right, Davis. Let me know how I can help you."

"Well, you see, sir, I ain't quite clear in my mind about the total abstinence pledge. There has one and another been to me along back, askin' me to join; but I always bluffed 'em off, for, says I, 'I ain't a-goin' to sign away my liberty. If I want to stop drinkin', I can do it without puttin' my name on a paper. I guess I know when I've had enough,' says I, 'and you needn't come to me with your pledge.' That's the way I talked it, sir. Well, a week ago last Thursday,—I remember the day, for toward night I began to have the horrors the worst way; in fact, I see snakes in my boots that mornin',—there was a few of us settin' round in Briggs' saloon, and this very subject came up. There'd been a temperance lecture over to Barton, and Crazy Joe was there, of course, and he came in to Briggs' to give us a lecture, and while he was talkin', in came young Riley, the deacon's son, with a total abstinence pledge. And Briggs, he cursed up hill and down, for Crazy Joe had just been sayin' some sharp things; and though he dursn't touch Joe, you know, he was well riled up. He hates the deacon, for he's interfered with his business more than once. Says Briggs, 'I'm opposed to totalities, to total depravity, and to total abstinence, and to all your other totals.'

Well, that brought up the whole subject. We had it hot for awhile. Riley talked strong, and Joe backed him with his queer, crazy talk. By and by says Briggs, 'The minister is on our side.' 'No, he ain't,' says Joe, as quick as lightnin'. 'I tell you he is,' says Briggs. 'If he ain't, why don't you have his name at the head of your paper? You can't get him to sign that pledge. The minister's a larned man,' says Briggs, 'and he's looked into the subject scientifically, and he's found out that the Bible goes square against teetotalism.'

"Well, young Riley, he never said a word, and I thought he looked rather down in the mouth, but Crazy Joe took up for you, sir, and said they was a-slanderin' you; that you was a kind man, and a good man, and tryin' to save souls from destruction, and was it likely you'd be in favour of what turned 'em into hell by thousands?

"Well, I sat and listened awhile, and then says I, more for the sake of seein' what would come of it than anything else, 'I'll tell you what I'll do, Riley,' says I; 'if you'll get Dr. Willoughby's name at the head of that paper, you shall have mine next.' 'Do you mean it?' says he. 'Yes, I do,' says I; 'I declare I do, and I ain't the man to go back on my word neither.' 'You are safe enough,' says Briggs, kind of sneerin' like. 'The minister won't sign; he's been tried before now.' By this time, Crazy Joe was all in a twitter. 'I'll go to him,' says he; 'I'll tell him he's wanted in the front ranks; I'll ask him to reach out his hand, and save a soul from goin' down to death; and so on. You know how Joe talks, and off he went. Well, we waited a spell, and by and by he came back, walkin' in slow, with his eyes on the ground. 'What did he say, Joe?' says Briggs. 'Parson Willoughby is in his study,' says Joe. 'Well, wont he step out to save a soul from goin' down to hell?' says Briggs, quotin' Joe's own words. 'Parson Willoughby 's in his study,' says Joe, and not another word would he say.

"I'm makin' a long story of it," said the sick man, pausing to rest a moment, "but I'm most through, sir. I gave that promise to young Riley without thinkin' much about it; but, Doctor, it's been on my mind ever since. She says I talked about it when I was the craziest. As I said before, I ain't a man to go back on my word. Dr. Willoughby, if you'll sign the total abstinence pledge, I will, and, the Lord helpin' me, I'll keep it to the day of my death."

More than once during this narrative, slight rustling was heard, and the half-closed door creaked suspiciously. Now it was thrown wide open, and John Davis's wife, her face flushed, and tears running down her cheeks, burst into the room.

"God bless you, John! God bless you for those words!" she cried, running to the bedside. "We'll be happy yet. Oh, Dr. Willoughby, he is saved at last! My husband is saved at last!"

Her warm tears rained down upon the sick man's hands, which she held fast in hers.

"She's just wild over it, Doctor," said John Davis. "She thinks if she once gets my name on that paper, it will all be right."

He spoke in a tone of apology, but his hollow eyes gathered moisture as he witnessed his wife's emotion.

"It will. Oh, it will," she said, eagerly. "This good man will support you, and my God will give you strength, John, to keep it."

"I am afraid you are both putting too much trust in a mere human instrumentality," said the minister. "The pledge is very good in its way, and a useful auxiliary. It is a help to many,—no doubt will be to you; but you must be careful not to give it undue prominence. It is not in societies, or pledges, or in any external machinery, that the hope of your cure lies, John Davis. You must go back of all these. If intemperance were merely a bad social usage, or a custom of ill manners, or anything not directly connected with duty to God, these voluntary human agencies might be sufficient for its control, and perhaps its extirpation; but it is a *sin*. My dear friend, your only sufficient remedy is that divine one which alone can conquer the sin of your evil nature. I pray God to make you a Christian, and then you will be safe indeed."

"Oh, Doctor Willoughby," said the wife eagerly, "he'd have got religion long ago if it hadn't been for drink.   In the last revival, when so many were brought in, he was wonderfully solemnized.   I knew the Spirit was striving with him, though he fought hard against it.   I tried to get him to some of he meetings.   One spell I thought I should, but he took to drinkin' harder than ever, and drowned all his convictions.   Oh, sir, if he'd signed the pledge he'd have been a Christian long ago.   His folks was all professors, and if there ever was a godly woman his mother was one.   Yonder's her Bible."

The sick man's eyes followed the direction of her hand.

"It's mighty queer, Doctor," said he, " the fancies sick folks get into their heads.   My old mother's body's been in the grave these ten years, and her soul in heaven, I know,—for, as wife says, she was a godly woman,—but I could swear she sat there by my bed one whole night since I've been sick, and sang to me just as she used to when I was a baby. Jennie, it was that night they said I'd die if I didn't go to sleep; and how was I goin' to sleep with ten thousand devils in the room all spirtin' fire at me, and droppin' live coals on my head?   Well, all of a sudden, and right in the midst of it, who should I see but my old mother in the white cap, with a broad black ribbon over it, she always wore after father died, sitting in 'her straight-backed rocking-chair, with her knittin'-work in her hands.   And, Doctor, she was singin' 'Mear.'   It made me think of a Sunday mornin' in summer time, and the old meetin'-house on the hill, and the bell tollin', and I, a little shaver in my clean white jacket, walkin' by mother's side. And I soothed right down. All the dreadful noises, that pestered me so, stopped, and I went right to sleep like a baby. And once when I roused up in the night all of a tremble, because I thought those critturs were back again, there mother sat rockin' away, knittin' her stockin', and singin' 'Mear.' She sung it all night; and the devil himself couldn't stand that tune, and he left me in peace. Poor old mother! she's laid awake many a night and cried, when I was down to the tavern drinkin' and carousin'."

"John, John!" said the wife, "she's looking down from heaven this minute, waiting to see what you'll do; and she'll sing louder than she ever sang before, and get all the angels to help her, when you put your name to that paper."

"Well, well, mebbe she will," he said. "Doctor, shall I do it?"

"By all means," said the minister; "and may your mother's God help you to keep the vow! You must go to Him, my friend. You will find your own strength perfect weakness in the hour of trial. Cast yourself upon the heart of love that will pity and save you."

"And you'll go with me, Doctor? It's going to be a hard pull. They'll all twit me with givin' up my principles, and signin' away my liberty, and all that; and I ain't the man I was to stand against it. Drink has taken all the grit out of me. I haven't any more heart than a baby. But, Dr. Willoughby, you are a good man and a strong. Nobody can make head against you. What you say is respectable *is* respectable; and what you do everybody else may do. Now just go with me, Doctor. Let me say when they run me, 'There's the minister,—he used to have his objections against the pledge, but he's signed it now. His name's right alongside of mine. Where I stand he stands.' I'll be proud to say that, Doctor. I'll be sure I am right, and I'll go ahead."

"Davis, you need no such support. Make up your mind what is the right thing to do, and, with God's help, irrespective of my course, or any other man's, go forward and do it. Your duty in this matter is not mine, neither is mine yours. What is right for you may be inexpedient and even wrong for me."

"I don't see it, Doctor. If it's a good thing for me, why isn't it for you? And if you'll excuse me, sir, for speakin' plainly, it don't seem to be just right to advise a man to do what you don't practise yourself."

"The cases are totally different, Davis. You have made a wrong use of one of the gifts of God, and to-day you are suffering the consequences of your sin. You realize your danger, and you feel so little confidence in your power to resist temptation, that you believe you are only secure by totally abstaining from all indulgence in those drinks that have caused your fall. *Your* safety lies in total abstinence, and you wish to solemnize this obligation by a written pledge. Very well, do it. Next to the higher duty of embracing the Gospel, and thus being saved from this and every other sin, it is the thing for you to do. But, because this is *your* duty, it does not follow that it is *mine.* Because total abstinence is necessary for you, who have injured yourself by hurtful excess, must I, who know how to use it with other good gifts of God, in moderation, deprive myself of an innocent gratification? This very gift is given me to use, not abuse. 'All things are yours,' says the apostle, 'the world is yours.' I must practise self-denial, of course. I must keep this appetite in perfect subjection, saying, 'Thus far shalt thou come, and no further,' making it my slave, and not suffering it to become my master. But I must not be a coward. Because you, and others like you, have been defeated, wounded, taken captive in the fight, must I turn and run from the enemy?

"I am not blaming you, my friend. You are weak, and your foe is strong. He has vanquished better men than you. The Saviour respects and tolerates your weakness; but He says to those who are stronger, 'Take unto you the whole armour of God, that ye may be able to withstand in the evil day, and having done all, to stand.' To stand is better than to fly, but to fly is better than to fall. Do you understand me, Davis?"

"I should be a fool if I didn't," he replied. "You mean to say that you are strong and I am weak. You can be trusted to go free, and I must have my hands tied to keep me out of mischief. You may walk in a pleasant path with your head up, and I must go grovellin' down in a ditch. Well, I won't dispute it The Lord knows I'm all you say, and more. I am weak, and poor, and miserable, and wicked enough, and despised by all; and you are rich, and happy, and good, with your praise in everybody's mouth. And you say, because there's all this difference between us, and you are· up there and I down here, that my duty isn't yours, and how can I expect you to come down to my level? Well, you'll say it's presumptuous in me, but it's just what I *did* expect. I thought, seein' as I couldn't come up to your road, mebbe you'd come down to mine. And if you look at it one way, sir, as high as you are, and as low as I am, we are in some sort on the same track; for I didn't get to be a drunkard all at once, Dr. Willoughby. What you do now I used to do once. I took a tumbler of whisky on election day, as you take wine at a weddin', or a hot sling when I was goin' out to work in the cold, as you take a little brandy and water on a stormy night when you go out to Brighton district to hold a meetin'. That's the way I began. I don't suppose you'll ever get a-goin' on the down track as I have; but I'll tell you this, Dr. Willoughby, if there wasn't any moderate drinkers there wouldn't be any drunkards. And now see what a hard spot you put us in. You say only drunkards need to sign the pledge, and you'd have us put our names down, and proclaim ourselves by that hard name to all the world. You say, ' Here, you poor, miserable sinners, sign the pledge and be saved;' and you won't so much as touch us with the tips of your fingers. Do you call that Christian? Dr. Willoughby, I ask *you* to do what you ask *me* to do. Put your name 'longside of mine on that paper. You give up your wine, and I'll give up my whisky. I know I'm a lost man, body and soul, if I keep on drinkin'. I've heard you say a deal, when I used to go to meetin', about the ' value of an immortal soul.' Ain't my soul worth makin' that little sacrifice for? or didn't it cost as much as some others?"

A group of little ragged children were playing in the next room, and in the pause that succeeded John Davis's appeal, a sweet, childish voice sang these words :—

> " Jesus died for you,
> Jesus died for me ;
> Yes, Jesus died for all mankind,—
> Thank God, salvation 's free !"

Dr. Willoughby rose and walked to the window; then he came and stood by the sick man's side.

" Davis," said he, " I will do anything in my power to help you—I mean, anything that does not involve the giving up of a principle. I will assist you to obtain steady work. I shall be glad to give you any pecuniary aid you may need. These children must have warm clothing. You shall not be left to struggle on alone, my poor fellow. Friends will gather round you, when they see you pursuing a different course. I hope to see you yet happy and prosperous, with the smiling faces of your wife and children gathered about you; and to hear you raise a prayer of thanksgiving to Him whose grace has set you free."

He paused, but John Davis did not speak.

"With regard to the request you so earnestly make, that I would take this pledge with you, I can only say that 'it is my carefully-studied and firmly-retained religious conviction, that wine, and other stimulating drinks, belong to the meats which God hath created, and which are not to be refused, but received with thanksgiving; and I value even more than meats the liberty wherewith Christ hath made me free.'* Therefore I reject the abstinence yoke. Anything in reason I will do for you, Davis, but this is a part of my religion, and I cannot in conscience give it up."

The sick man fixed his eyes steadily upon Dr. Willoughby's face while he was speaking.

"Do you hear that, wife?" said he. "It's a part of the minister's religion to drink wine! Shall I be wiser than my betters, or holier than the prophets? Hurrah! Send Tim to fill up the black jug. If it's his religion to drink wine, it's mine to drink whisky, and I will drink it till I die!"

Jennie Davis had stood all this time by her husband's bedside. Her glad look when she first entered the

* Thomason.

room changed to one of breathless anxiety, as she listened to the conversation, turning her eager face from one to the other of the speakers. When she heard these last dreadful words, she turned as pale as death, and, covering her face with her apron, burst into an agony of weeping.

"Davis," said Dr. Willoughby, sternly, "you forget yourself. My poor woman, don't cry so. Your husband will think better of this. He does not mean what he says."

"I *do* mean it," he said, "and I've got you to back me. Moderation! Liberty and whisky! that's the talk! The parson's principles are good enough for me. If I stumble, I'll stumble over him, and, if I go to hell, I'll tell them all the minister sent me there. Hurrah! Jennie, we'll fill up the black jug!"

"Davis," said Dr. Willoughby, "I will not listen to such language. I will talk further with you on this subject when you are in a proper frame of mind."

"Any time, Doctor; and we'll fetch out the jug, and have a drink together."

He said this with a laugh that made his face fiendish.

The weeping wife followed her minister to the door.

"We will pray for him," he said. "God alone can save him. I will see him again."

She answered him as well as she could for her tears.

"I thank you, sir,—but I am afraid—it will do— no good."

CHAPTER VI.

CRAZY JOE

> "Some strange commotion
> Is in his brain : he bites his lip, and starts;
> Stops on a sudden, looks upon the ground,
> Then lays his finger on his temple, straight
> Springs out into fast gait; then stops again,
> Strikes his breast hard; and anon he casts
> His eye against the moon; in most strange postures
> We have seen him set himself."—SHAKESPEARE.

GRACE WILLOUGHBY'S sewing machine was out of order one day, and, throwing a shawl over her head, she ran out to the back yard where Joe Martin, or Crazy Joe, as he was universally called in the village, was helping Dan to split up the great hickory log he had drawn from the woods a few days previous. Dr. Willoughby frequently employed this man when there was a press of work; and as he was skilful with tools, Grace hoped he might be able to assist her.

It was a bright day in early winter. The first snow of the season had fallen the night before, and lay upon the ground white and unsullied. The air below was quite still, but the upper branches of the trees that surrounded her father's house swayed to and fro, and from the tops of the pines came the pensive music of the winter wind. Joe stood, axe in hand, a rapt expression on his upturned face, talking softly to himself; and Dan, who had also suspended work, was watching him with a half-curious, half-contemptuous expression on his hard, Yankee visage. Neither of the men noticed the young girl's approach, and she stood quietly observing them, before discovering herself.

"There's a sound of going in the tops of the mulberry-trees," said Crazy Joe, "and it's like an army preparing for battle."

"*Them* ain't mulberry-trees," said Dan Taylor, following the direction of Joe's eyes; "them's young maples. What are yer talkin' 'bout, Martin? There ain't a mulberry-tree round here as I know on, nor hain't been since the *morus multicaulus* specelation. 'Nuff on 'em, then, more's the pity, an' some that owned 'em left with heads as cracked as yourn." (This last in a low voice.) "Don't ye know the difference between a soft maple and a mulberry, Joe?"

Joe did not answer him, or appear to notice the interruption, but went on talking; and his voice, always musical, though unpleasantly loud in his excited moods, was now very tender and soft in tone.

"The four angels stand in the four corners, holding the four winds of heaven," said he; "for my Lord commanded that they should not hurt any green thing, neither any tree, but only those men who have not the seal of God in their foreheads." He put his hand to his head with a troubled look. "The garden of the Lord is full of goodly trees, the palm and the olive tree, the pine tree and the box together, but in the midst of it, and on the bank of the river, is the tree of life." He began to sing:—

> "'Oh, my brother, are you sitting on the tree of life,
>   To hear when Jordan rolls?'"

"I can't say as I be, brother," said Dan. "I ain't clim' a tree these ten years. Use to go up wa'nut-trees like a chipmonk; and as for hearin' Jordan roll, I don't know as I ker about that kind o' music yet awhile. It's a hard road to travel,—hey, Joe?"

Joe answered him with great solemnity:—

"If thou hast run with the footmen, and they have wearied thee, how canst thou contend with horses? And if in the land of peace they wearied thee, then how wilt thou do in the swelling of Jordan?"

Then he continued his song:—

> "'Oh, my sister, are you sitting on the tree of life,
>   To hear when Jordan rolls?
>   Roll, Jordan, roll!'"

"Yonder she stands," said Dan, pointing to Grace, whom he had just discovered. Joe turned. "Ah, yes, Miss Grace," said he, with a smile, "*you* are on the tree of life. Jordan will roll for you. There's no flaming sword to keep *you* away. His mark is plain enough in your white forehead." Again he put his hand to his brow.

" Is your head very bad to-day?" she said, kindly.

" There is no change, Miss Grace.   You know there was power given to torment night and day for a season; but it's the time that frets me.   I think I could bear it better if I could reckon the time.   You know it says, ' It was permitted him to continue forty and two months, and a time, and times, and the dividing of a time.'   Now, Miss Grace, shall we count from when the angel with the key of the bottomless pit and the great chain loosed the old dragon that was bound for a thousand years; or from when the beast whose deadly wound was healed, rose out of the sea and put his mark, or the number of his name, in men's foreheads?   Miss Grace, do you think it was then, and why did he put *my* mark in a different place?"

He pointed to the scar upon his cheek as he spoke, —doubt, anxiety, and patient suffering mirrored in his face.

" What's the good of betherin' yer head 'bout it?" said Dan.   " Plague take the time, and times, and dividin' of times.   An' I'll tell you what 'tis, Joe Martin, if yer don't talk less an' work more, this ere hickory log won't git chopped up 'fore next April. Then there'll be a '*time*.'"

" ' Let him that hath understanding,' " said Joe, with great solemnity, " ' count the number of the beast; for it is the number of a man, and his number is six hundred threescore and six.'   Miss Grace, when you say your prayers to-night, would you mind asking that question about the time?"

"I will ask it," she said, "and I will ask the dear Saviour to take away all this trouble and confusion from your mind, and do for you, in His own good time, what He did when He was here on earth for a poor man as much worse than you are as you can think."

"With the mark on him, Miss Grace?"

"With the mark on him, Joe, so plain and so dreadful, that every one was afraid of him; and he never could live with his fellow-men, but went wandering night and day in the mountains, and among the tombs, crying, and cutting himself with stones, and when Jesus met him, all wounded and bleeding, He made him well."

"Made him well," repeated Crazy Joe, his hand seeking his forehead again. "It must have been down in the 'lonesome valley' that He met him, for you know the hymn says:—

> 'Down in the lonesome valley,
> My Jesus met me there.'

Oh, I've been there, Miss Grace, many and many a time; but I never met any Jesus. Yes, you may ask Him to do that for me, when the time, and times, and dividing of times is accomplished. Oh, if I could only count up that time!"

She hastened to divert his mind from this perplexing question by preferring her request, and was gratified to see how instantly the wandering look left his face, and was succeeded by one of grave attention, as she explained what she needed. He smiled when she had finished, made her two or three of the little fantastic bows peculiar to him, then drawing from a recess in the wood pile a bundle tied in a silk handkerchief, he produced the tools he needed, and set himself busily to work. Grace noticed, as he untied this bundle, the neatness and order that characterized the man's personal habits. His knife, chisel, screw-driver, and other simple tools, were in a box by themselves; his articles for the toilet in another; while a clean white handkerchief, a gay neck-tie, a bosom pin, and a bottle of perfumery, explained how he had gained among the boys of the village the name of "Dandy Joe."

While she stood watching his nimble fingers as he shaped the little wedge she needed, Katie called from the kitchen door, "Miss Grace, your gintleman has come," and her mother met her in the hall.

"It's Mr. Landon, dear," she said; "if you want to change your dress, I will entertain him till you are ready."

"Oh, no, mother, my dress is good enough," she said; and with a quick, light step entered the room where her lover awaited her.

Mr. Horace Landon rose deliberately from the arm-chair in which he was seated, wl en the young girl, her hand extended, and a smile of welcome on her face that brought every dimple in play, came forward to meet him. He was a tall man, with glossy black hair and beard, a high, straight forehead, eyes as black as coal, set deep in his head, and the other features of his face clear-cut, and in good proportion. But he was not handsome, and Frances Thayer flattered him when she called him young-looking. There were lines on his forehead, and about his eyes, that only time can make; the top of his head was quite bare, and the lower part of his face, when in repose, dropped like that of an old man. Standing side by side with Grace Willoughby, in her slender, girlish beauty, her fair skin, light hair, and dimples making her look younger than she really was; with his wrinkles, his baldness, and a certain weary, careworn expression that pervaded his whole face, he seemed old indeed.

"I called to give you the first sleigh-ride of the season," he said, when their greetings were over. "I am going to Barton to summon a witness. Will you ride with me?"

She joyfully assented, and a few moments later he handed her to her seat in the cutter, and with abundant care adjusted the robes to protect her from the cold. Mrs. Willoughby watched them from the parlour window.

"Grace has decided like a sensible girl," she said to her husband. "It is a comfort to think that matter is settled. What a position she will occupy! I declare I believe I smell burnt bread. If that Katie *has* spoiled another batch—."

Mr. Landon had taken his seat in the sleigh, and was gathering up the lines preparatory to starting, when his companion spoke.

"Wait a moment, please," she said. "Joe wishes to speak with me."

Mr. Landon turned, and saw coming toward them, through the yard, a man with curly gray hair, and an ugly scar on one side of his face.

"It is Joe Martin," she explained; "a poor, half-crazy fellow father employs for the sake of helping him. He has been doing some work for me this afternoon, and I suppose wants to show it to me. Well, Joe. Why, what is the matter with him?"

The man, who was by this time very near them, and with his axe upon his shoulder, and with one hand extended, had been making his curious little bows as he approached, stopped suddenly, the childish expression of pleasure on his face changing instantly to one of extreme terror and distress; then, dropping his axe, he rushed through the open gate, and extending both arms, appeared about to snatch the girl from her seat in the sleigh.

"Come away!" he screamed. "O Miss Grace, come away!"

"Stand back, sir," said Landon, sternly; "you alarm the lady. Grace, what does this mean?"

The sound of his voice seemed to increase Martin's agitation to ungovernable fury. He trembled all over. He clenched his fists, and stamped on the ground.   The veins on his forehead swelled almost to bursting, and the scar on his cheek turning a livid purple, added greatly to the frightfulness of his appearance.

"Let her go," he screamed. "You villain! you murderer! Let her go!" Then, as Landon started the horse, he sprang forward, and with almost incredible quickness, seized the animal by the head, holding him with an iron grasp.

"Come," said Horace Landon, angrily; "we have had enough of this. Let go my horse's head, you vagabond, or you and my whip will become better acquainted."

He raised the whip, but Grace caught his arm.

"Stop, Mr. Landon," she said. "Don't strike him. Joe, for shame! What do you mean? This gentleman is my friend."

He turned his face full of furious anger at the sound of her voice.

"Friend!" said he. "Is the wolf a friend when he crushes the lamb in his hungry jaws? Is the vulture a friend when he tears the little tender dove with his talons? Miss Grace! Miss Grace! he's got the mark of the beast on his forehead, and in the palms of his hands. Oh, come away!"

He loosened his hold on the rein, to stretch a hand imploringly toward her; and Mr. Landon, seizing the opportunity, touched his horse with the whip. The frightened creature sprang forward, throwing Martin with some violence back upon the snow.

"What are the authorities of your town about," said Mr. Landon, "that they suffer such a madman to run loose in the streets?"

Grace was looking back, and did not heed the question.

"Please drive slower," she said; "I am afraid he is injured."

He checked the speed of his horse, and turned to look.

"No, he is not hurt," he said. "See, he is getting up. It would have served him right, if my horse's heels had knocked the crazy brains out of his head. An ugly fellow, who ought to be put behind bolts and bars before he is an hour older."

"O Mr. Landon," she answered, "you would not say so, if you knew poor Joe. He is as simple-hearted and innocent a creature as ever lived. West Union people would laugh at you if you should tell them he is a dangerous citizen. He was never known to hurt a dumb animal, much less a human being. Why, the little children of the village all love him, and it is no uncommon sight to see a group of them about him, climbing his shoulders, and searching his pockets for candy. He is singularly mild and patient, hopelessly deranged, poor fellow, on religious subjects, but as harmless as possible. I cannot imagine what has occasioned this outbreak. I have never seen anything like it before."

She turned her head again. Crazy Joe had risen

and was standing motionless in the middle of the road. His gray head was bare, and both arms were extended towards the rapidly retreating sleigh.

"Who is he, and where did he come from?" inquired Mr. Landon.

"He was born and brought up in West Union," she replied. "His mother was an excellent Christian woman, a member of father's church. His father died when he was very young. Joe was her only child,— a bright, handsome boy, and fond of his books; and she was very anxious to give him a liberal education. She interested father about it, and he helped to prepare Joe for college. I was very young, but I can remember a rosy-cheeked, handsome boy, who came to recite Latin two or three times a week. Well, she found a place in a store in the city for him, till she could earn money to send him to Newhaven. She was a very industrious, smart woman, a tailoress by trade; and father says she worked night and day—in fact, killed herself—for her boy. On her death-bed she begged father to look after him, and he faithfully promised that he would. And now comes the strange part of my story. A few months after his mother's death, the boy disappeared strangely, unaccountably, leaving no clue to his whereabouts. Father was greatly disturbed about it, because of his promise to the poor mother. He set the police to work, and he advertised, but with no success. And, Mr. Landon, we heard nothing of him from that day, until three or four years ago, when the poor, gray-headed creature, who has just acted so strangely, came to our door one winter's night. Father did not recognize him at first, he was so dreadfully changed, but soon ascertained that it was poor Joe Martin He could give no account of himself, where he had been, or what he had suffered; and we soon ceased to trouble him with questions. Father got him into the asylum for the insane as a State patient, thinking he might be cured; but the physician soon pronounced it a hopeless case; and poor Joe, who had probably led a wandering life, was so very unhappy in his confinement, that it was thought best to release him. He lives in a little house by himself on the edge of the village, and earns a living by sawing wood, and clearing paths in winter, and by gardening in the summer. Every one pities him and treats him kindly. Even the boys of the village, though they have their jokes with him, are seldom rude. I believe he is truly a Christian. He knows his Bible almost by heart. He is never absent from church on the Sabbath, and walks his mile-and-a-half the coldest winter nights to attend the weekly prayer-meeting. He sings strange hymns and songs, that no one about here ever heard before. He attends all the funerals, and there can hardly be a town-meeting without him. He can preach and pray, to the great edification of the boys; but his forte is temperance. You should hear him talk temperance. He is a staunch teetotaler, and gives time, talent, and every cent of money he can spare, poor fellow, to help the cause."

" What did you call him, Grace?"

" Joe Martin. Have you heard the name before, Mr. Landon?"

" That, or one similar. A mere coincidence—nothing more." Then he turned to her, smiling. " Grace, when do you mean to drop the ' Mr.' from my name? Can I not teach you to call me Horace?"

Mr. Landon was a good talker. His mind was stored with knowledge, which his fluent tongue was capable of uttering with flowing grace and eloquence. He had the faculty of introducing old ideas in new shapes, clothing them in choice diction, and serving them up in brilliant style; and for the next two hours he exerted his conversational talents to the utmost to entertain the young girl at his side. Perhaps he wished to drive from her mind all recollection of the unpleasant incident at the commencement of their ride. If so, he was very successful. She laughed at his sallies of wit, till the dimples flashed in and out of her cheeks; blushed with innocent pleasure at his delicate flattery; or listened in rapt attention, her blue eyes moist with feeling, to his well-timed quotations from her favourite poet. Smiles and tears came to her at his bidding,— smiles that lit up her face with an ever-changing beauty, and tears that softened her eyes, and added tenderness to her flexible mouth.

" Mother," she said, standing by Mrs. Willoughby's chair that night—" mother, I am very happy."

" Yes, dear, and well you may be. Mr Landon is
one of a thousand,—so brilliant, so accomplished, and
able to give you every luxury that money can purchase.
You will have a good husband, Grace, and," she added,
as her daughter left the room,—" *and such a position!*"

CHAPTER VII.

THE WILMOT STREET CHURCH.

"Some go there to listen,
    Some to sing and pray;
    And not a few go there to view
    The fashions of the day."

THE Sabbath evening service of the Wilmot Street Church had just closed, and the well-dressed congregation thronged the aisles of the spacious edifice. Old Mrs. Barstow, wedging her capacious person through the crowd, stopped a moment to greet the minister's wife.

"My dear Mrs. Thayer, how do you do? Well, I am sure, with that charming colour in your face. My dear, what a sermon we have heard—so fervent, so eloquent, and so delightfully delivered. Really, such preaching lifts one quite above the things of earth, and gives a foretaste of heaven. Did you notice the Blairs of the Broad Street? I was charmed to have them hear it. I was thinking all the time—'You don't get such preaching as that at home.' Old Dr. Fiske may roll his r's, and pound his pulpit cushion to the end of time, but he'll never preach like that. And that reminds me of something Matilda said at dinner to-day. 'Mother,' says she, 'how splendidly Mr. Thayer

reads the Scriptures.   There's such a melodious fall
to his voice.   Why, he puts more religion into the
word Jeroboam,' says Matilda, 'than Dr. Fiske gets
out of a whole chapter.'   My husband says I make an
idol of my minister; but, dear me, I am so constituted
I can't help it.   That blessed man came down from the
pulpit last Sabbath, and walked out of church behind
me, and touched me on the shoulder to attract my
attention; and now, Mrs. Thayer, don't smile, but I
really have felt a particular regard for that shoulder
ever since."

Miss Irene Simpson, first soprano in the choir,
escorted home by Mr. Lawrence, first bass, thus expressed herself:—

"What a lovely sermon! and how *distingué* and
spirituelle Mr. Thayer looked, with his white forehead,
and his great, brown, melancholy eyes!   And his
teeth!   Did you ever see such beautiful teeth?   Oh,
I think he is perfectly charming!"

Mr. Peter J. Coleman, a prominent dry goods' merchant on Broad Street, gave his views to his brother
from the West, who was spending the Sabbath with
him, after this fashion:—

"Yes, we did a good thing for the Wilmot Street
Church when we settled that young man.   They never
would have got him but for me.   In fact, I have run
the machine for the last two years.   When they put
me in chairman of committee of supply, 'Gentlemen,'
said I, 'I am a better judge of muslins than of

ministers, though I believe I can tell an A No. 1 article in 'most any line.' Well, there was something about Thayer that struck my fancy the first time I heard him preach. You see he didn't come as a candidate. He was over at West Union last August, spending his vacation at his father-in-law's,—he married one of Dr. Willoughby's daughters, a smart woman, with a snapping black eye,—and our supply failed us one Sabbath, and he came and preached. I said to Barstow and Smith after church, 'If you want to draw from the Broad Street Church,' says I, 'there's your man.' Well, they went to see him, and they said he couldn't be got. 'Yes, he can,' says I; 'they all talk off.' So I rode over myself, but I found, sure enough, he didn't care to come. He was pleasantly situated, he said, with all the work he had strength to do, and wasn't inclined to make a change. I was about giving it up when his wife came in. I found she was on our side, and I took courage. Well, the upshot of it all was, we got him, and it's been a grand good thing for the Wilmot Street Church. Why, he carries all before him. They flock from the other churches to hear him, and Dr. Fiske preaches Sabbath evenings to a baker's dozen. We shall run up the sale of slips twenty per cent. the coming year."

Miss Bethiah Emmersly—a maiden lady, who paid for her seat under the east gallery, from her earnings in the paper-mill—climbed to her room in the third story of a brick tenement house on River Street. She lighted her lamp, carefully put away till next Sunday her black velvet bonnet and faded broché shawl, and sat down to write with much labour and care these words in her diary :—

"*Sabbath Evening, Dec. 15.*—My soul greatly refreshed and quickened this day through the preaching of the Word; feel to renewedly render thanks to God that He has sent His young servant to us, endowed with power from on high, to go in and out before us, breaking unto us the bread of eternal life. May the truth dispensed this day by him prove quick and powerful, and sharper than a two-edged sword. May his life and health be precious in thy sight! *Mem.*— In view of his paleness of countenance, to make it a special subject of prayer that his bodily health may be strengthened and renewed."

When Mrs. Thayer softly opened the door of her husband's study, half an hour after service that Sabbath evening, she found him with his head bowed upon the open sermon, on his table. At her light touch he lifted a very pale face, and looked at her with what Miss Irene Simpson had described as his " great, melancholy, brown eyes." His face was worn and troubled, hers very bright and sparkling.

"I felt very proud of my husband to-night," she said, her white hand still resting on his shoulder. " It was a grand sermon, Louis; everybody says so; but how tired you look! I am glad your day's work is over."

"If it were God's will," he said passionately, "I would it were my last."   .

"Louis!"

"Fanny, I am utterly discouraged. I wish I had never preached. I wish I never needed to go into a pulpit again. What have I accomplished these three months?"

Mrs. Thayer was too well accustomed to these dark moods of her husband to be greatly disturbed.

"You are exhausted," she said; "and no wonder, after such an effort; and you are not as strong as usual, for your cold has pulled you down."

She crossed the room to a small closet; and taking a cut-glass decanter and goblet, and a curious old-fashioned sugar-bowl of solid silver from one of the shelves, she proceeded, with a skill and despatch that proved it an accustomed service, to prepare a glass of the rich amber-coloured fluid that filled the decanter.

"It must be father's 'old cognac' to-night," she said. "'Strong drink to them that are ready to perish.'"

He stayed her hand as she was diluting the contents of the glass from the pitcher of water on his study-table.

"No more water, Fanny," he said. "Give it to me strong to-night."

He took the glass eagerly from her hand, and drained it at a draught. Then she came and took a low seat by his side.

"And now, my husband, that I have made you comfortable in body," she said, "I think I have earned the right to chide you a little. Louis, why will you allow yourself to feel, or talk, as you did just now? God has given you an extended field of usefulness. Crowds flock to hear you preach. You will not allow me to tell you half the good things I hear said about you,—' the well-meant though injudicious commendations,' as you call them,—or I could convince you that you have accomplished something in these three . months. Is it accomplishing nothing to satisfy a great congregation of intelligent people?—to send them away every Sabbath full of your praises?"

"I don't want their praises, Fanny; I want their piety. I don't seek their satisfaction, I seek the salvation of their souls. Yes; they come, as you say, in crowds to hear me preach, for the power of novelty is great, and 'I am to them as a very lovely song, of one that hath a pleasant voice, and can play well on an instrument, for they hear the words, but they do them not.' They go away not a whit better than they came. My wife, I am sick of it all. I preach Sabbath after Sabbath, on the danger of riches, to men surrounded by the luxuries of life, whose engrossing business from Monday morning till Saturday night is to make money, and whose souls are well-nigh eaten up with the love of this world; and they settle themselves on their soft cushions, and listen with such self-satisfied smiles, and never dream but that they have resisted and overcome all these temptations, and are ripe for heaven. And to gaiety-seeking, card-playing, ball-going Christians, I speak of the guilt of those who are lovers of pleasure more than lovers of God; and they listen well pleased, and count on their fingers how many balls and parties they are engaged to attend the coming week."

"Louis, you remind me of a poem translated from the German that father often quotes. It is called 'St. Anthony's Fish Sermon.' It seems the holy father

> ' Went down to the river,
> A discourse to deliver,'

and the carps, and the pikes, and the crabs, and the eels all came,—

> ' Their mouths widely reaching,
> To swallow the preaching.'

They thought it the best sermon that ever was preached; but

> ' When the sermon was ended,
> To his business each wended,—
> The pikes to their thieving,
> The eels to good living;
> The crab he walked crooked,
> The carps were still stupid;
> *The sermon found favour,*
> *They remained just as ever,*'

"So, my dear husband, your experience was St. Anthony's, and many a good, faithful minister's before you. Take that for your comfort."

"It is a hopeless field," he said. "I should preach, with more expectation of success, to a congregation of Hottentots, or South Sea cannibals, than to a rich city church dead in self-righteous worldliness. And the popularity you speak of for my encouragement is proving a curse to me, and I feel it. It affords me no pleasure, yet it is becoming a necessity of my life. It feeds nothing but pride, and it is dearly purchased,— how dearly, you can never know. Fanny, you said the other evening you sometimes thought I wished myself back in our New Hampshire parish. I do, indeed. I believe it was an evil day for me when I left that quiet village among the hills. Dear old Gloverton! I had no such trials there."

She looked at him with scorn in her black eyes.

"No," she said, "for your people were not discriminating enough either to praise or blame. Louis, I admire your taste. I think I see you in that old pulpit nearly up to the ceiling, and your choir of singers opposite, led off by a cracked melodeon, and the row of ear-trumpets levelled at you from the front slip, and your congregation of greasy operatives, and sleepy-headed farmers, and wizened old women, and boorish boys, and apple-faced country girls. Oh, that was infinitely superior to the Wilmot Street Church, with its velvet-carpeted platform, and its five-thousand dollar organ, and quartette choir, and the *élite* of the city for your listeners! Yóu never had any trials up there,—had you? Old Deacon Larkins never wore out your patience with his long-winded exhortations to his 'poor, dyin' feller-critturs,' and Sister Blinn never wanted to 'speak in meetin',' or Brother Carter to have an anti-slavery gathering once a fortnight? The singers never quarrelled—did they?—till you threatened to leave if they didn't behave? You never came home on Thursday night discouraged, because your brethren all stayed away from prayer-meeting in haying-time? They didn't go to sleep under your best sermons—did they?—or take a month to make up their minds about a new measure? And when Brother Miller refused to come to communion, till Brother Gates was turned out of the church—."

"Fanny, stop!"— he spoke reprovingly, but half laughing. "Of course, they were not faultless, and every minister must have his troubles; but they were a simple-minded, grateful, and affectionate people. You know how they clung to me to the last. I loved them, Fanny; I loved them."

"I know it, dear," she said, more gently, "and I only wished to remind you that there was human nature up in Gloverton as well as here. Every one to their taste; but to my mind, there is a pleasanter phase of it in the Wilmot Street Church than in that little one-horse town among the New Hampshire hills."

"It was my first parish," he said, "and I carried

another 'first love' there,—a dark-eyed girl, whom I called wife.   Do *you* wonder that I love Gloverton?"

The allusion touched her, and she sat silently for a few moments with her hand in his.

"You are feeling better," she said, when she rose to leave him.

"Yes; but wretchedly tired still," he answered.

"Nevertheless," thought Frances Thayer, "I have

laughed you out of your dumps for this time, and now I may go to my babies."

There was no shadow of a coming sorrow on her handsome face. Pride, and gratified ambition, and untiring energy to tread an upward path, were all written there, but not a trace of impending disgrace and shame.

When she left him, her husband rose and filled his glass from the decanter. He drank hastily, and, returning to his seat, buried his face in his hands.

CHAPTER VIII.

A LITTLE FOR MEDICINE.

" Fill high the bowl with fusil oil!
    With tannin let your cups be crowned;
If strychnine gives relief to toil,
    Let strychnine's generous juice abound!
Let oil of vitriol cool your brains,
    Or animated atoms brew,—
And fill your arteries, hearts, and veins,
    With glee—and infusorial glue!"

R. BARSTOW called to see his minister the next day. He was a round, portly gentleman, with whom the world had gone well for sixty years; a merchant, and one of the moneyed men of the Wilmot Street Church. In the course of the conversation, he said:—

" I have laid aside for you, Mr. Thayer, a couple of dozen bottles of my choice wine, which, with your permission, I will send my man round with in the morning. My wife has a good deal to say about your looking pale lately, and I have noticed it myself. So I said to her, 'When Brown's package comes to hand,' —it was shipped the 9th, and I knew it couldn't fail to be here the last of the week,—'I will send our minister some wine that *is* wine.'"

" You import it, then?" Mr. Thayer said.

"For my family use, yes, sir. I must have an article that I can depend upon, and I have no confidence in the wine sold by the dealers in this country. The greater part, sir, is a vile compound—lead, and cocculus, and everything else that is bad. I want port, and claret, and sherry—good, honest, official wine, to promote digestion, stir up the heart and arteries, raise the bodily heat, and exhilarate the animal spirits,— not cognac oils, sugar colourings, gypsum, arsenite of copper, sugar of lead, &c. I want to be *graped*, sir, not *griped*. Why, if this business of manufacturing imitation wine goes on, in a few years there will not be the slightest occasion for vineyards, or the cultivation of grapes. The vineyards of the American people, sir,—why, they are not in Medoc or Frontignon. They are in the garrets and cellars of our large cities. It makes a man shudder to think of it."

"I suppose there is an immense quantity of wine manufactured in this country," said the minister.

"Why," said Mr. Barstow, "look at the one article of port wine. My agent tells me, and he has good means of knowing, that the Oporto wine is sold in England at thirty dollars a dozen, and we have a superior article, a *superior article*, Mr. Thayer, offered in the New York market at just half the price. How do you account for that, sir? And there's champagne; there's a firm in New York city to-day, manufacturers of champagne wine—I speak that I do know—that does a business of sixty thousand dollars per annum.

And of the hundreds of gallons sent out from that house every year, not one of them ever saw a pint of grape-juice, and if called fortieth cousin to a vine, would deny the relationship."

"Have you been behind the scenes, Mr. Barstow," said the minister, "that you speak so positively?"

It was a random shaft, but it hit the mark.

"Ahem," said Mr. Barstow, "I— the fact is, I had a friend in the liquor business some years ago, and— well, as you say, I have been behind the scenes, and understand some of their tricks."

"And may I ask," said Mr. Thayer, "how you manage to procure the genuine article? Your friend's champagne, manufactured in New York, has, I suppose, the foreign mark on it?"

"Of course; and much of our imported wine is as great a humbug as the home manufacture. Brown tells me there's a house in the city of Lyons, where they ship eighty thousand bottles a year of what they call champagne wine. Some chemists analized it one day. What do you suppose it contained? Gypsum, arsenite of copper, and sugar of lead. Ugh! But, sir, there *is* a way of getting pure wine. It costs time and money, but it pays. Perhaps you are not aware of the extent to which wine-worship is carried in England. We know little about it in this country. The rich landed proprietors, and men of large means there, take great pride in their wine cellars, and put themselves to a deal of trouble to stock them. And

the sale of a lot of wine belonging to deceased gentlemen is almost as common as sales of their libraries.
Well, Brown is in London the greater part of the time,
and when he sees the sale of such and such a gentleman's
cellar containing valuable wine advertised, he is sure to
be on hand, and I have given him *carte blanche* to
purchase for me. Of course he exercises his discretion,
for some of these wines sell at almost fabulous prices.
Think of port at five, seven, and even nine pounds per
dozen; sherry at twelve guineas per dozen; claret at
eight, and so on. Brown says, at one auction sale he
attended there was wine sold to the value of *five
thousand pounds.* Think of it! Not less than thirteen thousand bottles of wine in one man's cellar."

"How do you know this is pure wine?"

"How do I know? Because they exercise the
greatest care in its selection, attending to it personally.
Why, sir, those gentlemen keep their cellar-books, as a
merchant keeps his ledger, putting down all desirable
information respecting each kind of wine he possesses.
I will give you only one instance. In this lot just
sent there are four dozen of port, of which Brown
writes:—'According to Mr. Cockburn's cellar-book,
this was selected from the hill country as the finest
port, from the best grapes, bottled in 1846.' This
wine costs money, Mr. Thayer, but it pays. It's the
genuine article—the simon pure. I want you to try
it, sir, and if you don't find it goes to the right spot,
and works like a charm, my name's not Barstow.

And when it's gone, Mr. Thayer, there's more where it came from."

He shook his minister's hand with genuine cordiality, and took his departure.

Later in the evening, Mr. Coleman dropped in. "He couldn't stop a moment," he said; "he was driven to death—led a dog's life—tired all the time; but no help for it. Business must be attended to."

"Leave your business to your clerks, Mr. Coleman," said the minister, "and give yourself more leisure. A man of your means ought not to be confined so closely to business."

"I know it; but can't help it. Must be on hand myself,—can't leave the concern to boys. But I didn't come here to grumble. I have worked hard all my life, and expect to. A man in good health ought to work. And that brings me to my errand. You look a little worn, Mr. Thayer. Nothing serious, you know, but just a trifle under the weather. You must drink ale, Mr. Thayer. . Nothing like it, depend upon it. I know all about it, for I've been there myself. A dozen years ago, everybody thought I was going into a consumption,—cough, night-sweats, and all the rest. Doctor ordered cod-liver oil,—no good. Somebody told me to drink ale. I concluded it would do no harm, so I tried it. It did the business for me, sir,—cured my cough and. my night-sweats; gave me strength, appetite, and ten pounds of flesh in a month; strung me right up, you see. Depend upon it, it's

just what you need. I keep a barrel of the best
Canada ale in my cellar, and bottle it myself. I'll
send one of the boys round in the morning with some,
if you'll promise to drink it. Ah, good evening, Mrs.
Thayer; I hope you are well. No, thank you, I
mustn't sit down. I called on professional business.
I'm a doctor as well as a drygoods man; ha! ha! I
deal in medicines as well as muslins. I have been
prescribing for your husband. Such sermons as he
gives us require considerable head-work, and tell on a
man after awhile. Try my medicine, Mr. Thayer,
and you'll be all right in a month. Good-night, sir."

Bethiah Emmersly, after praying earnestly one
evening for the restoration and establishment of her
young pastor's health, resolved to add to her faith
works. She drew from under her bed an old hair-
covered trunk, thickly studded with brass nails—the
same in which she stored her earthly possessions, and
brought with her from the Vermont farm-house years
ago, when she was left almost penniless to push her
solitary way through the world. There were secrets
hidden in Bethiah's trunk with which a stranger may
not intermeddle. We have nothing to do with the
relics of bygone days, which she reverently lifted, one
by one, from their retreat; but we may look over her
shoulder as she turns the leaves of an old recipe-book
she has drawn from the bottom of the trunk. Some
of the writing is pale with age; the paper worn with

long use, and disfigured by ancient stains; little splashes of egg, or bits of crusted sugar, or the print of the housewife's finger,—all bringing to Bethiah's remembrance the kitchen table at the farm-house, where the balls of yellow butter, the bowls of cream, the wooden spice-box, and the bucket of sugar, could as well have been dispensed with as "mother's cook-book."

Bethiah turned the leaves slowly, holding the book close to her dim, old eyes; but she did not stop at "Mother's Election Cake," or "Sister Jane's Sweet Pickles," or "Mrs. Deacon White's New-Year's Doughnuts," but in the back of the book, between "A Salve for Old Sores," and "A Sure Poison for Rats," she stayed her hand at a recipe headed "Spiced Wine for a Weak Stomach." She studied it long and carefully; then she opened her green morocco purse, and counted its contents.

"There's the missionary money," said Bethiah to herself; "but no; I promised it to the Lord for His servants in a foreign field. I must manage it some other way." She thought a moment, and her face brightened. "I'll wear the brown merino another winter," thought Bethiah. "Dear suz! what does an old woman like me want of a new gown, and that godly man carrying his pale face into the pulpit every Sunday?"

She put a mark carefully between the leaves of the recipe-book, donned her bonnet and shawl, and went out. Half-an-hour later, when she climbed the three flights of stairs leading to her room, her rheumatic joints creaking at every step, she carried under her shawl a quart bottle of Madeira wine, and various small packages that emitted a spicy smell. And all that evening, with painful exactness, and with a hand that trembled a little at the responsibility of the task before her, Bethiah weighed, and measured, and stirred, and shook, and a perfume pervaded her apartment suggestive of the delicious vintages of Italy and the sunny South.

"Eh, woman," said Jean Maghee, Miss Emmersly's Scotch neighbour across the hall, "'gin I didna ken ye were a guid temperance buddy, an' na gien to drinkin', I'd say ye had speerits on ye the nicht."

The next evening, when her frugal supper was cleared away, with a radiant face Bethiah took the precious bottle from her "corner cupboard," and wended her way to the parsonage. But when her modest request was granted, and the door of the study thrown open, she paused on the threshold, her heart beating like a timid girl's, and half-repented her purpose. She would fain have taken the shoes from off her feet before entering this sacred retreat—for must not the place where those fervent discourses on which her soul feasted were written, where the minister knelt at his private devotions, and received the rich supply of ministerial gifts and graces, that made him so faithful and successful a labourer in

Christ's vineyard, be quite on the verge of heaven? And he, the godly man, bending over his sermon, the light from his shaded lamp surrounding him like a halo, and leaving the rest of the room in shadow, did he require the nourishment of common mortals? or had he meat to eat we know not of? and how should she offer *wine*, though it was the blood of the tropics, and flavoured with the spices of Araby the blest, to one whose drink, perchance, was " wine on the lees well refined," of which he had been bidden by his " beloved " to " drink abundantly ? "

While these thoughts passed through Bethiah's mind, the minister was writing down the last few words of a sentence in his sermon. Then he rose to greet her, drew her forward to the light, and by his simple, kindly manner, endeavoured to set her at her ease. She found it difficult to do her errand, until, raising her eyes to her pastor's face, all the motherly feeling in the lonely woman's heart burst forth.

" You do look dreadful pale Sabbath days, Mr. Thayer; and I heard the doctor said you had dyspepsia and a weak stomach, and mother was a master hand to nurse sick folks,—they used to send for her ten miles round the country,—and she said there was nothing so good for a weak stomach as spiced wine ; and I've fixed up some according to her recipe, Mr. Thayer, and I've made bold to fetch it, sir,"—here she produced the bottle,—" and if you'll go to the trouble of taking a large spoonful three times a day, sir,—I've writ the directions and pasted them on the bottle,—and eat your victuals regular, it will be sure to help you. Mother used to say it was Bible medicine, and meant

for ministers; for St. Paul says to Timothy, "Take a little wine for thy stomach's sake" (1 Tim. v. 23).

Bethiah's voice trembled a little while she was

speaking; but the minister received her gift so kindly, expressing his thanks more than once for her thoughtful remembrance, that the good woman was reassured; and when he had comforted her heart by a few words of Christian counsel, she went home superlatively happy. She was, to use the words of her diary, "greatly assisted in prayer that night for my dear pastor, was blessed with much freedom, and received in my soul the assurance that the means used for his recovery would, under God, be blessed to the establishment of his health; for which mercies I desire, O Lord, 'to render unto thee the calves of my lips'" (Hosea xiv. 2).

CHAPTER IX.

A FIGHT WITH THE RUM-SELLERS.

"This should teach us not to fear the face of men; no, nor the faces of the mighty; not to fear them in the matters of God, though they should run upon us like a giant. We must not be afraid of Og, the king of Bashan, though his head be as high as the ridge of a house, and his bedstead a bedstead of iron. Persecution, or the appearance of the giants against the servants of God, is no new business."—BUNYAN.

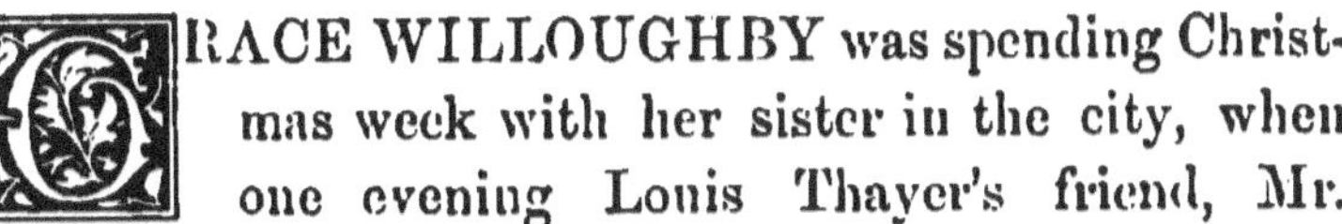

GRACE WILLOUGHBY was spending Christmas week with her sister in the city, when one evening Louis Thayer's friend, Mr. Richmond, called at the Wilmot Street parsonage. Then Mr. Thayer knew he must at once withdraw the encouragement he had given his friend of winning the young lady for his wife; and on pretence of showing his library, he got Mr. Richmond away to the study, and told him of her engagement.

"If he were a good man," thought Allan Richmond, as he returned to his hotel—for he had resisted all entreaties to spend the night at his friend's house—"if he were a good man, and in any respect worthy of her, I could bear my own disappointment, and rejoice in her happiness; but to see an innocent, pure-minded Christian girl thrown away upon that—," The expression used in describing Grace Willoughby's lover was not ministerial, and is best omitted.

He paced his little room on the fourth floor of the hotel for an hour, in burning indignation.

"Are they blind?" he said; "her father and mother, and her sister so happily married, and Louis too? Is it possible they do not know what that man has been, and would be still, but for motives of selfish prudence, stopping in a course of dissipation only because he must stop or die? Ought I not to tell Louis what I know of him—what every one knows who has heard Horace Landon's name? But he knew what he was in college—what he had been since. My depreciation would naturally be ascribed to unworthy motives. Has Grace Willoughby sold herself for money? No. I will never believe that."

He paced his room with a quick, unequal step, and his face was flushed and agitated with conflicting emotions. He was young; he had hitherto met with no serious disappointment in life; and with his Scotch blood he inherited a warm, passionate temperament, and a strong will. But he was a Christian; and the hour that followed this burst of angry feeling was spent in a struggle with his own heart.

"I will take the first train," he said; "I cannot stay another day in the city. I shall learn to 'accept the inevitable,' but I cannot look upon her sweet face again." Yet in the morning he decided that it would be uncourteous to leave town without calling to bid his friend good-bye; and at eleven o'clock he was ushered into Mrs. Thayer's parlour, where Grace sat alone at her sewing.

Of course, Frances Thayer had told her sister, at the first convenient opportunity, the intelligence imparted by her husband, the evening of the ministers' meeting, concerning his friend's unspoken love; and of course Grace had blushed, and said, "Nonsense! it is one of Louis's jokes;" but of course, in her heart of hearts, had believed it all the same, and in her treatment of Mr. Richmond she was governed by the gentleness and almost tenderness of feeling a true woman experiences toward a rejected lover. Quite unconsciously, too, she bestowed upon him, from time to time, pitying glances from her blue eyes that well-nigh drove him frantic. She rose this morning to receive him, greeting him in her artless, girlish way, thrilled him with the touch of her hand, and, during the few moments that elapsed before Mr. Thayer made his appearance, so bewitched him with the magic of her presence, that he forgot everything, except that he was with the woman he loved.

Louis Thayer, when he came in, drew his chair close to that of his friend, and, looking straight into his honest eyes, began to question him about his parish.

"Tell me the whole story, Allan. You are in hot water—you know you are. I have heard something about it, and it is just what I expected. There was a Grantley man in the bank the other day, a rough fellow, talking loud and fast about the ———— teetotal parson (it is not necessary to repeat the adjective he used in describing you), who was splitting the church all to pieces with his (more adjectives, of which 'cursed' was the mildest) doctrines. Now, what was it about, Allan? Must you always be running a tilt against people's pet sins? Preach the Gospel, man. Attack drunkenness and every other sin by preaching a personal Christ."

"So I will, Louis; and as I firmly believe that intemperance is the Gospel's bitterest enemy, I will fight it to the death; for I believe the battle to be God's battle."

"Well, and how are you conducting this campaign, —this 'battle of the Lord'—in Grantley?"

"I am having a hand-to-hand fight with the rum-sellers, Louis."

"Now, may Michael and all his angels help you," said his friend; "for you have Beelzebub and his host on the other side."

"You have passed through Grantley village, Louis. You know what a compact town it is, lying snugly in between the hills, with two thousand inhabitants in the radius of three-quarters of a mile. There are fourteen places in that town, including hotel and drug store, where liquor is sold in open defiance of the law. Saturday night, when the workmen in the factories are paid off, these places are *full;* and a large proportion of the earnings of those hard-working men, every cent of which in these days of high prices is needed to feed and clothe their families, goes into the rumseller's till. I talked faithfully with the men engaged in this business. They felt greatly abused by my strictures, declared that they regulated their business with discretion, that no man got drunk on their premises, and that they were censured for other people's sins, &c. But as they all put forth the same claim, and every day there were drunkards in our streets, their professions amounted to little.

"Well, I looked up the temperance men in the church and community, and tried to organize them for action, that we might enforce the law, and break up some of these dens. And here I utterly failed. They were timid, or they were time-serving, fearful of making enemies, or of injuring their business. The evil was thoroughly ingrafted into the social life of the place ; families had intermarried, or were associated together in business, or real-estate owners rented their buildings to those engaged in the traffic. If I touched one man, I touched a dozen. I believe there are not twenty men in my church, of two hundred members, who are not in one way or another implicated in this wretched business. Then, worse than all the rest, the minister of North Grantley failed me. He talked temperance zealously and loudly in a general way ; but when he found there was difficult and dangerous work to be done, he fell away, and left me to do it alone.

"When I found these methods failed, I tried yet

another. I gathered the statistics of intemperance in the place, and wrote them out in the form of a lecture, gave notice that I would deliver it on Sabbath evening, and invited all to attend. Of course, I had a crowd to hear me. I designated by name the different places in our midst where liquor was sold in violation of the law. I stated such reliable facts as I could gather relating to these places: how the wives of the 'iron men' (as the hands in the foundry are called) came with babies in their arms, and begged that no more whisky might be sold to their husbands; how one of these iron men, too much intoxicated to find his way home, was kicked out of doors the coldest night last winter, and found frozen to death, not a dozen yards from the place where he obtained his liquor; how an Englishman who had signed the pledge eight years before in his own country, and kept it till he came to our village to work, whose young wife was on her way across the ocean to join him, and whose snug cottage, fitted by his skilful hands, was all ready for its mistress, was tempted by a companion to enter one of our saloons, tasted, and called for more, and drank day and night till he died; and how—and this happened only the week before I delivered my lecture—a lady in the village went one night successively to every place where liquor was sold, putting her pale face in at the door with the sad question, 'Is my Bertie here?' Her Bertie, a fair-haired boy, sixteen years old, lay in a drunken sleep behind the counter in one of those saloons.

"I had plenty such facts to give, and I did not spare them. It was a dark picture: I meant it should be. I gave the number of the men in our midst who were known to be in the constant habit of using intoxicating drink; and I told them there were not a dozen young men in Grantley who were growing up to habits of sobriety. Then I appealed to the moral strength of the community, to their Christian principle, and to their political wisdom; and called upon them, as they valued the favour, and feared the judgments, of Almighty God, to see to it that this most righteous law was vindicated and enforced."

"Did the liquor dealers tar-and-feather you, or horsewhip you out of town?" said Mr. Thayer.

"They were nearly all present. Two left the house in the middle of the lecture. One shook his fist in my face as I came down from the pulpit. They call my list of drunkards ' Richmond's string,' and twit each other with being on it. But they cannot dispute one of my facts; and I have thus far accomplished my object; for the community is awake,—the subject is talked about from one end of the town to the other."

"And your church, Allan?"

"Is shaken to its foundations," he replied. "The men I attacked personally were some of them pew-holders; their wives and daughters members of my church. They have given up their slips, and withdrawn their subscription. Two of my strongest men financially—one connected by marriage, the other by business relations, with the liquor dealers—talk loud, and threaten to leave us. Still another, who rents his building for a saloon—and this last has been an active church member—passes me every Sabbath on his way to a neighbouring church, where, my landlady says, 'he will be troubled neither with temperance nor religion.' I have told the society to deduct from my salary all they lose. What the result will be, it is impossible to tell."

"How dare you take the responsibility of bringing discord into the church of God?" said his friend. "What if that hitherto peaceful and prosperous society, torn and weakened by contention, should not be able to stand this storm, and should go down?"

"If the church stands on rum, let it go down," said Allan Richmond.

"It is a pity," said Louis Thayer. "And you are so pleasantly situated there; and now, of course, you cannot remain. You have cut your own fingers, Allan. The rumsellers will move heaven and earth to be rid of you."

"I won't go," said the minister.

His friend looked at him, half-laughing.

"I should think you would be afraid of personal violence," he said.

"Do you really think one of those fellows would dare attack me?" said Allan Richmond, with sparkling eyes; "because you know one may defend one's self when attacked, if one *is* a minister. Oh, the inexpressible satisfaction it would be to give a rumseller a *knock-down* argument! But no, I shall never have the opportunity. If I owned a barn, they would set fire to it; or a hen-roost, they would rob it; but as for attacking a man in fair fight, they are too mean and cowardly ever to venture it. No, Louis," said the young minister mournfully, "such good luck will never happen to me."

Louis Thayer surveyed the six feet of muscular Christianity before him with honest admiration.

"I like your courage, Allan," he said, "better than your cause. It is a serious thing to break up the harmony of a community, and turn the church of God into a bear garden."

"So it is," he returned. "I have done nothing rashly. I have asked God's blessing upon every step. Louis, I *must* fight this evil, whether in the church or out, and be known as the avowed and uncompromising enemy of a traffic that is only evil. And the Grantley church will not go down. God will take care of His own. We shall come out 'as gold that is tried in the fire,' all the brighter for the dross that is purged away."

With these hopeful words on his lips, he crossed the room to say good-bye to Grace Willoughby. She looked up earnestly in his face, when she gave him her hand.

"I believe you are right," she said, "and that God will help you. I am going to pray that He will; and oh, Mr. Richmond," her blue eyes moistening, "do try and save that poor mother's Bertie."

Louis Thayer followed his friend into the hall. He could not help seeing the look of passionate, regretful tenderness on the young minister's face.

"Allan," said he kindly, "I am sorry. I wish from my heart it could have been otherwise."

"God bless her!" said Allan Richmond, and hurried away.

"Fanny, dear," said Grace that evening, when the sisters sat alone together by the nursery fire, "how did you feel when you were engaged?"

Mrs. Thayer smiled at the question, put with a directness and simplicity of manner that was peculiar to her sister.

"How did I feel, child?" she answered; "why, happy, of course, as every girl does who marries the man of her choice. Why do you ask, Gracie?"

"Did you have no doubts and fears, Fanny? Didn't you feel sometimes as if you were on the threshold of a great unknown future? Weren't you afraid, Fanny?"

"No, indeed," said the young wife. "I loved and trusted Louis perfectly. I knew I should be happy with him anywhere. Why should I be afraid?"

There was a little pause, and then the younger sister said sadly, "I wish Horace was a Christian."

"He will be, Grace," said her sister. "He told

Louis that his opinions on religious subjects had changed materially of late years. My dear girl, with your influence over him, you can make him what you please."

"He is so much older and wiser than myself," she answered, "that I am more likely to be changed by him than he by me. And I am not dignified and womanly like you; and, Fanny, sometimes he treats me like a little girl. Before you were married, when you used to try and talk seriously with Louis, did he laugh at you, and turn everything you said into a joke?"

"My dear, the cases are very different. Louis was a minister, and, of course, we talked about serious things. Why, I was obliged to hear all his sermons, as fast as he wrote them. Think of it! And I never dared go to sleep, lest he should discover it. You haven't that trial, Grace."

"I think I should rather like it," she said. "Of course it would be tiresome, you know; but I would like to feel that I was helping, and that my opinion was worth something."

"You ought to have married Louis's friend, the country parson," said Mrs. Thayer. "Did he give you a temperance lecture this morning? I thought he would never go."

"I like him; Fanny, of course," said the young lady, blushing a little, "not as I like Horace; but I think he is good and noble. You should have heard him tell what a work he is doing over in Grantley, quite alone, too, trying to save the young men of the place from intemperance.   It made me long to do some good in the world. My life seems very useless and selfish to me."

"You were always an enthusiast, dear. When you were a little girl you used to talk about going on a mission; and I am not sure now, but if some good missionary from the South Sea Islands, or the Gaboon River, lately bereaved by ship-fever, or small-pox, of his third partner, should appeal to you, you would consider it a call of Heaven, and give up all your hopes of happiness in the path Providence has marked out for you, to make victim number four on his list. My dear sister, let me tell you your mission. You will occupy, as Horace Landon's wife, a high social position. You will have wealth at your command, and you may wield all this power for good. I don't like to hear you talk of doubts and fears. A girl with your brilliant prospects should anticipate nothing but happiness. You do not appreciate your success, Gracie. Half the girls in the city are envying you. Mr. Landon is considered a great catch; and he has been so long in society, and is so much of a ladies' man, that every eligible girl in his set has had hopes at one time or another of securing him."

"Fanny," said Grace, abruptly, "did Louis love any one before he loved you?"

"No, indeed," she said, laughing; "and the funniest

thing about it was, that he was principled against ministers marrying young; thought they ought to get well settled in their profession, and all that; but during his last year in the seminary he saw me—I was visiting Aunt Benson, you know, that winter—and he not only forgot all his good resolutions, but was in such haste to marry, that he did not even wait to find a parish, and we boarded two months at father's before he was settled in the ministry."

The recollection of those early days brought a very soft light to the young wife's eyes; and Grace, watching her, gave a little sigh. Then she came and sat on the carpet at her sister's feet, and laid her head in her lap.

"I am going to tell you something, Fanny," she said. "When Horace says the sweetest, tenderest things to me, I cannot help thinking that he has said them to other girls before me; and one night I asked him, Had he ever loved any one as he loved me? and he tried to turn it off at first; and when I pressed him, he seemed almost angry, and said, 'Let the dead past bury its dead,' and was a little moody the rest of the evening. I have no 'dead past' to bury," said the girl with a sob, "and I do want my husband's whole heart."

"Now, Grace," said Mrs. Thayer, "you are making yourself foolishly unhappy. Not one girl in a hundred has her husband's heart in the sense in which you mean it. Boys have their foolish fancies, and their first loves, as they have the measles and the hooping-cough ; and when they come to man's estate, with their judgment mature, and their taste cultivated, they know far better what they want than in the flush of boyish passion. A man often makes for his first choice a foolish one, which he regrets all his life."

"Did Louis?" said her sister, mischievously.

"Grace, you know what I mean. I am speaking of what often occurs. Ours was an exceptional case. Do talk common sense."

"Wouldn't that be taking an unfair advantage of you, dear?" she replied. "Now, Fanny, don't be vexed. I did not mean to be sharp. Yes, I know I ought to be a happy girl, and I am. Good-night, dear."

"I wish they were married," said Mrs. Thayer to her husband. "Grace is peculiar. I am almost afraid she will change her mind."

"I wish she would," said Mr. Thayer.

"Louis!"

"I never liked the match, Fanny. He is brilliant, and rich, and talented. I have heard him argue, on the wrong side of the question, with an acuteness of sophistry and sarcasm that Dr. Johnson himself might envy. But I have no confidence in his principles. Grace is a dear girl, and she deserves a better husband."

"Yes," said Mrs. Thayer with some bitterness, "you

would like to have her throw herself away on that poor country minister."

"I should like," said her husband, "to see her the wife of a good man."

CHAPTER X.

THE DRUNKARD'S CURSE.

"Will it not grieve thee to see thy whole parish come bellowing after thee to hell, crying out, 'This we may thank thee for?' I say, look to thyself, lest thou cry out when it is too late, 'Send Lazarus to my people, my friends, my children, my congregation to whom I preached, and whom I beguiled through my folly. . . Send him to the town in which I did preach last, lest I be the cause of their damnation.'"— BUNYAN.

WHEN Mr. Landon brought Grace home, after her week's visit in the city, he narrowly escaped a second encounter with Crazy Joe. The man was at work in the front yard, under Dr. Willoughby's direction, protecting some shrubbery from the severity of the season. He was talking softly, now to himself, and now to the plant which, with strong, skilful hands, he tenderly wrapped from the cold, the minister standing by, when the sleigh stopped at the door. Joe looked up, and, recognizing its occupant, began to exhibit signs of angry excitement, when Dr. Willoughby caught his arm.

"Joe," said he, very sternly, "stop it instantly. I heard of your treatment of this gentleman the other day. Now, I want to say to you, once for all, if ever again, by look, or gesture, or word, you behave discourteously to him, you will incur my severe displeasure. Do you understand me, sir? Mr. Landon is my friend, and my daughter's friend, and shall be treated with the greatest possible respect. Unless you want to make me very angry, you will never give me occasion to mention this subject again."

This reproof, administered in Dr. Willoughby's most dignified manner, struck terror to the culprit's heart. All the respect and awe the curly-headed boy felt years ago in his instructor's presence, all the shame and confusion he experienced when reproved for an imperfect lesson, the gray-headed man underwent now at this rebuke. He put up both hands entreatingly, and his face expressed bewilderment and fear.

" Parson Willoughby," he said, " don't you be angry with me; I couldn't bear that, you know. Oh, I couldn't bear that. I will do all you say. I would bow down and worship the beast with the seven heads and the ten horns, if you should bid me, for you know you are going to speak for me in the great day. You promised. You will never forget. Whatever I do, you will never forget that, Parson Willoughby."

" I shall not be angry with you, Joe, unless you give me cause," he replied. " Come, to show your repentance, bow respectfully to Mr. Landon as he passes."

Dr. Willoughby, as he spoke, stepped forward to meet his daughter and her companion as they approached; and Joe, endeavouring to comply with his patron's wish, advanced a step, made a horrible contortion of face, in his attempt to smile, then shuddered from head to foot, and ran round the house as fast as he could go. Mr. Landon seemed disconcerted at the man's second appearance.

"Why do you keep that crazy fellow about the place?" he said to the Doctor. "He looks very much to me as if he had been in State's prison; and that cut on his jaw tells of some desperate fight he has had with his keeper. Depend upon it, he is a dangerous man. He will do mischief one of these days."

"I can control him with a look, Mr. Landon," the minister answered. "His unaccountable attack upon you, the other day, I will take good care shall not be repeated. You are naturally prejudiced against him on that account, but I assure you poor Joe is as innocent a creature as ever lived. He has been cruelly treated, no doubt, and they have much to answer for who have made him what he is."

"Father," said Grace, that evening, "I believe Horace is actually afraid of Crazy Joe. How ridiculous! as if he would hurt anybody."

It happened that for some reason Joe slept at Dr. Willoughby's that night, occupying a small chamber at the back of the house. Going to her room late in the evening, Grace heard him at his devotions, and standing at the head of the kitchen stairs she could easily distinguish the words.

"Oh my Lord," said Joe, "thou knowest that when

thy servant David kept his father's sheep, there came
a lion and a bear, and took a lamb out of the flock,
and thy servant went after him, and smote him, and
delivered the lamb out of his mouth. And now, oh my
Lord, help me, thine unworthy servant, to deliver this
little white lamb out of the paw of the lion, and out
of the paw of the bear, and out of the hand of this
uncircumcised Philistine, even as did thy servant
David when he smote him, and slew him, so that he
fell upon his face to the earth. Do this, O Lord, and
get great glory to thy name for ever and ever. Amen."

"What does he mean?" thought Grace—a vague
feeling of uneasiness stealing over her at the solemnity
and earnestness of the petition. Then he broke out
singing in his clear, sweet voice :—

> "He caught him straightway by the beard;
> 'Now die, thou dog!' he cried.
> So perish all God's enemies
> Who have His name defied."

Grace shuddered, she knew not why, and stole away
to her room.

She went the next day to carry a basket of provisions to John Davis's family, who were again in
great destitution. This man's ruin was complete
and dreadful. He rose from his sick-bed, with
just strength enough left in his rickety, half-palsied
body, to be driven by a slavish will to the gratification
of his appetite, seeking every day, in one and another

of the places in the village where liquor was sold, for the poison that was hurrying him to his grave. Filth, and poverty, and disease, and guilt, were all that remained to this being created in God's image.

There was no answer when Grace knocked at John Davis's door, and she entered softly. The room, bare and fireless, was deserted, but in the small bedroom beyond, where a few weeks before Dr. Willoughby had talked with the husband and father, she found the children playing about the bed where their mother lay.

"Mrs. Davis," said Grace, hastening to her side, "I did not know you were sick."

Jenny Davis turned her head, and drew up the sheet so as to cover a part of her face.

"My head aches," she said. "Tim, put down the baby, and set a chair for Miss Willoughby."

"Let me help myself, Mrs. Davis. Will you bring me the baby, Tim?"

The small boy, who had recently effected an entrance into Mrs. Willoughby's kitchen in so unprecedented a manner, came forward at the young lady's call, and put the baby in her lap. Recognizing Grace the instant she entered the room, with a great appearance of secrecy he was endeavouring, in dumb show, to impart to his brothers and sisters the fact of his previous acquaintance, and its happy results. The baby, pale and puny, and so lank and long that the small boy could hardly carry it without dragging some part of it on the floor, taking its poor little blue thumb from its mouth, and not liking the change of position, set up a dismal wailing.

"Did it want its own bubby?" said Tim, and the patient arms opened again to receive their burden.

"He's a dretful good baby, if you please, ma'am," said Tim, apologetically, and fondly stroking the scant, white hair on the baby's head; "but he wants his dinner so bad, and ma can't nurse him, 'cause—."

"Bub," said Mrs. Davis, hastily, "fetch me a drink of water."

"You are very thirsty," said Grace, as she saw how eagerly the sick woman drank. "Would you like a cup of tea?"

"We have no tea in the house," said Jenny Davis.

"I have some in my basket," she replied, and going to the table she began to take out the provisions she had brought. She was instantly surrounded by the children, who pushed and scrambled over each other in their eagerness to see.

"There's bread," said one,—"white bread!"

"And cakes, and butter, and meat!" cried another.

"And 'lasses!" screamed Bub Davis, as Grace opened a small pail and displayed its contents.

"Miss Willoughby," said the mother's weak voice, "never mind about the tea, if you'll give the children a bite of something. They didn't have a hearty break- fast, and I wasn't well enough to cook them any dinner."

"Ma," said Bub Davis, "you know there wasn't anything to cook, only the sour meal, and it's *so* sour."

"Run and get me a knife quick, Bub," said Grace.

She cut thick slices of bread and meat, and distributed to the hungry group. They ate like famished wolves, tearing with teeth and nails, and quarrelling for the fragments they scattered in their unseemly haste. The baby choked itself, and grew black in the face, but Tim, in his frantic hunger, did not heed his charge. Grace took the little creature in her lap, and, dipping morsels of bread in the pail of molasses, she fed the hungry child. A sound from the bed drew her attention, and she saw that the poor mother was crying, very softly at first, then with irrepressible emotion, until her sobs shook the crazy bedstead on which she was lying.

Grace put the baby in his brother's arms, and, going to the bedside, laid her hands on the sick woman's head, and smoothed the thin hair that was already turning gray, though Jenny Davis was a young woman.

"God knows all, Mrs. Davis," said Grace.

"My starving children!" said the poor woman, and broke into fresh sobs, and while Grace stood at her side, striving by the gentle touch of her hand to express the sympathy she knew not how to put into words, the drunkard's wife lifted her face, and showed the mark of the cruel hand that laid her on her sick-bed in the midst of her famishing children. Then there came a noise at the outer door. Bob Davis caught up the baby, and ran with it to the recess behind his mother's bed. The others followed quickly, and the sick woman hastily dried her eyes, and drew up the sheet so as to hide her bruised face, and all was explained in two words uttered under Tim's breath, "Pa's coming!"

A moment later, John Davis entered the room. Grace had seen this man often in her father's house. He was a carpenter by trade, and when he was a steady, sober man, Dr. Willoughby used frequently to employ him to fit a lock, or mend a refractory door. She remembered him as a quiet, inoffensive man, somewhat silent and unsocial; but perfectly civil and respectful in manner. Once, she remembered, he brought with him a little red-headed boy, and, setting the little fellow on a heap of shavings in the barn, gave him his rule to play with, and turned round from his work now and then to chirrup and whistle to his baby boy. He stood in the doorway now, ragged, filthy, bloated, and heavy-eyed, and looked about him in a sullen and ill-tempered way, till his eye fell upon Grace.

He knew her instantly.

"What's she doing here?" he said to his wife with an ugly scowl.

"She came to help us," the wife said, timidly, "to bring some things for the children."

"I'll have none of her help," he said. "Do you

hear?"—to Grace—"we want none of your help. Go home, and never darken my doors again. Your father's a cantin' old hypocrite, and I'll tell him so to his face, if I get the chance. He can preach, and pray, and whine over rich sinners, and slip them all into heaven with his priestcraft; but he'll see a poor man go down to hell before he'll lift a finger to save him."

Dr. Willoughby's daughter rose from her seat, pale and trembling; but the furious man stood in the doorway, and she dared not pass him.

"Curse him!" said John Davis, "curse the proud old aristocrat, that calls it religion to drink wine and brandy, and a sin for a poor man to take his pint of whisky now and then. Curse him, I say, and make him feel in his grand house, and under his shiny broadcloth, every evil he threatened me with in my rags. I want he should drink the cup I'm a-drinkin'; I want he should feel in his own flesh and blood, and in his body and bones, the curse he's left me to bear; I want he should be humbled and disgraced, and ashamed to show his head among decent folks—that's what I want. And when the pit opens its mouth to take me in, I'll tell every soul there, that a cantin', hypocritical old parson, named Willoughby, sent me there."

He stood aside to let her pass, when her basket and the food that remained on the table caught his eye.

"Did you bring those things?" he said.

She made him no answer, for she was too much frightened to speak. He was throwing the fragments into the basket, when Bub Davis crept from his retreat.

"Oh, if you please, pa," said the child.

With one kick of his heavy boot, he sent the boy half across the room.

"For shame!" said Grace, forgetting her fear. "Oh, I wish I was a man, just for one minute!" and then to prove that she was very much of a woman, she began to cry, and ran out of the house as fast as she could.

CHAPTER XI.

WHO'S TO BLAME?

" At everybody as passed that road,
  A stick, or a stone, this old cove throwed ;
  And venever he flung his stick, or his stone,
  He'd set up a song—' Let me alone,
  Let me alone, for I loves to shy
  These bits of things at the passers by ;
  Let me alone, for I've got your tin,
  And lots of other traps snugly in.
  I'm a quiet old cove,' says he, with a groan,
  ' All I axes is—Let me alone.' "—BROWNELL.

JOHN DAVIS died in his next fit of *delirium tremens*. When the small funeral procession, with Dr. Willoughby at its head, passed into the cemetery, a group of idlers were sitting upon the piazza in front of Briggs's saloon just opposite.

" Well," said one of them, taking his pipe from his mouth, " we've seen the last of poor John. I little thought, when I worked alongside of him at the same bench, that he'd come to this. A strong, hearty young fellow he was in them days, as ever handled a saw. But John was his own worst enemy. Well, yonder he goes on his last journey. What will he do where he's gone if he can't get any whisky? They say he called for it with his last breath."

"No, he didn't," said an old man in the company, "for my Bill was there the night he died, and he said he held up his right hand and cursed the minister just afore the breath left his body. And there couldn't nobody have been kinder to him all through his sickness than Dr. Willoughby and his folks. Miss Willoughby, she fixed up all kinds of notions, and Miss Grace couldn't do enough for them children, and they say the Doctor went in and tried to have some kind of good talk with him afore he died; but John swore at him awful, and wouldn't have him in the house. It does beat all, the spite he took to that good man."

"Well, if you look at it," said the first speaker, "it ain't so strange after all, for it does seem plaguey hard in the Doctor to refuse to put his name alongside of John's on that paper. Why, I don't pretend to any religion myself, and I like my glass of grog as well as the next man; but if John Davis had said to me, 'Larkins, if you'll quit drinkin', I will,' how long do you reckon it would have been before my name went on to that paper? And I've heard the minister go on by the hour, about Christian charity, and brotherly love, and all the rest. Practice is better than preachin', I say, and it looks to me as though the minister was somehow responsible for poor John Davis's death."

Briggs, the keeper of the saloon, listened, well-pleased, to this speech, and nodded his head approvingly at its conclusion.

K

"That he is," said Mr. Briggs.   "I told 'em when John made his offer, sittin' in that very chair, says I, 'You won't get the minister to sign that paper;' and they didn't.   'It ain't them that preaches and prays the loudest,' says I, 'that's the most willin' to make sacrifices for other people's good.'"

"No, no," cried the voice of a new-comer,—for the brief service was concluded, and several, who had followed the drunkard to his grave, joined the company on the piazza,—"No, no; it's Briggs that makes the sacrifices, when he takes the children's shoes for whisky, and the old woman's best bed-quilts to fill up the empty jug."

The laugh that followed this sally was not agreeable to Mr. Briggs, and he scowled angrily in the direction of the speaker; but the young man happening to be a good customer, he swallowed his rage from motives of policy, and answered him with a bland smile.

"You must have your joke, Mr. Clapp," said the rumseller; "but I put it to this 'ere company if I haven't always conducted my business on principles of equity and justice.   A trade's a trade, and I'm an honest man, earnin' my children's bread in an honest way; but I don't never sell liquor to a man when he's had as much as is good for him.   I've had a long experience in the business, gentlemen, and I've learned to be very careful."

"Go it, Briggs!" said the young man again.   "Nobody ever gets drunk on your premises.   Oh, no!

You are a dreadful abused man, ain't you? Folks get their liquor somewheres else, and come to your place drunk, and you have to take all the blame. Come, what's the use of talkin' that way? You might as well own up. If it wasn't for your place, and more in West Union just like it, the sexton wouldn't be fillin' up that grave yonder. It's a mean business, and you know it; but folks will drink, and you might as well make money out of it as the next man. Ain't that so?"

"On my honour, gentlemen," said Mr. Briggs, "I've told Davis, time and time again, he took more than was good for him. In fact, I've sold it to him for the last six months under protest, and often sent him away without a drop when he has come here beggin' for it."

"Of course you have," rejoined Clapp, "when he hadn't any money, or old shoes, or bed-quilts to pay for it with."

Mr. Briggs grew very red in the face, and a party of schoolboys, attracted by the loud tones of the talkers, joined their shrill voices to the laugh that followed. When it subsided, the man who had first introduced the discussion again took his pipe from his mouth, and spoke in defence of his friend.

"Now, look here, Clapp," said he, "you are too plaguey hard on Briggs. He's an honest fellow, and he's followin' an honest calling. He's just as good a right to sell whisky as Deacon Riley over the way has to sell grain and groceries. He gives you an honest meal, don't he, for an honest penny? You ain't obleeged to buy his liquor. You can take it, or you can leave it. I believe in free trade. I done all I could to oppose a law that interferes with the personal rights, and individual liberty, and reputation, and property of the citizens of this 'ere glorious republic. And I'm glad to say, gentlemen, that that law is a dead letter in the town of West Union to-day. There ain't a man that voted for it dares to enforce it. That's so. And now I say again, what I said afore, Davis was his own worst enemy. If he drinked himself to death, I don't see as 'twas Briggs's fault, allowin' he got all his liquor here, which he didn't. If there's anybody besides himself to blame, it's the man that refused to put his name alongside of his on that paper. As I look at it, 'twas the turnin'-pint in Davis's life, and the one that wouldn't help him up was the one that kept him down."

There was a stir in the crowd, and Joe Martin pushed his way toward the speaker.

"Here's Joe! Give us a speech, Joe," the school-boys cried.

"Yes, a speech! a speech!"

With great gravity, Joe mounted a pile of boards conveniently near. He was dressed in his holiday clothes to attend the funeral, and was really gorgeous in his gay neck-tie and perfumed handkerchief.

"Friends, countrymen, and lovers," said Joe, "hear me for my cause—."

"Now, Joe, that ain't fair," said one of the schoolboys. " We don't want Shakespoke to-day ; we want a real blood-and-thunder, tiptop, teetotal temperance talk—."

" Be quiet," said another. " Joe knows what he is about."

Not at all disturbed by the interruption, Joe commenced again.

" Friends, countrymen, and lovers, hear me for my cause, and be silent that you may hear. There be some present, who have called a good man's honour in question this day. Is there in this assembly any dear friend of John Davis? I say to him that Parson Willoughby's love was no less than his. Then, if they ask me why he refused to save him, I answer, it was not that he loved Davis less, but that he loved his principles more. When this man was virtuous, he honoured him; when he was unfortunate, he pitied him ; when he was in error, he admonished him. There's honour for his virtue, pity for his misfortune, and reproof for his error. My noble patron rejects the abstinence yoke, as made by men who would bring him into bondage. Who is here so base that would be a bondman? If any, speak, for him has Parson Willoughby offended. He believes wine to be one of the meats which God has created, and which is to be received with thanksgiving. Is any here so vile that he would not be a Christian ? If any, speak, for him has Parson Willoughby offended. I pause for a reply—None?"

"Nary one, Joe," said a voice from the crowd.
"Then none has he offended—

Do any ask the cause of this man's death?
I answer, poison, liquid fire, and twice-distilled damnation,
Which, swallowed, takes away the senses, drives one mad,
And makes a man a block, a beast, a fool,
And turns him down to hell.   But who's to blame?
Not Briggs!   Briggs follows but an honest calling,—
A useful citizen, a good, hard-working man,
Whose little ones lie warm beneath the drunkard's quilt;
Grow plump and strong, fed on his children's bread!
Moreover, Briggs doth tell us, on his honour,
(And we all know Briggs is an *honourable* man,—
So are they all *honourable* men,)
He gave this poor man poison under protest;
Yes; many times has served him sore against his will;
And often (when there were no quilts, or children's shoes)
Turned the poor devil, thirsting, from his door.
He tells you on his honour,—*honourable man!*
Whose long experience in this honest trade
Has taught him wise discretion,—he will give
To no man more, when he has had enough.
Good friends, though you be raging with the thirst of hell,
You'll find him iron, adamant, and steel—
(Unless, indeed, you bring the goodwife's quilt, the little
    children's shoes)."

Mr. Briggs here interposed.
"You quit that!" he shouted, advancing menacingly
upon the speaker. "Gentlemen, will you allow this
crazy fellow to insult me on my own premises?"
"Fair play!" said Clapp. "Free trade, and free

speech. That's the talk! Joe Martin has as good a right to proclaim his sentiments as Briggs has to carry on his business. Go it, Joe! I'll see you through!"

The speaker stood quiet, and apparently unmoved during this conflict of feeling, his face relapsing into the troubled expression habitual to it. When called upon, he roused himself, and thus continued:—

"Good friends, sweet friends, be quiet, pray!
They that have done this deed are *honourable* men,
And will, no doubt, with reasons answer you.
Yet bear with me; my heart is yonder in the graveyard.
You all did know this man, who, lying there,
Despised, dishonoured, in his lonely grave,
With none so poor to do him reverence,
Once walked these streets erect and strong.
Oh, what a fall was there, my countrymen!—
My masters, if I were disposed to stir
Your hearts and minds to mutiny and rage,
I'd tell you what he was, and what he is.
Oh, I would take you to the drunkard's home!
Show you a woman, sitting in her rags,
Some little children, wailing in their sleep
For cold and hunger,—and anon,
Lead you to where, in the brilliant-lighted room—
(Good friends, not *here*,—this place is kept
By such an *honest, honourable* man—
But, somewhere)—where a fiend in human shape
Takes all a poor man's earnings in exchange for rum;
Ay, gives him poison, for his children's bread.
If I should show you this, oh, what would come of it?
You are not wood, you are not stones, but men,

And, being men, it would inflame you, it would make you
    mad;
You'd rise in fury, rush to yonder den—
(Nay, pardon, friends, the word slipped unawares,
 These walls enshrine an *honest, virtuous* trade)—
I say, you'd go armed with a righteous law,
No matter where,—where'er such deeds are done,
Drag out the wretch (not Briggs, you know,
An 'honest,' '*honourable*,' 'hard-working' man,
But him I spoke of,—he who coins his gold
Out of the groans of children, and the tears of wives),
You'd drag him out, I say, to public shame,
Unbind his barrels, stave his hogsheads in,
And bid the unwilling earth drink up his rum."

He bowed with great gravity, descended from his
elevated position, and walked slowly away.

CHAPTER XII.

PREACHING WITHOUT NOTES.

> " Only men in their extremity
> Prove what they are,—what their ability."—DANIEL.

T was a warm Sabbath evening in early summer. The bell of the Wilmot Street Church was tolling for evening service, when Mrs. Thayer entered her husband's study.

" Not ready, Louis," she said, " and the bell tolling ? I thought you would be waiting for me in the hall."

He rose hurriedly from his chair.

" Is it so late ?" he said. " I have been sleeping, I believe. I have not heard the bell."

She watched him anxiously, as he threw off the study-gown in which he had been sitting, caught his sermon from the table, and made other hasty preparations for departure; and she noticed his unsteady hand, with an indecision and lack of purpose in his movements, which she attributed to nervous haste. But in the hall, he searched about the rack for his hat, though the gas was lighted, and it hung upon its accustomed peg. She handed it to him with an exclamation of impatience, gave him a keen searching look, and hurried him into the street. A moment later, at some inequality in the pavement, he stumbled, lost his balance, and only saved himself from falling by leaning heavily against her shoulder. She stopped short then, and turned to him in a quick, excited way.

"You will have to go back, Louis," she said. "There is no help for it. You are in no condition to come before an audience to-night. I must tell Mr. Barstow you are taken suddenly ill."

"There is nothing the matter," he said; but as he spoke he stumbled again.

"Louis," she said, in great distress, "I beg you not to attempt to preach to-night. You cannot do it. Oh, what shall I do?" for he did not heed her, and they turned that moment from a side street into the main avenue of the city, thronged with people going to the different churches.

"Now, husband, we are not so late, after all," said old Mrs. Barstow, as, puffing and wheezing with the haste they had made, the worthy couple came up close behind them, "for here is our own dear minister, who we all know is a pattern of punctuality. Mr. Thayer, I am delighted to find myself in your company. My husband has been fretting all the way, because I kept him waiting a moment after the bell began to toll. But, dear me, if we keep with the minister, I think we shall walk straight."

The minister's wife at that moment was exerting all the strength of her woman's arm to uphold the crooked steps of their spiritual guide. She hastened to reply for him.

"Mr. Thayer was so deep in his meditation," she said, "that he did not hear the bell, and for aught I know, would still be in his study if I had not called him."

"Ah," said Mr. Barstow; "see what it is to have a good wife to supplement a man's deficiencies. Well, it always frets me to be behind time; but we are safe to-night, that is certain."

The house was full. The bell had ceased tolling, and a deep stillness pervaded the waiting assembly. Mrs. Thayer felt, as they walked up the aisle, that every eye was upon her husband. She could no longer uphold his steps, but she kept close to him till she reached her own seat. Then she watched him breathlessly as he went on alone, walking very slowly. She trembled when he reached the two or three steps leading up to the platform where his desk stood; but he ascended them in safety, and dropping into his chair, buried his face in his hands, while the great organ swelled, and quavered, and pealed forth its triumphant tones. Mrs. Thayer leaned forward in her seat to request Mr. Coleman, who sat just before her, to see that the sexton opened every ventilator in the house, explaining that Mr. Thayer was not well, and would feel the closeness of the air. She put into his hand— her own trembling a little in spite of her self-control —her bottle of smelling-salts. Would he send that up to the desk? She had forgotten to give it to her husband at the door.

While Mr. Coleman was absent on her errand the organ ceased playing. The minister had not changed his position, but sat motionless, his face covered by his hands. To Frances Thayer, the silence that succeeded was horrible. She wondered if the people in the next slip could hear her heart beat. Was he asleep? too far gone to arouse himself? what did it mean? At length, when others began to think the interval of silence long, Mr. Thayer raised his head, and came forward to the desk. His wife dared not lift her eyes to his face, and she heard no sound, but knew by the bowed heads around her, that, by the motion of his hand, he had called the assembly to prayer. Then, that sweet, rich voice, which was one of Louis Thayer's peculiar charms, came to her ear, tremulous, almost broken in tone, but so distinct as to be heard to the farthest corner of the house. The wife listened as she had never listened to a prayer before; and when she found that the few brief sentences were coherent and well expressed, she thanked God and took courage. But her heart sank again when she saw him turning the leaves of the Bible in an uncertain and purposeless manner, and she knew the portion of Scripture he had intended to read that evening had gone from his mind. When his voice broke the stillness again, though he chose the Psalm at random, there was to her a strange significance in the second verse.

"Truly God is good to Israel, to such as are of a clean heart.

"But as for me, my feet were almost gone, my steps had well-nigh slipped."

Of the song of praise and the prayer that followed she heard very little. She prayed herself, and more earnestly than for many a day, that her husband might receive help in his hour of need, for she knew the great trial of the evening was at hand. She saw how closely he bent over his hymn-book, hesitating more than once, remembered his indistinctness of vision in the brightly lighted hall at home, and trembled as she thought of what was to come. "For he will never be able to read his sermon," she said to herself. It seemed for a few moments that all her fears were to be realized, for Mr. Thayer, after giving out his text, and slowly repeating the two or three opening sentences of his sermon, hesitated, repeated his last words, stumbled in his speech, put his hand to his brow with a con fused look, and while his wife, in an agony of apprehension, was waiting for what was to come next, deliberately laid aside his manuscript, and closed the Bible.

Dr. Willoughby, in kindly counsel with his son, had frequently urged him to accustom himself, while a young man, to occasionally preach without notes, alleging it to be a mistake in his own professional career, that he had never practised extemporaneous speaking, but had strictly confined himself to a written discourse. This advice the young minister had not followed, and it was, therefore, with unmingled surprise that Mrs. Thayer listened this evening, as, standing in an attitude of perfect ease and self-possession, one hand resting upon the closed Bible, and looking down with a strange light in his dark eyes upon the multitude of upturned faces, her husband went on with his sermon. There was no uncertainty of purpose now, no hesitation, no faltering. The tones of his voice, always sweet and melodious, and charming his audience by their mere cadence and flow, to-night fell upon their ears with a peculiar power. Now rising, now falling, through many gradations of sound, and as the medium of the eloquent language, and wave after wave of thought that succeeded each other in this strange sermon, they were irresistible.

His audience listened almost breathless, and at times bowed as one man ; and when the voice at length ceased, there was a stillness as profound as if an oracle had spoken. And one and another said, as they came out of church, in half-hushed accents, for the spell was still upon them, that the minister had never preached like that before. Surely, if ever inspiration breathed through mortal lips, they had listened to God's teaching that night.

Bethiah Emmersly, in her garret, remained so long upon her rheumatic knees in grateful prayer to God, that she lay awake half the night with the pain, but solaced herself with happy thoughts. "For he must be a great deal better," thought Bethiah ; "with his eyes so bright, and that beautiful colour in his lips,—

and if he's took it regular, it's time the spiced wine did him good."

When the minister, at the close of the service, joined his wife at the door of her slip, Mr. Coleman bustled up to return to the lady her bottle of salts.

"I did not send it up," he said; "for the service commenced before I found the sexton. That man's always out of the way when he's most wanted. But I rather think that sermon was pungent enough without salts. A most excellent discourse, Mr. Thayer. And see here, I told Barstow the other day, we should have to put a couple more burners to that drop-light by the desk, or some night our minister would complain that he couldn't read his sermon; but I concluded to-night to do nothing about it, and perhaps turn the gas down a trifle now and then. Mrs. Thayer, your husband needs to be put in a tight spot occasionally, to bring out his reserved force."

Near the door stood an elderly gentleman in spectacles, evidently a country clergyman, waiting to speak with Mr. Thayer. "He was taking an old man's liberty," he said, when he had introduced himself. "The interest he felt in young men of his profession must be his apology. He had listened with delighted attention," &c. "Under any circumstances, the discourse would have been a remarkable production; but considering the fact that it was called out on the spur of the moment, it deserved unlimited praise. But, my dear young friend," said the old gentleman, with great solemnity, "listen to one piece of advice. I noticed that the sermon you found it impossible to read this evening was written upon blue paper. Mr. Thayer, burn every quire of blue paper in your possession. Write your sermons on clear, white paper, with a wide margin, and on every other line. If you do not, sir, by the time you are sixty years old, they will be utterly useless to you. I am a living witness to the truth of what I say—a warning and example to my young brethren in the ministry. I am wearing green spectacles to-night, sir, because, when I was a young man, I wrote my sermons on blue paper."

Mr. Thayer and his wife walked home in silence. She felt the arm upon which her hand rested tremble; but his steps did not falter. She followed him to his study, instead, as was her custom, leaving him alone a few moments while she went to the nursery to see that her little ones were safely settled for the night. Her mind at rest on this point, it was her habit to come to him, and talk over the events of the day; give her own and others' opinions of the sermons, and beguile him by her presence and words of cheer, from the despondency that was apt to settle upon him after the labours of the day.

But to-night she went with him to the study. He sank wearily in his chair as soon as he entered the room, and his wife, carefully closing and locking the door, came and stood by his side. She glanced at the table on which an empty glass was standing.

"Oh Louis!" she said, and burst into tears.

Frances Thayer was not given to the melting mood. To her sister's blue eyes the tears came almost as readily as the smiles to her mouth and the dimples to her cheeks; but during their four years of married life Louis Thayer had seldom seen his wife weep. The sight disturbed him exceedingly. He raised his face, very pale and weary, now that·the excitement of the occasion was over, and looked at her with great tenderness and sorrow.

"Fanny," he said, "it shall never happen again."

"Oh, I hope not. I think I could not live through such another hour of anxiety and fear. When you faltered and stopped, and put away your sermon, I thought it was all over, and felt ready to sink through the floor; then when you overcame the difficulty, and you did it splendidly, the surprise and reaction were so great that I could hardly control my feelings. I felt frightened and ashamed, and proud and triumphant, almost in the same breath. Louis, how did you do it? God helped you, I am sure."

"I am afraid my help came from another source," said the minister, bitterly.

She looked at the empty glass again.

"Promise not to be vexed if I speak plainly, Louis."

"Was I ever vexed with my wife for her plain speaking?"

"Oh, no; but this seems like an interference in a matter of which every one is his own best judge. But, once or twice before, I have felt afraid of the very thing that came near happening to-night, because you are so easily affected by stimulants. I think you should never touch wine or brandy, Louis, before going into the pulpit. You have such a peculiarly sensitive organization, that you cannot bear what most men would scarcely feel. I do not know how much you drank to-night; but I presume the same quantity would not have affected father in the least; but now that you know your own weakness, and especially after to-night's experience, I am sure you will agree with me that you cannot be too careful."

"You have expressed my own convictions, Fanny; and I agree with you so perfectly, that I believe my safety lies in my never drinking a glass of wine or brandy as long as I live."

"Louis, you know I meant nothing of the sort. You jump to the other extreme. Because you have made a single mistake, there is no reason that you should punish yourself the rest of your natural life. Of course you will drink brandy and wine, as you have done, in moderation. They have been very beneficial to you. I counselled abstinence before going into the pulpit, because you are so easily affected. After your day's work is over, and you can sit here quietly in your chair and doze off the effect, it is quite another thing. You know father takes his glass of wine after the evening meeting, and calls it his 'Sunday night-cap.' Do you suppose he would do it if it was wrong?"

"I entertain a great respect for your father's opinion, Fanny, and I have no disposition to judge him; but for *me*, after to-night's experience, is there any safe course but total abstinence?"

"I hate that word. Louis, don't go back to those crude notions you entertained when we were married. I am afraid the next thing you will propose to do will be to sign the pledge."

"Why not?"

"Why not? Because I hope my husband has moral strength enough to exercise reason and self-control in the regulation of a mere bodily appetite, without the help of a written pledge. Because I hope he is courageous enough, when he is tempted by a sin, to give it battle, and not to run from it. Brave men fight. Cowards fly. And because, when as a Christian he vowed to keep the body under, to be temperate in all things, and to let his moderation be known to all men, he took upon himself a more binding obligation than any total abstinence pledge."

Frances Thayer was never more her father's daughter than when she repeated these arguments, which she had many times heard from his lips.

"I think I see you," she said; "*you, Louis Thayer*, putting yourself on an equality with reformed drunkards—miserable creatures rescued from the gutter—proclaiming to the world that you cannot govern your

appetite, and must resort to total abstinence. Think
of being obliged to refuse an innocent glass of wine at
a wedding, or a social gathering, with holy horror
depicted on your face! I am only a woman, but I
should despise myself if my reason, and common sense,
and Christian principle, were not sufficient helps in
the maintenance of any virtue, without resorting to a
pledge.   But I have wearied you nearly to death, dear,
with my lecture.   I am sure I have said enough, and
more than enough, to deter you from any rash purpose you may have formed respecting that hateful
total abstinence pledge."

CHAPTER XIII.

WILL HE COME, MOTHER?

" With patient eyes fixed on the door,
    She waited, hoping ever,
Till death's dark wall rose cold between
    Her gaze and you for ever.
She heard your footsteps in the breeze,
    And in the wild bees' humming,—
The last breath that she shaped to words
    Said softly, ' Is he coming ? ' "

R. COLEMAN rang his minister's door-bell one day with a hurried peal, and, hastening after the girl who admitted him, met the lady of the house at the parlour door. His usually neat dress was a little disordered, and his face bore marks of watching and grief. He inquired eagerly for Mr. Thayer.

" We want him immediately at my house," he said. " She has asked to have her minister pray with her once more. She is failing fast, Mrs. Thayer,—we are going to lose our little Alice."

" O Mr. Coleman, is it possible! We thought she was better; that the symptoms were all favourable. There must have been a very sudden change."

The usually voluble man could not speak. His lip quivered, and he turned his face away.

"You have my deepest sympathy," she said. "Sit down a moment while I call my husband, and he will return with you."

She ran upstairs to the study. The minister was leaning back in his chair with his eyes closed. The paper he had been reading was on his knees.

"Louis, come quick," she said; "Alice Coleman is dying, and they want you immediately. Her father has come for you. Don't keep him waiting a moment. Why, Louis!"

She stopped suddenly, for her husband did not in any way seem aware of her presence. She went to him, and, laying her hand heavily upon his shoulder, tried to rouse him. He opened his eyes, looked vacantly at her, muttering a few unintelligible words, then his head dropped, and he sank helplessly back. She made no further effort to waken him. Mortification, anger, and contempt followed each other rapidly on her expressive face, and she turned and left the room.

She found Mr. Thayer, she told his afflicted parishioner, too ill with dizziness and headache to leave his room. It was a sudden attack; she hoped it would soon pass off, and he would come the moment he could do so with safety. She spoke calmly, adding many regrets and expressions of sympathy; but when, sorrowful and disappointed, Mr. Coleman went away, she hurried to her room and wept tears of mortification and anger. Toward evening, ascertaining that Alice

Coleman was still living, she went to the kitchen, and prepared with her own hands a bowl of strong coffee, which she took to her husband. He was dozing in his chair, but roused up readily at her summons, drank the refreshing beverage she brought him, and was sufficiently himself to understand the necessity for exertion. Then with soft, cool hands she bathed the aching head, and assisted him to arrange his disordered dress. He accepted these wifely attentions very gratefully and humbly, and professed himself able to go upon his sorrowful errand.

The young girl, who lay dying in her home of luxury that night, had endeared herself greatly to her pastor. An only daughter, and the pet and darling of her father's heart, she had received every advantage that affection and wealth could furnish. She was lovely in every sense of the word, beautiful in person, amiable and affectionate in disposition, and a devoted Christian, but singularly timid and shrinking in her nature. During the last few months, owing partly to this constitutional tendency, and partly to bodily weakness,—for she had gradually failed in health,— she was troubled with distressing doubts respecting her spiritual state. It had been the young pastor's office to administer comfort to her during these seasons of religious despondency,—an office for which he was peculiarly fitted, inasmuch as, through a painful experience of his own, he was familiar with a similar case of mental distress. He had been taught, by a very trying process, and at how vast an expense of suffering and conflict was known only to himself and his God, how to speak a word in season to him that is weary, to be a "guide to the blind, a light to them that are in darkness, a teacher of babes." In Alice Coleman's case, he recognized all the symptoms, and could apply the needed antidote.

He had spent many hours in her sick-room, and a very pleasant relationship existed between the two—of clinging trust and confidence on her part, with reverential love and gratitude for the counsel and comfort he had given her, and upon his, the protecting love of an elder brother, and the regard a faithful pastor feels for the tenderest lamb of his flock. He hurried to her bedside with no common emotions. Such was the sense of power he was conscious of possessing over this virgin soul, that he knew he could dispel any lingering doubts which might oppress her, lead her by the hand to the brink of the river, and make a safe and easy passage for her to the other side.

Alas, it was too late! The eyes that had so eagerly looked for his coming were covered by their veined lids, and the long lashes lay upon her marble cheek. The voice that many times that afternoon had repeated in plaintive tones, "Will he come, mother? O mother, will he come?" was stilled for ever, and the little restless hands he had held in his own many times, soothing her nervousness by the magnetism of his touch, lay folded on her breast.

"O Mr. Thayer!" the mother said, "she wanted you so much! She could not give it up. We explained to her again and again that you were too ill to come, and she would appear satisfied for a few moments, but her mind wandered a little, and she would forget, and go back to it again and again. She thought we were cruel not to send for you; that we had not told you how much she wanted you to come. She never once blamed you, sir. Oh, how she loved you! Your name was on her lips only a few moments before she died."

The minister knelt beside the dead girl, and, dear as Alice Coleman was to her father's and mother's heart, there had been no such bitter tears shed over her as the remorseful man shed that day.

"How he loved her!" the mother said,—"our dear minister. What a tender, affectionate heart he has!"

"You found her living?" Mrs. Thayer said, anxiously, when her husband returned from the house of mourning.

He shook his head, for at that moment he could not speak. Then Frances Thayer thought it her duty to improve the occasion. The cruel words she said need not be repeated here. There came a time when she remembered them only too well herself, for by reason of after events they burned themselves deep into her soul; but she felt no pity then. She knew her husband well, his delicate sensibility, his tender conscience, his love of the truth, and hatred of all that savoured of hypocrisy and deception, and his scrupulous anxiety to fulfil the duties of his high calling. But this one trusted friend, to whom he should have confided all the remorse, the agony, and the deep repentance of that hour, with the certainty that her woman's heart would love, and pity, and forgive, only used her power to torture him afresh. Her pitiless eyes looked into his inmost soul. She saw every wound his sin had made, and she probed them till they throbbed again with agony. She put into language the bitter self-condemnation he felt when he knelt by the bedside of the dead girl. She did not hesitate to accuse him of acting a lie, inasmuch as Sabbath after Sabbath, from the sacred desk he taught a religion that enjoins upon its followers to keep themselves pure, unspotted from the world, to abase the flesh, and exalt the spirit, while yielding in secret to the indulgence of one of the lowest appetites of our poor fallen nature.

She used his brilliant popularity to wound him. She demanded how he dared stand in his high place and turn his face to heaven; how he could accept the reputation of sanctity his people gave him, and hold himself up as their pattern and guide, enslaved as he was fast becoming to such a vice!

She verily thought she was pursuing the right course; that it was necessary to say these cruel words, to rouse her husband to a sense of his danger, and induce him to throw off the habit that had gained such power over him. She grew weary of the sound of her own voice at length, and perhaps relented a little at the utter dejection and misery his face and attitude expressed.

"I am all you say, and more," he said, when she had finished. "My wife can never think half as meanly of me as I think of myself. I would to God that my sins and my sorrows might soon be buried in the grave with me."

She saw him no more that night, but hour after hour, lying awake in her bed, she heard his monotonous tread as he paced his study floor.

"He feels badly," she thought, "and no wonder; my plain talk will do him good. Poor Louis, if he only had father's force of character, what a man he would be! I declare it is provoking to have him so mild and amiable. If he had only answered back tonight now, it would have been a comfort. One hates to have all the scolding to one's self."

Then she fell asleep, thinking she would say some kind things in the morning. She was alarmed when she awoke at daylight to find him still absent, and hastened to the study. She found her husband lying upon the lounge in an uneasy slumber. He was moving his head restlessly from side to side, and talking in his sleep. She bent over him, and heard the words, "unfaithful shepherd;" and then Alice Coleman's dying call, "Will he come, mother? O mother, will he come?" She put her hand upon his wrist, and felt the bounding pulse; then he opened his eyes, and saw her standing by his side,

"I can go," he said, struggling to rise; "I will go at once; there is not a moment to be lost."

He looked wildly about him, and then, full consciousness returning, sank wearily back upon the pillow. But during the three weeks of fever and delirium that followed, amid all the varied delusions that troubled his brain, none gained so strong a hold upon his imagination, or caused him half the distress, as the fancied neglect of parochial duty, and the seeming to be what he was not. His wife, standing by, heard, with what feelings may be imagined, her own reproachful words repeated again and again, mingled with exclamations of despair, or prayers for pardon. He fancied himself at times confessing his sin from the pulpit, and, painfully raising his weak voice that all might hear, denounced himself as "the worst of sinners, a hypocrite, a false teacher, a lying prophet, a thing of horrible iniquity, a creature utterly vile and polluted, not fit to live." Then he called upon the godly men and saintly women of his congregation to come and drag him from the holy place he had defiled; but cried out in the same breath, that he could not leave his post; that, unfaithful sentinel as he was, he must not desert, he must stay out the dreary watch, though it ended in death and shame.

While his brother clergymen of the city were taking their summer vacation, and gathering strength for a winter's campaign in the life-giving air of the hills, or the cool sea breezes of the coast, the young minister of the Wilmot Street Church lay in his darkened chamber, his body wasting with burning fever, and his diseased brain, preternaturally active, struggling and toiling under the fancied stress of labour to be done. There were many sermons thought out and delivered on that bed of suffering, it may be with an impulsive flow of thought and emotion that had accompanied no real discourse. He was driven on, perhaps, in a kind of ecstasy of inspiration that he had never known in health; but the glow, and the fervour, and inspiration were all accompanied by a painful consciousness of weakness, and even the most triumphant strains sometimes ended in a cry of human pain.

Hour after hour, day and night, through the closed door came the muffled tones of the minister's voice. His anxious parishioners, coming to inquire for him, heard, in the hall below, that strange murmur, low and sweet, and very plaintive in tone, and went away with sad faces, and a presentiment of coming ill. And Irish Annie, stopping on the stairs to cross herself, called on the Holy Mother of God to save him, "for shure," said Annie, "an' it's the death-song he's singin'."

His wife scarcely left him night or day. With gentle hands she cooled his temples and supplied his every want; and her calm voice soothed his troubled fancies and quieted his fears. She seemed to feel little weariness or need of repose, and would yield her post to no one.

Louis Thayer came back to life again at last, pale, and thin, and his voice tremulous with weakness. But

when the family physician recommended him to take with his beef-steak and mutton-chop a glass or two of

wine, " to aid digestion and give tone to the system,"
he quietly but steadily refused.

" I understand my own constitution, Doctor, and I
am fully convinced that stimulants do not agree with
me."

When Dr. Willoughby urged the young minister's
former experience to the contrary, he replied that
there had been a change in his system, and he could
no longer bear wine.

" Then," said his father-in-law, a little impatiently,
" you stand a fair chance for a relapse. It is all but
impossible for a man in your state of weakness, with
little or no constitution to back him, to get up from a
fever without stimulants. I tell you, Louis, you must
drink wine, or you will die."

" Then I will die," said the minister.

CHAPTER XIV.

THAT STUMBLING BROTHER.

"It is good neither to eat flesh, nor to drink wine, nor anything whereby thy brother stumbleth, or is offended, or is made weak."

WHEN the cool September days came, and ministers and people were returning to their city homes, Louis Thayer was just creeping into the sunshine of the outer world again. Then his people arranged for himself and wife a trip to Saratoga, and Mr. and Mrs. Barstow, who had spent all the summer on the sea-shore, expressed an earnest desire for an inland journey. And when the party found themselves comfortably settled in one of the large hotels of that beautiful village, the height of the season passed, and the company that still remained composed of very quiet, orderly people, it seemed that no better arrangement could have been made for the invalid's speedy restoration to health.

He drank the healing waters of the springs, and walked and rode in the invigorating air. He renewed old acquaintances and formed new ones, with intelligent and companionable men, principally outside of his own profession. Perhaps it was quite as well for him that the ministers had mostly returned to their work. He found it a change and a relief to hold converse with a class of men in whom he recognized intellectual cultivation of no common order, but who looked at the world in a different way from his own; whose ideas had a freer range, and who delighted in speculation and theory. He was conscious of a healthy mental friction and exhilaration while he combated their arguments and opposed his well-established belief to their flimsy and fanciful imaginings. And, slowly and almost imperceptibly at first, the melancholy that for months had enshrouded him began to disappear. His wife more than once heard his low, pleasant laugh on the piazza of the hotel, saw him one in a group of animated talkers, and her spirits rose and all her hopes revived.

He marvelled most himself at the change. " Do I dare to be happy?" he said to himself. " Can it be that God has forgiven me, and is sending me out to a new life?" He found himself laying plans for the future, looking forward with real pleasure to his return to his people. A sweet sense of pardoned sin, and an earnest desire to retrieve the errors of the past, took possession of his soul.

And all this time not a drop of wine passed his lips, But in an evil hour there came to Saratoga, returning from a northward tour, a venerable city minister,—a man whose praise is in all the churches, whose ministry has been blessed to the saving of many souls, whose voice and pen have for half a century been busy in his

Master's work. This distinguished divine, sitting near Louis Thayer at the dinner-table, pointed him out, with words of high commendation, to his wife.

"I heard that young man preach an ordination sermon two years ago," said he, "over in New Hampshire. I was stopping in D—— at the time. It was a remarkable sermon, though it contained no great learning. There were a dozen ministers present far better versed in theological lore than the speaker; men of stronger mind, keen and shrewd in debate, and better able to sustain themselves in theological discussion; but there was a wonderful power in what he said, and he had one of the sweetest voices I ever heard. He possessed the power of conveying great truths in very simple language. He spoke directly to the hearts of the people, and the whole audience—and it was composed in part of uncultivated country people—was moved by his eloquence. I predicted great things for him then, though he was settled over a small country church; but very soon after, he was called to the city. I understand he is very popular. I should like to pay the young man some attention. John,"—to his own servant, who attended him in all his journeys, and now stood at a respectful distance from his master's chair,—"John, draw the cork of this bottle of Burgundy, and take it, with Dr. ——'s compliments, to the gentleman sitting opposite us, four seats from the foot of the table."

When the servant, with his noiseless tread, came

round to Mr. Thayer's chair, and offered this delicate piece of attention from one whose slightest notice was highly esteemed by the younger members of his profession, the minister extended his hand to take the bottle, then he hesitated and seemed about to speak; but his wife, bowing and smiling, received it from the man, poured a little of its ruby red contents into a glass, and gracefully presented it to her husband, saying, in a hurried whisper, "You must drink his health, Louis."

It was a small bottle, containing not more than a pint, and when they left the table it was empty. Mrs. Thayer congratulated herself that, in the exigency of the moment, her husband had yielded his tectotal principles; "for I half expected he would decline the Doctor's civility," she thought, "and make himself ridiculously conspicuous before the whole company. *But how like a gentleman he took his wine!*" said this daughter of a wine-drinking minister.

When she joined the ladies of her acquaintance in the parlour, while her husband sauntered off for his after-dinner talk, she was the gayest of the gay. "So brilliant, so fascinating," Mrs. Barstow said confidentially to an acquaintance. "I assure you, my dear, the Wilmot Street people are proud of their minister and his wife." Mrs. Thayer spent a pleasant evening; but after Mr. and Mrs. Barstow, who were old-fashioned in their habits, and retired early, left her, and an hour slipped by, she grew uneasy that her husband did not make his appearance. "Perhaps he is visiting some friend at one of the other hotels," she thought, and presently went to her room to await his coming. As she sat a little weary and impatient, she heard steps on the stairs; and going into the hall, looked over the railing. Coming up the second flight—Mrs. Thayer's room was on the third floor — she saw two of the coloured waiters of the house bearing a man between them. They were in a jovial humour; and the fragment of a joke, as one rallied the other on the weight of the helpless burden they carried, reached her ears. She retreated instantly. "They are taking some poor, drunken wretch to his chamber," she thought.

The steps came on, ascending the third flight of stairs. No laughter and joking now. A little way through the hall, and stopped. Not at her door! "Was it 44?" one whispered. There came a low knock, and the wretched woman, even then thinking there was some mistake, opened her door to receive the senseless form of her husband.

The blow was so unexpected that she uttered a frightened exclamation, and turned as pale as death; then pointed to the bed without speaking, and the men laid down their burden. They were quietly leaving the room, when, overcoming her repugnance to question a servant on such a' subject, in her anxiety to know the worst, she caught one of them by the arm.

"Where was he?" said she.

"Below, ma'am, in the office," he answered.

"It was public then," was her thought, "in the bar-room of a hotel!"

She packed their trunks that night, and, late in the morning, when her husband woke from his feverish sleep, she begged him to leave Saratoga that very day. She gave no reason for this sudden change of plan, and he asked for none, but assented to her wishes with a reckless indifference of manner very unlike himself. She excused their departure to their friends as well as she could, persuaded the kind old people who came with them, and who were loath to leave their comfortable quarters, to remain another week, and started with her husband for home.

At the first stopping-place, a small way-station, Louis Thayer left his wife's side for a few moments; and when he returned, she saw that he had been drinking.

"Louis," she said, "are you bent upon your own destruction? Are you determined to kill yourself body and soul?"

He looked at her with a strange evil light in his dark eyes.

"It is all over with me, Fanny," he said, "and now I shall drink till I die!"

And the white-headed minister,—the good, wise, temperate old man, who knows how to use his liberty, "not as an occasion to the flesh," but drinks his choice wine as one of the meats "which God hath created, and which is not to be refused, but received with thanksgiving,"—what of him?

He lingered a few days at the fashionable watering-place, commanding, by his well-earned reputation, and his dignified and unimpeachable habits and deportment, the respect and veneration of old and young, and then departed, leaving an honoured name behind him. And going back to his work with a heart full of love to the souls of his fellow-men, and a determination to toil in his Master's vineyard till the close of the day, he is fulfilling amid the infirmities of old age the arduous duties of his profession. There is no lack of self-sacrificing effort. The lamp in his study burns late into the night. His printed words of consolation, coming from one who has known what it was to sorrow, " but not as those without hope," have brought peace and comfort to many a bereaved parent's heart.

He gives liberally of his large income for the spread of the Gospel. He searches out the poor of his congregation. He has caused many a widow's heart to sing for joy. No weather is so inclement as to keep him from the bedside of a sick parishioner. He visits the prisoner in his cell, the pauper in the workhouse, the dissolute and abandoned in their haunts of vice, that he may preach Jesus. We cannot doubt his singleness of motive, his steadfast, ardent piety, and if God's promises mean anything, his reward is sure.

But, oh, that stumbling brother! What if the temptation presented in hospitality and friendship, as a flattering tribute offered by age to youthful talent, bring sin, and sorrow, and wretchedness, and ruin, upon that precious soul for whom Christ died?

If the contents of that glass, red, and sparkling, and fragrant, cause the half-reformed man to grievously fall again, who caused him to stumble? He would have fallen, you say, without another's instrumentality. Yes, for the horrid greed was strong upon him. "It must needs be that offences come, but woe to that man by whom the offence cometh."

"In that he did it ignorantly, he shall obtain mercy." That good man would have cut off his right hand sooner than have knowingly injured his young brother, for he is tender of the feelings, and watchful of the interests of his fellow-Christians, and zealous for the church of God with a godly jealousy.

But he believes his moderate use of wine to be right. Infallibly safe himself, he offered it to his neighbour, whom he supposed also to be strong.

A great ship tempts a small vessel into deep and dangerous waters; and while the one, with her massive hulk and iron-ribbed sides, defies the elements, and floats majestically in mid ocean, making safe harbour at last, the weaker vessel loses her bearings, is driven hither and thither, and her anchor lost, her masts gone by the board, she drifts onward, a dreary wreck, until with one awful plunge she goes down. Oh, the desolated firesides! oh, the blighted hopes! oh, the bleeding, broken hearts that lost vessel leaves behind!

"It is good neither to eat flesh, nor to drink wine, nor anything whereby thy brother stumbleth, or is offended, or is made weak."

CHAPTER XV.

THE BIBLE WINE QUESTION.

"I was the song of the drunkard."

"WAL, neow, if it ain't the curusist thing," said Dan Taylor, looking up from his Bible one Sabbath evening; "I've read that story of Jacob an' Esau more'n twenty times, an' there's one thing I never noticed about it afore to-night. It beats all tew, for I allers paid peticelar attention to what Jacob done, bein's as he's a great favourite of mine. Seems though he was easier to pattern arter than some of the rest of 'em in the Bible; for, as I used to tell mother, if there was ever a feller that looked cont for number one, 'twas father Jacob. I allers thought he was 'cute, but neow I think he was cuter'n ever."

"Why, what discovery have you made about him, Dan?" said Grace, who, passing through the kitchen, stopped to hear this speech.

Dan was seated at the kitchen table, arrayed in his Sunday suit, his hair as smooth as bear's oil and brushing could make it. He looked up with a queer smile on his Yankee face.

"Wal, yer see, Miss Grace, it was allers a puzzle to me heow Jacob came it so easy over the old gentleman when he passed himself off for Esau; for it seems as though a man must be a born nataral if he couldn't tell the woolly side of a sheep from a man's skin, if he was ever so hairy. But this 'ere passage lets in daylight; for, yer see, Miss Grace, he fetched the old man *wine* 'long of his soup, an' then he pulled the wool over his eyes easy! Neow, that stands tew reason, don't it? I'm oncommon moderate myself in the use of speerits; but time an' time agin, arter takin' a horn or two, my fingers has been all thumbs, with no more feelin' in the eend on 'em than so much cotton wool. I say for't, 'twas too plaguy hard on Esau, warn't it, Miss Grace? Wal, the Bible's a wonderful book. Seems as though folks could prove most anything they was a mind to, eout on't. Why, I've jest been a-runnin' over in my mind the names of them that drinked more'n was good for 'em,—what yer pa would call 'abusin' the good gift.' If there ain't a lot on 'em! Noah, an' Lot, an' Elah, an' Benhadad, an' Nadab, an' Abihu, an' Uriah, an' Nabal, an' Nebuchadnezzar, an' Belshazzar, an' Herod, an' I don't know heow many more; an' that ain't countin' the moderate drinkers like David, an' Solomon, an' Nehemiah, an' sich like. I tell yer, Miss Grace, the Bible's a wonderful book."

"Have you just found it out, Dan?"

"I never seemed to have sich a realizin' sense on't afore," he said. "In fact, I've been considerable tossed up an' deown in my mind 'beout it by spells, there was so many cur'us things I couldn't see inter;

but I overheerd a conversation t'other day between yer pa an' Deacon Riley's son, that had a very settlin' effect on my mind. Yer pa has a way of puttin' things, Miss Grace, that there can't nobody get reound, an' he 's made me love this 'ere Bible more'n I ever expected tew, that 's so."

"I am very glad to hear it, Dan."

" Yer see, Miss Grace, comin' hum from Rocktown t'other day, yer pa an' I got ketched in a shower, an' I turned up agin the south meetin'-'us, to wait in the horse-sheds till 'twas over. And pretty soon Deacon Riley's son and another chap driv in, an' they went ter talkin' Bible temperance 'long with yer pa. I didn't take much notice long at fust; but arter a spell I tuk ter listenin'. Sez yer pa, sez he, 'There 's no sich thing as teetotalism as a rule of dooty in the Bible,' sez he. 'Wine is spoke of as a blessin' an' a symbol of marcy; an' they used it for sacrifice, an' gin it to the guests at the passover, an' the Lord's supper, an' the weddin' feast.' 'Yes, sir,' sez young Riley; 'but the Bible condemns it tew, don't it? an' calls it a symbol of wrath, an' sez kings nor priests mustn't drink it. Neow, what does that mean?' sez he. 'Is the Bible a-contradictin' itself? Is the same thing good an' bad, a symbol of wrath an' a symbol of marcy?' 'Not at all,' sez your pa. 'Them good vittles you ate for yer dinner,' sez he, 'would make a man awful sick, if he ate too much on 'em; an' I've heern tell of folks killin' themselves drinkin' tew much cold water. It 's use, an' not abuse, Mr. Riley,' sez yer pa; 'that's the Bible doctrine. Now, look over yer Bible,' sez he, 'an' see heow many times the word *rich* is used to praise, an' heow many times to blame. Some of the best men in the Bible was rich men,' sez he, 'an' yet the Bible sez, " Woe to them that are rich." There's jest as much sense,' sez the Doctor, sez he, ' in my takin' a veow of poverty, as there is in my bein' a teetotaler; 'caus' if I don't use riches I shan't abuse 'em, that's sartin.' (I don't begin to give all his big words, Miss Grace, only jest the sense on 'em.)

" Young Riley kinder flared up at that. ' Doctor,' sez he, ' does the Bible anywheres say, I mustn't *look* at gold when it glitters, an' that I mustn't so much as tell a feller where ter put his 'arnin's ? It does tell me not tew *look* on the wine when it's red, an' sez 1 mustn't teach my neighbour to drink.'

" Wal, I didn't see heow yer pa was a-goin' ter git cout o' that, but he done it slick, I tell yer. He had a sight ter say 'bout *look* bein' an intense varb, an' that ter *look* on the wine meant we wasn't ter look on it to *gloat* on it, an' ter long for it, an' said he'd seen a pictur' somewheres, of two old topers, with bottles an' glasses, one holdin' up his glass tew the light, an' lookin' at it mighty lovin', an' the other screwin' up his mouth for another dram, an' he said that was all that are text o' scriptur' meant. Wal, you'd better believe I was glad ter hear that! It tuk a weight right off my mind, for, yer see, I allers felt skittish over that text,

it's writ eout so plain, an' kinder stud in the way o'
my habits, an' I couldn't git reound it noheow.   I
never shall forget heow once when I was a leetle shaver,
mother she feound that are passage o' scriptur' on the
back side of a tract, with a pictur' underneath of a
pizen sarpint squirmin' reound in the bottom of the
glass.   An' she pinned it right over the shelf where
father kep' his rum-bottle.   Father was awful mad.
He tore it down, an' hove it inter the fire, but some-
heow I couldn't git that pictur' eout o' my head, an'
it's pestered me by spells ever sence.   But yer pa's
driv it all away with his larnin', Miss Grace; it don't
trouble me no more.   It was a grand sight ter see that
old gentleman sit there an' *explain away the Scriptur'.*"

"What did Riley say?" Grace inquired.

"Oh, he talked farce enuff on his side.   Yer pa's
reasonin' didn't seem ter hev no effect on him at all.
He hung onter his own way o' thinkin', jest as Mose
Pike hung onter the bull's tail."

"How was that?" said Grace.

"Miss Grace, didn't I never tell yer that story?
Wal, yer see, Squire Pike's son Mose was an easy,
good-natured kind of a body, but dretful weak in the
upper story; saft, yer know.   Wal, he was deown in
the medder-lot one day with the old man, when a
young critter the Squire owned poked a gap in the
fence, an' made tracks for the next pastur'.   'Stop
him,' sez the Squire.   What does Mose dew but run
an' ketch that critter by the tail.   Away went the

bull, an' Mose a-hangin' on behind. He rid reound the pastur' a spell, the bull a-goin' it like the dragon, then he flung out behind, fetched Mose an awful kick in the stomich, an' laid him sprawlin' in the ditch. ' Yeou great fool yeou,' sez the Squire, ' why didn't yer let go?'—'Let go, father!' sez Mose, sez he, blubberin' away to kill,—' let go! 'Twas all I cud do to *hold on.*' An' that was jest exactly the case with young Riley. He didn't stand no more chance of gettin' the best o' your pa on the Bible wine question, than Mose Pike did of stopping that crittur by hangin' outer the cend of his tail.

" Why, he tried ter prove to yer pa that the wine the Bible praises ain't the wine that makes folks drunk, and the Doctor come down on him with so much Greek an' Hebrew, it made my hair stand right up on cend. He talked about *Tirosh* an' *Yain*, an' somebody's ' death principle.' I can't remember half on't, but 'twas so larned it was terrible, an' he showed heow if grape-juice warn't fermented, there couldn't be no wine 'beout it, an' it would gin folks that drinked it the colic awful, an' heow if they'd had it at that weddin' in Cana the bridegroom an' all the rest on 'em would have been in a sufferin' sitiwation. ' An',' sez young Riley, sez he, ' Dr. Willoughby, dew yer think the guests at that weddin' was intoxicated?' —' I say,' sez yer pa, ' that nobody that uses their common sense ken read that second chapter o' St. John, without believin' that the wine the Lord Jesus

Christ made was intoxicatin' wine, not "must," ' sez
he, 'nor sickish grape-juice, biled down to a jel.'—
'An' yer think they were well drunk?' sez Riley.
'From what one o' the company said,' sez yer pa, 'the
implication is that all present had drinked freely of
wine that would intoxicate; that Greek word,' sez
yer pa, 'that the governor of the feast uses, means
drunk, an' yer can't make nothin' else cout on't.'—
'An' did the Lord Jesus Christ make eighty or ninety
gallons more, for men in that sitiwation?' sez young
Riley, sez he.—'So it reads in my Bible,' sez yer
pa.

"Miss Grace, when I heerd that, I come near
jumpin' right cout o' the waggin. Seems as though I
couldn't hold in nohcow, but must throw up my cap
an' shout halleluyah! 'Caus', yer see, it made the
path o' dooty so plain afore me. 'Why,' sez I to
myself, 'talk abeout the Bible goin' ag'in drinkin','
sez I, 'in the face o' this 'ere fact, the Doctor jest
brought eout! Why, look at it! Here was a lot of
folks more'n half-corned, with their tongues so thick
from what they'd drinked, that they didn't know good
wine from bad, an' the Lord Jesus Christ, the Saviour
of the world, comes an' makes 'em a lot more, eighty
or ninety gallons, ter steam on. Why,' sez I, 'they
had a gay old time at that weddin', you bet! I'd like
ter been there myself!' An' sence I heerd that talk,
Miss Grace, I ain't had no more trouble 'beout the
'Bible wine question.'"

A few evenings after this conversation, as Dr. Willoughby was returning from his weekly lecture, he found Dan measuring his length upon the ground near the front gate. His feet were braced against the hitching-post, and his head reclined easily in a mud-puddle. His stone bottle lay at his side. The minister helped him to rise, and guided his stumbling steps to the house.

"Th-thank yer, Doctor," said Dan, at the kitchen door, "*I-I'll do the s-same for yeou s-some night.*"

He received the severe reprimand the Doctor gave him the next morning very humbly, expressed the deepest penitence, and, begging not to be sent away, promised earnestly to do better; but when Dr. Willoughby made it one condition of his remaining, that he should keep away from Briggs's saloon, Dan remonstrated.

"Why, Doctor," said he, "I've been deown there time an' time ag'in, to hold religious-conversation with Briggs. I've reely been a-laborin' for his soul. Seems as though I wanted ter see him brought in. I know I'd oughter get religion myself, Doctor. I'm sinnin' ag'in great light an' privilege; but I dew feel a consarn for the welfare o' Zion. And it's my opinion that Briggs would be a bright an' a shinin' light, ef he cud be made ter see his dooty plain afore him. He's oncommon exercised in his mind; but yer see there's been this 'ere stumblin' block in his path. He was afeared, if he got religion an' jined the church, 'twould interfere with his bizness. 'It won't do no such thing, Briggs,' sez I. 'It'll help it. Rum-sellin's gittin' to be right respectable,' sez I, 'an' ministers an' church-members are upholdin' it.'—'Is that so?' sez Briggs. 'Wal, it is,' sez I; an' then I told him what I heerd you say, Doctor, t'other day, 'how we hadn't no right

to condemn liquor-sellers, good and respectable men, a-doin' their dooty in the station it pleased Providence to call 'em, an' a-worshippin' God an' performin' the dooties of a Christian, as sartinly as yeou dew when yeour a-preachin' the Gospel.'—'Did Dr. Willoughby say that?' sez Briggs. 'Them's his very words,' sez I.

'Then I'll go an' hear him preach next Sunday,' sez
Briggs, 'for he's the right kind of a parson for me.
Why,' sez Briggs, sez he, 'I don't see nothin' to hinder
a minister with sich principles from takin' his grog
with the rest on us.'   'That's so,' sez I, 'an', Briggs,
yeou talk 'bout its interferin' with yer bizness ter git
religion; let me tell you somethin' that happened over
here in Rocktown a spell ago.   The chap that plays
the organ in the South Church keeps a drinkin' saloon
for the factory hands,—jest like yourn, Briggs.   Some
o' the church-members got riled up 'beout it,—one in
peticelar,—'caus' the rum-seller told him, 'he'd sell his
son as much liquor as he'd pay for, in spite of him or
any other man.'   Wal, they called a meetin', and
drawed up a set o' resolutions ter turn him cout of his
place; but the church voted 'em down by a thunderin'
big majority; an' this 'ere 's the present state o' things
in Rocktown,—the minister *preaches* at one eend o'
the church, an' the rum-seller *praises* at t'other." *

* Fact.

CHAPTER XVI.

GOD BLESS OUR MINISTER.

> " He was enthusiastic too.
>   Now, whether they were false or true,
>   Or good or bad, must be referred
>   To the fixed meaning of the word.
>   If to be warm and wisely zealous
>   Be what is meant, then plainly tell us,
>   Did not the state of things require
>   The ardour of this heavenly fire?"

 FEW days after Mr. Thayer's return from Saratoga, he was transacting some business in one of the city banks, when he heard the word " Grantley" uttered by a stranger standing near, and stepping round to the cashier's desk, he inquired the gentleman's name.

" That is Mr. James Otis," he replied, " of the firm of Otis, Brown, & Co., Grantley Iron Works. We do business for him, and he is in the city every week or two. One of the heavy men of the county, sir."

" Will you introduce me, Mr. Pearce?"

" With the greatest pleasure. Mr. Otis, the Rev. Mr. Thayer of the Wilmot Street Church."

When the gentlemen had shaken hands and exchanged a few commonplace civilities, the minister said :—

"Mr. Otis, I have solicited the pleasure of your acquaintance, that I might make inquiries concerning a friend of mine, now a resident of your village. I refer to the Rev. Mr. Richmond."

"God bless him!" said Mr. Otis, warmly.

The answer was unexpected, and Mr. Thayer's face expressed surprise.

"He is my pastor, sir," said Mr. Otis; then in a lower tone, "I owe a very happy change in my feelings, under God, to Mr. Richmond. I united with the church last Sabbath, Mr. Thayer."

"Indeed, I am most happy to hear it. Is there much religious interest in my friend's congregation?"

"Oh, sir, the whole town is moved. There was never such a work of grace in any place before."

He spoke with the enthusiasm of a young convert in the warmth of his first love.

"Sit down and tell me about it," said the minister. "You are welcome as one that bringeth good tidings from a far country."

They went back to a retired part of the room, where they could converse with more freedom.

"I saw my friend," said Mr. Thayer, "in last December. He was then in difficulty; his church shaken to its foundation, in consequence of strong ground he took on the temperance question. I have felt curious to know how the struggle would end. I thought I should see him in the city, or that I would run out on the train some day, or write to him. But multiplied

dutics and a tedious confinement by sickness have
prevented me. How did the church come out of the
conflict ?"

" You know Mr. Richmond gave us a very practical
temperance lecture ?"

" Yes."

" Well, it opened the eyes of some of us to the true
state of things in our midst. I, for one, had been
careless and indifferent on the subject. I knew we
had a good many dram-shops and drinking saloons in
Grantley village; that our hands in the foundry were
a hard set. I used to be annoyed at their drunken
quarrels, and 'laying off' so frequently for a spree;
but it never occurred to me that any of the responsibility of the thing rested with me.

" I was opposed to the prohibitory law. It seemed
to me it was nonsense to attempt to make liquor-
selling a crime, and punishable accordingly, when
spirits are a commodity, recognized as such by the
laws of every nation; and, besides being used for
drinking purposes, valuable as a medicine and for
many scientific and mechanical purposes. You see, I
took the ground that so long as liquor is used, it must
and will be sold, and what the law has a right to take
cognizance of is its abuse, and, like many good temperance men, I advocated a stringent licence law,
instead of a prohibitory statute. And, I must confess,
I felt a little wicked triumph after the ultra-temperance men carried the day, and their Maine Law had

been on the statute book a year or so, to find that there was more drunkenness and unrestrained liquor-selling in our place under the new law than the old. For it was just a dead letter. Nobody was afraid of it. Nobody enforced it.

"Well, as I said, Mr. Richmond's lecture set us thinking; but the week after, something occurred in my own family that made me terribly in earnest. There was a church festival held in our town hall, and under that hall was a drinking saloon,—a bad place, one of the worst in town. Mr. Thayer, the man's son who kept that place enticed my two boys,—mere children, Sunday school scholars, the oldest not seventeen years old,—into that vile place, and made them both *drunk*.

"I went to the minister the next morning. 'Mr. Richmond,' said I, 'if there's any efficient way of putting down this evil in our midst, let's set about it. If your prohibitory law will do it,' said I, 'though I voted against it, and was president of the largest Anti-Maine liquor-law meeting held in —— County, I am ready for one to enforce it. These dens must be broken up somehow,' said I. 'You know how to go about it better than I do. I'll stand by you, Mr. Richmond, with my money and my influence ; only go ahead !'

"You should have seen his eyes sparkle. I thought he would shake my hand off. (Our minister is a Samson in body, you know, as in strength of will.)

Well, we worked like Trojans. We looked up every temperance man in the community, and organized for action; and we were so still about it, that the blow fell on the rumsellers like a bolt from heaven. We cleaned them out handsomely, sir. We shut up nine grog-shops, and drove some of their proprietors out of town."

"And what has this to do with the revival?"

"I am coming to it," he replied. "The two are so connected, that I could not well tell the last part of the story without the first. Well, you know how much personal feeling against Mr. Richmond that lecture excited. Some of his strongest church members fell away; in fact, those that stood by him were of the poorer class. He hadn't a single man of wealth and influence on his side. I must say, before I espoused his cause I respected him for his independence and boldness of speech. They were bound to get rid of him. Deacons, rumsellers, and, worse than all the rest, a pack of chattering women, who talked themselves hoarse with pious cant about sowing dissension among brethren, &c. They sent two or three committees to wait on him, and he heard all they had to say, and bowed them politely out, and paid not the slightest attention to their request."

"Do you mean to say," inquired Mr. Thayer, "that his people requested him to resign his charge, and he refused?"

"Certainly. They told him so many had withdrawn

their subscriptions that they could not give him a
support. 'Give me what you please,' said he. 'I can
live on as little as any man in Grantley. I have a
work to do here. When it is done I will go; not
before.'—'We'll call a council,' said they, 'and make
you go.'—'Try it,' said Mr. Richmond. 'See if you
can get a council of ministers in this county to dismiss
a man for preaching temperance.' For, you see, they
could not bring a single charge against him. He
preached splendid sermons. He was the most faithful
pastor they ever had. His Band of Hope made his
Sabbath school so attractive, that the lecture-room was
too small to hold it. And the trouble in the church
made so much talk, that people not in the habit of
going to meeting came to hear the 'teetotal parson,'
as they called him, out of curiosity; and some

'Who came to scoff, remained to pray.'

"The rumsellers formed a league against him, and
threatened to take his life. 'I have but one life to
give,' said our minister, 'and I could not give it in a
better cause.' He was perfectly good-natured, never
lost his temper; but was as immovable as the granite
hill. He always had a keen answer to give them.
One day, when he went to the polls to deposit his
vote, one of his church members said to him, 'I am
very sorry to see you here, Mr. Richmond.'—'Why?'
he inquired. 'Because,' said the other, with a long
face, 'Christ said His kingdom was not of this world.'

'Ah!' said our minister, 'have only those a right to vote, then, who belong to the kingdom of Satan?'

"Well, all this time he was working among the operatives in the foundry, the 'iron men,' as we call them. I told you what a hard set they were, drinking and godless. I don't know how he got hold of them. They hated him at first. They used to curse and swear when they saw him coming. But one and another of them he picked out of the gutter—literally, Mr. Thayer—and made men of them. He's gained a marvellous power over them. They twit each other about it, and declare it's no use to fight against the parson. If he singles a man out, he may just as well give in first as last, for he'll get no peace of his life till he signs the pledge. With these reformed drunkards, he formed the nucleus of a total abstinence society, and called it the 'Iron Club.' I wish I had time to tell you the good that 'Iron Club' has accomplished, and is accomplishing; but I shall keep you here all day with my story.

"Much of what I have told you happened before we struck the blow that broke up so many of our dramshops. For months before this the preaching on the Sabbath had been listened to with marked attention, and the evening meetings were largely attended and very solemn. Mr. Richmond was encouraged to hope for a revival; but there were no conversions, and the work did not progress till the Sabbath evening after we struck that blow, and then the blessing came down upon us like a flood.   It seemed as if the Spirit of God was waiting till those evil spirits were cast out, and the house 'swept and garnished.'   There have been over a hundred hopeful conversions, sir, in Grantley village,—three of our leading business men are among the converts, heads of families, gray-headed men and women, and my two boys, Mr. Thayer."

Grateful tears filled the father's eyes as he spoke.

"Tell me about yourself, Mr. Otis."

"Well, sir, up to this time I had no personal interest in religious matters.   I hired a seat and attended church generally half-a-day; but that was all.   I kept away from the meetings at first.   I was shy of Mr. Richmond too; but we had so much temperance business on hand, that I could not avoid him altogether. But he said not a word to me on the subject of religion, till one morning he came into my office, his face all a-glow, and shook my hand till it ached.   'What is it?' said I, for I knew he had good news to tell.   'Has Bart Tyler signed the pledge? or Deacon Risley promised to give up his cider?'   He shook his head. 'Your two boys, Mr. Otis.'—'What of them?' said I, quick enough.   'They were at the inquiry meeting last night,' said he.   'They are both indulging hope.   Mr. Otis, will you let them begin a Christian life alone?' He touched me just where I live, sir.   If I desire anything in this world, it is to see those boys grow up good Christian men.   I had Christian parents.   I had lived under the sound of the Gospel all my life; but I

neglected to seek the Saviour when I was young—was
Gospel-hardened, you may say; but those boys,—well,
you can imagine what he said to me. He persuaded
me to seek religion for my children's sake. I prayed

in my family that very night; but I could not pray
again for a week, only to cry to God for mercy. Well,
He *was* merciful, sir; and last Sabbath I took my two
boys by the hand, and we promised, in the presence of
angels and men, to devote the rest of our lives to God's

service. And, sir, it was the happiest day of my life."

The "iron man" broke down here, and Mr. Thayer pressed his hand in silence.

" You don't wonder that I said God bless him," said Mr. Otis. " Why, I thank God every day of my life that He sent us such a minister."

" And what of his opposers?" said Mr. Thayer.

" They haven't a word to say, sir; they don't dare to peep. This ingathering makes the church so strong, that their opposition would not be worth minding. Why, sir, we are a church by ourselves; and if they make us any trouble, and annoy our minister, we'll go off in a body, and build him a church, where he can preach temperance to his heart's content. God bless him !" said the "iron man" again. " We are going to stand by our minister."

CHAPTER XVII.

SOUL TORTURE.

"Abstain! I have known one in that state when he has tried to abstain but for one evening—though the poisonous potion had long ceased to bring back its first enchantments, though he was sure it would rather deepen his gloom than brighten it—in the violence of the struggle I have known him to scream out, to cry aloud for the anguish and pain of the strife within."—CHARLES LAMB.

RACE WILLOUGHBY'S wedding-day was fixed, and dressmakers and seamstresses were at work upon moire antique, Lyons velvet, *gros grain* silks, and other costly materials that went to make up the bride's *trousseau;* for the country minister's daughter was to have what Mrs. Thayer called an elegant outfit; and this lady, who undertook to superintend the preparations, spared neither time nor money. She was in her element, tossing over silks and satins, sitting in private consultation by the hour with fashionable dressmakers, and displaying her excellent taste in the choice of trimmings and the blending of colours.

To add to her happiness, Mr. Landon requested her advice and assistance in furnishing the stone-front mansion built for him during the summer upon

Clement Avenue, the fashionable street of the city; for it was Mr. Landon's purpose to commence married life under his own roof-tree. "He had dragged out a miserable existence," he said, "long enough in hotels and boarding-houses, and now intended to commence living with a wife and a home." He peremptorily refused Dr. Willoughby's offer to furnish his daughter's future residence, and proceeded to prepare it for his bride, in a style of lavish expenditure that would have drawn largely upon the Doctor's bank stock. In the arrangement and ornamentation of the rooms, he found he needed a lady's taste; and he called upon Mrs. Thayer, who was only too happy to lend her assistance.

It was necessary at this time for Grace to spend much of her time in the city with her sister. There were dresses to be fitted, and important decisions to be made respecting points and scallops, plaits and gathers. But every few days Dr. Willoughby's bay horse stood at the parsonage door, and Grace was summoned home upon some pretext. "Your mother wants a little help on her sewing machine," or, "Your mother is in trouble with Katie; you must come and straighten matters out between them;" for Grace, with all her girlishness, had that firm, sweet temper which controls, without seeming to dictate. The fact was, the old people missed her sadly, and wondered every day, when they sat down to their solitary meals, what they would do when this dear child left them.

The doubts and fears that troubled Grace Willoughby

during the early part of her engagement had apparently all disappeared. Every one told her she was a fortunate girl; and to all appearance she believed it. She knew that her parents and sister were superlatively happy in view of her prospects; her lover was thoroughly devoted to her; she was proud of his talents, and the position they gave him among his fellow-lawyers in the city; and she very often assured herself that she loved him. But she was in no hurry for her wedding-day. When Mr. Landon fretted over the delays in building, and feared the house would not be ready at the time appointed, Grace suggested, with a bright face, the expediency of postponing the marriage. She looked upon the grand preparations going forward with almost a childish wonder and delight.

She visited the house one day in company with her sister and Mr. Landon, and ran through the spacious rooms, opening and shutting doors, and peeping into closets, with a look of girlish curiosity on her face that Mrs. Thayer thought very unbecoming in the future mistress of this stately mansion.

"Fanny," she called out with great animation from the next room, "I've found the dearest little closet— just the nicest place for to make a soft bed for my kitten."

Mrs. Thayer looked at the grave, careworn face of the man at her side.

"I wish she were a little more womanly, Mr. Landon," she said, "for your sake."

"I like her very well as she is," he returned. "Her freshness and enthusiasm please me, Mrs. Thayer. One of your sister's chief attractions in my eyes is her youthfulness of feeling. She retains all the buoyancy of childhood, while she possesses the judgment of riper years. We are fond of contrast, you know, and to a world-worn, world-wearied man, the spring and newness of her life are refreshing."

It did not occur to either of the speakers that youth, and freshness, and enthusiasm, might not find congenial companionship in the world-worn and wearied,—that a rose tied to a withered branch will be likely to fade and die.

Mr. Landon and Mrs. Thayer were excellent friends; and the long walks and rides she took with him to visit furnishers and upholsterers, the hours she spent in the house on Clement Avenue, arranging and re-arranging, with her frequent shopping expeditions, so delightfully occupied her days, that home duties for the time were neglected. She knew that all was not right with her husband. She could not fail to perceive the gloom that darkened his face, and kept him silent and sad, save that now and then his eyes were lit up with a strange fire, and the melancholy was exchanged for a brief season of hilarity, which left him gloomier than before. She understood perfectly well the cause of these sudden transitions of feeling. She knew he kept his study locked at times, when even *her* voice and knock failed to effect an entrance, and that he came out with a pale, haggard face, and a look of gloom and terror in his eyes. She could not forget his desperate words, after the shameful affair at Saratoga; but with the hopefulness of her enthusiastic nature, and the feeling so natural in view of a threatened calamity, that something will prevent, or the thing is too dreadful to happen, she put the fear from her. Her mind, too, was thoroughly preoccupied. "I have no time," she thought, "to watch Louis now. When this wedding is over, if there is no change, I will tell father all about it. He has great influence over Louis, and will make him realize the danger he is in, if any one can. Oh, how can he be so infatuated! My husband a—no, it will never come to that."

For the two or three Sabbaths after their return from Saratoga she watched him closely, but soon found she had nothing to fear. Louis Thayer never entered the pulpit again under the influence of liquor. Perhaps he recognized as a positive precept the commandment to the Aaronic priesthood, "Do not drink wine or strong drink when ye go into the tabernacle of the congregation, lest ye die," and feared the fate of those who offered strange fire and died before the Lord; or perhaps he dared not again test the power, heavenly or of another origin, that stood him in his sore hour of need. However this may be, the sermons he preached, rich and powerful, terrible sometimes in their threatenings and denunciations, but more frequently full of sad and persuasive eloquence, were all his own.

There was no second lifting out of the written discourse. No flow of ideas and freedom of language, as marvellous to the speaker as to those who listened.

But when the day's work was over, and, refreshed and strengthened for another week of toil, the godly members of his flock thanked God, in their evening prayer at home, for the words of heavenly wisdom they had heard, and invoked every needed blessing, spiritual and temporal, upon their young pastor's head, what was he doing then? The study door was locked on the inside, and he was alone. His wife never went to him on Sabbath evenings now. The horror of this man's sin lay partly in its solitude. There may be a shadow of an apology for one who, in mistaken hospitality, gathers his friends about him, and passes the sparkling wine-cup; but what shall be said for the man who, turning his key, deliberately sits down to selfish and solitary indulgence? There was no self-deception about it. He had a thorough understanding of the enormity of the sin he was committing, an utter loathing of the vice and its consequences. He looked to the very bottom of the abyss down which he was gliding, saw the ruin that awaited him, all the horrors of the death below, and could not, or would not stop.

At this time he neglected no outward duty. He visited his people from house to house, seizing the most favourable opportunity to urge upon the impenitent the claims of religion, with a simplicity and directness, and a persuasive tenderness of manner, that were well-nigh irresistible. He was particularly careful to ascertain who were sick. The scene in Alice Coleman's death-chamber was never repeated; and dying believers, listening to the young pastor's words of assurance, forgot their fear, and, with the song ot triumph on their pale lips, stepped boldly into the flood. His faintly-uttered Amen was the last sound of earth in many a dying Christian's ear.

"Courage, my brother!" he said to an aged member of his flock, in the agony of the last struggle. "Courage! It is but a moment, and you shall be singing the song of redeeming love around the throne."

A look of tender recognition lit up the old man's dying eye.

"We will sing it together, my dear pastor," he said, "when *you* come."

Then the minister turned away his head, and an expression of the keenest anguish crossed his face.

Perhaps none of his services were so peculiarly blessed as those at the communion-table. He came to this sacred feast, his people said, as one who had " seen the Lord;" and with his soul melted into tenderness and compassion, dwelt upon the love of a suffering Saviour with a touching pathos that melted his audience to tears. He set forth the Son of God crucified, making Him incomparably attractive to the eye of the believer. And he led them to feel that in sinning against this Saviour they had wounded their dearest friend.   Making sin appear very hateful in their eyes, he called upon them, while sealing their vows with the consecrated symbols of Christ's body and blood, to renounce it, and in renewed and unreserved dedication give themselves soul and body to God.

His hand visibly trembled when he took his share of the sacred feast; and when the sexton swept the church the next week, he found a piece of bread which had somehow fallen behind the minister's chair.

The senior deacon came to his pastor the week following this precious communion season, to consult as to the expediency of holding a church-fast; "for we feel," said the good man, "that the Lord was made known to some of us last Sabbath, 'in the breaking of bread;' and that 'He showed us His hands and His feet.' Who can tell, if we humble ourselves with prayer and fasting before our God, confessing our sins one to another, He will not 'open the windows of heaven and pour us out a blessing, that there shall not be room enough to receive it.' In conversing with a Christian woman of the church to-day, Miss Bethiah Emmersly, she tells me that she has been wonderfully drawn out and assisted in her prayers lately for a reviving of God's work in our midst."

The fast was appointed; and when the large assembly, gathered in the audience-room of the church that Friday morning, noticed the pale face and listless, despondent manner of their pastor, as he passed up the aisle, they looked upon him with reverence and pity.

"He is wearing himself out for us," they said—"the faithful minister! Such devotion to study! Such scrupulous fulfilment of parochial duty! *He* has no need to fast. The dulness of the flesh will never dim *his* spiritual lamp."

He offered a short introductory prayer, read the fifty-first Psalm, and, coming down from the desk, took his station immediately in front.

"I wish," he said, "to put aside the minister, to place myself on a visible equality with the humblest disciple present; for in the sight of God I feel myself to be less than the least,—a great sinner,—the vilest of the vile; needing the forgiveness of my church, and that God would have mercy on my soul." Then he sat down, and, bowing his head upon his hands, burst into tears.

There was nothing of stage effect in this. No imposing attitudes or gestures, or canting, whining tone, no extremes of intonation, no affectation of tears. Not a person present doubted his heartfelt sincerity. But how did they receive the confession?

The senior deacon rose, and, in a voice tremulous with age and with emotion, said :—

"If to our dear pastor, dwelling, as we believe he does, in intimate communion with his Saviour from day to day, is vouchsafed so clear a view of the exceeding sinfulness of sin, that his own heart appears vile in his sight, what depths of iniquity, my brethren, must the all-seeing eye of God behold in yours and mine!"

While the good man was speaking, the minister shrank and cowered in his seat, and would gladly have sunk into the ground for shame.

But his hardest task was among the children. Is there a sweeter sight upon earth than that of the faithful pastor, standing with his Bible in his hands, surrounded by the little ones of his flock, leading them into " green pastures, and beside the still waters?" What choicer fruits can a minister reap, what riper harvest of golden sheaves, what sweeter addition to that great multitude which no man can number, than these dear lambs whom he has led to the Saviour? Louis Thayer, by his gentleness and almost womanly tenderness of manner, was peculiarly fitted for this part of his work. In the early years of his ministry he loved it. He hated it now. He dared not look into the sweet, earnest faces and honest eyes of the children.

> " O Christ! to think of their white souls,
>   And mine so black and grim!
> I could not lead in evening prayer,
>   Or join in evening hymn.
> Like devil of the pit I seemed,
>   'Mid holy cherubim."

He was called one day to visit a murderer in his cell. The day of execution was fixed—the man must surely die.

" I am the worst wretch alive," he said. " I don't deserve any mercy from God or man,"

"Oh, no," said the minister, very earnestly; "you are not the worst. You have confessed your guilt to your fellow-men certainly—to God, I hope. You are, to suffer the penalty of your crime. Christ died for sinners who confess and forsake their sins. There is mercy even for you. Tell me, now, are you not happier in this cell to-day, and knowing that you must die next week, than when you were going about seeming to be what you were not; acting like an honest man, but all the while bearing about with you your horrid secret, like the dead corpse of your victim?"

"I haven't seen him," said the man, looking fearfully over his shoulder, "once, since I told of it; and every night afore that, as soon as it got dark in the corners, he used to come and show me the gash in his throat, and the blood runnin'." He shuddered at the recollection. "Well, I do suppose, if I swing for it, it'll make it even with my fellow-men; but they say there's another bar where I've got to be tried."

Then the minister preached Jesus to this "spirit in prison." With all the earnest desire he felt in his inmost soul to comfort the forlorn man doomed to die, he told him of the infinite love and compassion of Him who conquered death and hell upon Calvary,—who died even, as this murderer must die, on the gallows, only without sin. His thrilling tones filled the gloomy cell with music, and the condemned man listened with solemn attention.

Louis Thayer spent many hours with this prisoner

in his cell, went with him to the place of execution,
and heard him offer at the foot of the gallows the
prayer of the dying thief, "Lord, remember me when
thou comest into thy kingdom."   And in view of his
sincere penitence, and entire surrender of his sin-laden
soul to Him " whose blood cleanseth from all sin," the
minister felt warranted in giving him the blessed
assurance, "This day shalt thou be with me in para-
dise."   He saw the body placed in its rough coffin,
and laid away in an obscure grave.

"Next summer," said he, " the grass will cover
him, and the daisies wave as sweetly above his head
as over the body of that sinless child buried yonder;
for, though he was a *murderer,* he confessed his sin,
and was forgiven; but methinks no grass will grow
above *his* head who is false to himself, to his fellow-
men, and to his God."

CHAPTER XVIII.

THE RELENTLESS JUDGE.

"The quivering flesh, though torture-torn, may live;
But souls, once deeply wounded, heal no more."—ELLIOT.

"Can we forget our own behaviour?
Can we for all our sins atone?
Let him who needs no blessed Saviour
Be first to scourge or cast the stone!"—BUNGAY.

"IS Louis ill again to-day?" Grace said one morning, when her sister came to the break-fast-table alone. "Fanny, I wonder you are not alarmed about him. These violent headaches, accompanied by such depression of spirits, must mean something. I think he suffers more than he tells us, for when I was awake so long the other night, I heard him walking his study for a long time. I thought I would go to his door, and ask if I could be of any service; it was the night baby was so troublesome, and I knew you could not leave him."

"I am glad you did not," said Mrs. Thayer. "Louis does not like to be disturbed when he is poorly. The pain wears itself off after awhile."

"But why not consult a physician, Fanny?"

"Louis says he wants no medicine," his wife replied,

"and indeed you must not trouble your head about him now, Grace; you have quite enough to think of for the next fortnight. When you are married and off my hands, dear, I shall turn my whole attention to my husband. A little good advice, which I can give him quite as well as a physician, with nursing and care, will soon cure him."

She spoke with forced gaiety, and immediately changed the subject.

One night, Grace, lying wide awake on her bed, heard a door softly open, and footsteps in the hall. She rose hastily, and, looking out, saw the gleam of a lamp carried by some one going downstairs. She waited till she heard the steps returning, threw a cloak about her, and stepped into the hall. It was Louis Thayer. The lamp he carried shone full upon him, and she noticed, as he came toward her with a hesitating, unequal step, his disordered dress, his flushed face, and matted hair. She also saw that he had a bottle in his hand.

"Louis," she said, "are you ill?"

He startled violently at the sound of her voice, for he did not see her till he was close upon her, and, in his nervous agitation, nearly dropped the bottle.

"I heard your step in the hall," she hastened to explain. "I felt afraid you were ill again. Can I do anything for you, Louis?"

He looked at her vacantly, as though but half understanding what she said.

"No, no," he said, at length. "You can do me no good. Go back to your bed, Grace."

His manner and look troubled her, and she passed a sleepless night. He did not breakfast with his family the next morning, but about noon came down to the dining-room, drank a cup of tea, and went out. Then Grace stole up softly to the study. As she opened the door, she met the sickening odour of stale spirit. In the closet were bottles and glasses; among them the bottle she had seen in her brother's hand the night before. It was labelled "Old Cognac Brandy." She took it in her hands, and then immediately replacing it, went to the room where her sister sat in earnest consultation with a dressmaker.

"Fanny," she said, "will you come here? I want to speak with you."

"In a moment, dear," said Mrs. Thayer, without looking up. "The silk should be cut at least two inches in width, Miss Pierce, and perfectly bias, and the satin piping as narrow as possible. Your sample is altogether too wide, and the upper trimming—."

"Fanny," said Grace, impatiently, "do come. Let the trimming go till another time."

Mrs. Thayer rose reluctantly.

"Really, Grace," she said, as she followed her sister through the hall, "you are a little unreasonable to hurry me so, when you see how busy I am, trying to make that stupid woman understand what I want. I declare, I am worried to death, they are all so slow,—

the pearl satin scarcely touched, and the white *moire
antique* to be trimmed, and the *gros grain*—. Why,
Grace, where are you going?"

Her sister did not reply. She opened the study
door, and entered. Mrs. Thayer, following her, looked
greatly surprised. Her first move, after entering the
room, was to raise a window.

"The air is very close here," said Mrs. Thayer.
"Louis keeps his room too warm." She turned to see
Grace with the bottle of brandy in her hand.

"Fanny," she said, speaking in a low, frightened
tone, "I saw Louis bring this upstairs last night. I
am sure it was full then. See here!" She tipped the
bottle to show that it was nearly empty. O Fanny,
those headaches! I have suspected something for
more than a week. What shall we do?"

Mrs. Thayer's face flushed to the temples. "I must
say, Grace," she replied, quickly, "that you take
strange liberties in my husband's private apartment.
He hardly requires your assistance as inspector of his
medicines. You know very well his physician orders
brandy for his neuralgia."

"Fanny, don't talk so to me. Oh, it is dreadful!
Poor Louis! What is to be done?"

She began to cry. The proud woman at her side
stood silent a moment, then she laid her hand upon
her sister's shoulder.

"Grace," said she, "listen to me. You are giving
yourself needless pain. You are distressing me very

much. You have in some way discovered what I never intended you should know; but since this cannot be helped, I ask you in all sisterly kindness to let the matter rest just where it is. You can do nothing. You greatly exaggerate the trouble. It will all come out right in the end. My dear sister, you are touching a very delicate matter. Will you promise me to let it alone?"

"Do father and mother know, Fanny?"

"No," said Mrs. Thayer; "and neither would my sister, if she had not meddled with what does not concern her."

She took no notice of the taunt.

"Father must know it at once," she said. "He has almost unbounded influence with Louis. Fanny, he will be in town this afternoon. You will tell him."

"I shall do no such thing," said Mrs. Thayer. "When I see fit to disclose what concerns me personally, I can do it without the advice of a younger sister."

"This is not a personal matter, Fanny," said Grace, very seriously. "It concerns us all. It concerns the whole church of God. You are strangely blind if you do not see the dreadful danger Louis is in. *You do see it.* There is not an hour to be lost. All the influence his friends possess should be brought to bear upon him in this crisis. Fanny, I am sure you can save him. He loves you with all his heart, and it is a very gentle and loving one. With your arms about him, and father's strong will and influence over him for good, there is everything to hope."

"I have entreated, and chided, and expostulated with him," said Frances Thayer. "He is strangely infatuated; but I have no serious apprehension as to the result. He will wake by and by to realize the sin and the shame of the course he is pursuing."

"Fanny," said Grace, "a new horror seizes me. Are you sure no one suspects this? The servants,— have they seen nothing, or people outside?"

"It is not known," said Mrs. Thayer, again colouring; but even as she spoke, came the recollection of the senseless form borne to his chamber, in the arms of menials, from the bar-room of a hotel. But Saratoga was a long way off. There was not, to her knowledge, a person there from the city beside their own party. Of Mr. and Mrs. Barstow's ignorance of the matter she had long since assured herself, by their continued cordiality, and the reverential regard they manifested for her husband.

So she repeated, "No, it is not known; and, Grace, I cannot do anything about it till after the wedding. Husband, and children, and everything else, must be set aside till that is over."

"I wish it *was* over, or was never coming," said the bride elect.

"Grace!"

"Fanny, I am so tired of hearing about it. What is the use of making such a fuss over a little country girl's wedding? I should be much better pleased if they would let me put on a plain travelling dress, and be married some morning in the old sitting-room at home, with only you and Louis for witnesses."

"So you might have been, my dear," said Mrs. Thayer, "if you had married Deacon Riley's son, or that school-teacher who was so much in love with you, or Louis's dear friend, the country parson."

"Fanny," she said, "I wish Mr. Richmond was here. I think he would know better what to do for Louis than any one else."

"He is the last person I should desire to consult," she said coldly. "And now, Grace, go to your room, and bathe your eyes before dinner. What a fright you are, to be sure, and Mr. Landon coming this after-noon to take you to ride!"

"You will tell father all about it, Fanny?"

"No, not at present."

"Then I must."

"Grace!"

"Fanny, he ought to know it. If you do not tell him, I shall."

Mrs. Thayer saw that her sister was fully resolved, and she yielded as gracefully as she could. It was not the first time that the impetuous spirit of the elder sister had bowed to the quiet, steadfast purpose of the younger.

"She must not be crossed," thought Frances Thayer, "so near her wedding-day. It is as well for father to know, perhaps, but I dread to tell him. He will despise Louis for such a weakness."

Dr. Willoughby listened to his daughter's story—and she kept back nothing—with grief, indignation, and shame; and his fine features assumed their sternest expression. There was much of the severity of his Puritan ancestors in the character of this good man.

"I would not credit the tale, my daughter, from other lips," he said. "How a man in your husband's high social position,—with his powers of mind, with his Christian principle, a teacher of the Word, a minister of Jesus Christ,—how he can stoop to so low, so sensual a vice, is utterly beyond my comprehension. I confess, Frances, I do not know what to say to him. If his moral perception has become so obscured, and his conscience so blunted, that he can do the thing you say—return from serving his God at the altar to the beastly indulgence of this low appetite—I fear no argument I can present will move him."

"Father, you will plead with him?"

"Yes, Fanny, for your sake, and for the sake of his children, and the church of God, which he has dishonoured."

In the heat of his righteous indignation, Dr. Willoughby sought a private interview with his own son-in-law.

He found his task exceedingly painful, but he did not flinch. If he had lived in those stern old days under the Jewish dispensation, when it was commanded that "the drunkard shall be stoned with stones till he die," he would have gone out beyond the camp, with the elders and the men of the city, and hurled his stone at the victim with a calm and deadly aim, though related by as tender ties as to the wretched man before him to-day; and the blow would have been merciful in comparison with the soul-torture he inflicted; for the crushing weight and ragged sides of the cruel flint never left a ghastlier hurt in the flesh of its victim than the weight of his words upon a heart already well-nigh wounded to death.

He brought the law from Sinai in thunder tones to rouse to a sense of guilt one whose remorse was already too dreadful to be borne. He held up the picture of a suicidal wreck to one who bore about with him continually the piteous spectacle of his own ruin; who could not forget what he had been, what he was, and whither he was hastening.

"I might plead with you," said Dr. Willoughby, "in behalf of a beloved child, who left father, and mother, and home, for you, and ask you how you are fulfilling the vows you took upon yourself when you made her your wife. I might speak of your children, and the inheritance of shame you will leave to them if you go on in this evil course. But I have higher claims to urge. You have taken holier vows upon yourself. My son, angels will weep, and Satan will laugh, over the dishonour you are bringing upon the church of God."

This and much more he said, and the wretched man, crouching rather than sitting in his chair, his face and

attitude expressing utter despair, attempted no apology, put in no plea for mercy.

But when **Dr.** Willoughby ceased speaking, he rose to his feet.

·' Father," said he, " no tongue can reproach me as my own conscience reproaches me. No punishment can be greater in this life than the remorse that gnaws my soul. If you could look within, you would see sin, and corruption; but you would see anguish and repentance too. Oh, father, all goodness has gone out of me; but I cannot forget when it was not so. I am not only afraid of the justice of my God, but of the mercy of my Redeemer. I curse the day of my birth, and long for a night of death that shall know no waking. I make my bed in hell, and point out to others the road to heaven. I dare not ask you to pity me—I dare not ask you to pray for me—for there is a sin unto death for which you may not ask the mercy of Heaven. I would to God that I had never been born!"

CHAPTER XIX.

A WOMAN'S STRATAGEM

> " A maiden never bold,
> Of spirit so still and quiet, that her motion
> Blushed at herself."

" She is of so free, so kind, so apt, so blessed a disposition, that she holds it a vice in her goodness not to do more than she is requested."—SHAKESPEARE.

THE day after the interview recorded in the last chapter, as Grace sat in her room, with the door open a little way, her brother came out of his study, and as he passed through the hall she heard him say, with a sigh, "Oh, Allan! Allan!" She was seized with a sudden resolution. "He needs the counsel and companionship of his friend," thought Grace; "and he shall have them, if I can bring it about." She opened her desk, and wrote the following note :—

"WILMOT ST. PARSONAGE, *Dec. 4th, 18—.*

"MR. RICHMOND,—Your friend, Louis Thayer, very much needs your counsel and presence. Will you come to him immediately? As he does not know that I have written to you, and as it is desirable for me to see you before you go to him, will you first seek an interview with your friend,

"GRACE WILLOUGHBY.

"REV. ALLAN RICHMOND,
"Grantley Village, —— Co."

She posted the letter herself. "He will certainly get it to-morrow," she thought, "and will take the first train. I shall tell him all I know. Fanny will not be pleased, but she cannot help herself. It will be hard to tell him; but he is very kind and gentle, and loves Louis dearly."

"Grace," said Mrs. Thayer at the tea-table; "you and I will ride over to West Union to-morrow. I want to talk with mother about the wedding-supper. If she has not given her orders, I shall advise her to go to Blanco's instead of Salter's. Mrs. Barstow says they are considered much more stylish. She employed them at her last party, and felt no more responsibility about the entertainment than any of her guests."

"I cannot go to-morrow, Fanny, possibly, because—because—well, you know I am to go to Madam Passao's in the afternoon to try on the *gros grain*, and—well—I don't care to go to-morrow. You go without me, Fanny, and you and mother can settle it all between you."

"I thought you were always glad of an excuse to go home," her sister said; "but just as you like, though I should be glad of your company."

"She will certainly stay all day," thought Grace; "for there will be no end to her consultations with mother. It has happened beautifully!" And this young lady, within ten days of the time appointed for her wedding, anticipated, with no little agitation, a private interview of her own appointment, with a gentleman who was not her affianced husband.

Allan Richmond, returning from his morning walk about ten o'clock, stopped at the post-office for his mail. There was a package of "The Child's Paper," a "Missionary Herald," a communication from a Bible agent, and Grace Willoughby's letter. He read this last, standing in the door of the post-office, and hurried to his lodgings to make preparations to take the noon train to the city.

When he entered Mrs. Thayer's parlour, Grace was nervously awaiting his coming. She had been thinking all the morning how she should tell her story, expecting to be embarrassed in its recital ; but the earnest interest of Mr. Richmond's manner, his quick inquiry, after the first greeting, "Is Louis ill?" gave her the necessary introduction, and in a few moments she was sitting beside him, and talking to him as freely as to a brother, telling him all she knew, and all she suspected.

"It is a great relief to tell you this," she concluded. "It was kind in you to come so soon. He needs you, and you can help him, can you not?"

He heard her with grave and sympathizing attention. He tried to hide from her how much he was moved by the recital, but he could not disguise his eagerness to go at once to his friend, and Grace liked him none the less for his impatience to leave her for such a purpose.

She led the way to the study, knocked once, and opened the door. Louis sat at his table writing.

The expression of weariness on his pale face changed
to glad surprise at the sight of his friend. She waited
to see them clasp hands, and went out softly.

"I have done what I could ; and now," said Grace,
with unbounded faith in her ally, "Allan Richmond
will do all the rest."

In the long conversation that ensued, neither by
word nor look did the visitor lead Mr. Thayer to sus-
pect the object of his coming. He was shocked by the
change he instantly perceived in his friend, but he
took good care not to show it. He talked of his parish, and the work still going on there, and the minister
tried to rouse himself to listen and reply. When the
afternoon was nearly gone, Mr. Richmond said :—

"I must go back to-night, Louis, and I want you
to return with me. Your people can spare you a
week. The change will greatly benefit you. Come,
take a vacation with me among the Grantley hills. I
have a quiet boarding-place, with plenty of room all .
to ourselves, and I want you. Don't refuse me, Louis.
Indeed, I cannot go home alone."

"But my pulpit?"

"Can be easily supplied. There are half-a-dozen
ex-ministers in the city, any one of whom will be glad
to earn his twenty dollars next Sabbath. Just step
round with me to Barclay Street, and get Raymond.
Your people like him, don't they? or Judd, or Sud-
bury? It will do your congregation good to hear
another voice. Louis, you will not disappoint me.

You promised me a visit long ago, and I want it now."

His persistence prevailed; and the young men went out together, found a supply for the pulpit, and on their return, while Louis went to his room to pack his valise, Mr. Richmond sought Grace in the parlour.

"He is going home with me for a week," he said. "You may be sure I will do what I can for him. Grace—Miss Willoughby, I thank you more than I can express for sending for me."

Then he turned the subject, but retained the seat he had taken beside her to make this confidential communication.

Grace presided at the tea-table, for Mrs. Thayer, greatly to her sister's satisfaction, had not returned from West Union. The young lady was eager to send them away before the mistress of the house came home. "I will make it all right with Fanny," she had said to Louis, when they were talking the matter over. "She will be glad to know that you can rest for a few days;" but, notwithstanding this confident assurance, she was not certain of Mrs. Thayer's approbation of the plan, and wished to put it beyond the possibility of change. They took the evening train at seven o'clock, and fifteen minutes later Dr. Willoughby's bay horse stopped at the parsonage door, and Grace, with a face as innocent and demure as her own white kitten's, just after it had played a particularly sly trick, informed her sister that Mr. Richmond had

called and taken Louis to Grantley with him for a
week's visit.

After the first surprise at the suddenness of the
flight was over, Mrs. Thayer accepted the fact of her
husband's absence very quietly. Indeed, everything
seemed of minor importance to her now in comparison
with the important event for which she had so long
been preparing.

"It will be convenient," she said, "on some accounts,
to have Louis away at present; for we can take a
lunch down town, and not trouble ourselves always to
be at home at dinner-time; and, Grace, mother says
we must come on Tuesday and trim the parlours. She

says it will not answer to do it later, and—did I tell you?—Mrs. Barstow has promised me some of her pressed fern, and your myrtle-bed is as green as in summer!—I looked yesterday to see. Dear me! such a busy day as I have had! and to think how much we have to do, and so little time to do it."

CHAPTER XX.

LOOK UP, BROTHER!

" Whoso aids a sorrowing, struggling brother,
 By kindly word, or deed, or friendly token,
Shall win the favour of our heavenly Father,
 Who judges evil, and rewards the good,
And who hath linked the race of man together
 In one vast, universal brotherhood."—MACKAY.

THE hour's ride between the city and Grantley village was taken almost in silence by the two young men. Louis Thayer, absorbed in his own gloomy thoughts, seemed to have forgotten the presence of his friend, and Allan made no attempt to rouse him from his reverie. But long after the sober village of Grantley was wrapped in its midnight slumber, the two sat talking in Allan Richmond's study.

In trying to recall this conversation, Louis Thayer could not remember how he was led to reveal, that night, the whole story of his fall. He only knew that, having told it, with all its sin, and sorrow, and shame, he felt a sense of unutterable relief. And when he dared to raise his eyes, he saw in the face of this dear friend no reproach, no bitterness, or scorn of his weakness; only love, and compassion, and a look of yearning tenderness such as the Saviour might have given when he beheld the young man in the gospel and loved him. But for a long time Allan Richmond sought vainly to inspire hope in the despairing man's soul. With a peculiarly sensitive organization, a tender conscience, and an inborn love of the truth, and hatred of a lie, he inherited a constitutional predisposition to melancholy. Under any circumstances Louis Thayer would have been subject to seasons of great mental depression; and perhaps a part of his power lay in that unobtrusive, but soul-subduing melancholy, which has nothing repulsive in its character, yet attracts and melts the beholder into sympathy and love. With this tendency, and his health seriously impaired by too close attention to the labours of his profession, the young minister had fallen into a deadly sin, the heinousness of which was ever before him, for his conscience was not blunted, but rather quickened into new life, and kept in a preternatural state of activity by every repetition of his crime. Loathing himself for a sin which he yet had not found strength to conquer, he was the victim of black despair. From this state of mind his friend laboured long to rouse him.

"It is of no use," he replied to the young minister's words of hope. "You bid a man, who has fallen to the ground for very weakness, rise and run a race. You ask me to fight an enemy under whose conquering power I lie bound hand and foot. Allan, Allan, my strongest resolutions are broken, 'as a thread of tow is broken when it toucheth the fire,' for I have an appetite within me more ravenous than a wild beast of the forest. I am like the man in the old Persian fable, who permitted an evil spirit to kiss his shoulder, when instantly there sprang out a serpent, who, in hungry fury, attacked his head and tried to get at his brain. And, when he strove to thrust it away and tear it from its hold, he found it was a part of himself, and he was torturing his own flesh. Such a monster have I created and nourished by my sin, and it gnaws me! it gnaws me! I shall feel its pangs till I die. Allan, I have fallen too low ever to rise again."

"'A just man falleth seven times, and riseth up again,' Louis. With God's help, you will destroy the power of that monster, and tread the serpent under your feet."

"'A just man!'" he repeated, bitterly. "Was I ever *that?* Was I ever anything but the miserable hypocrite I now am—'a whited sepulchre full of all uncleanness'?"

"I will not hear you talk so," said his friend. "You are no hypocrite. You are a deeply repentant man; and as you preach salvation through Christ to the vilest sinner, so I preach it to you to-day."

"If he repent and forsake his sin."

"Yes; and of deep and sincere repentance there is enough. For the power to resist temptation in the future, you must trust in God. The Master, for whom it has been your delight to labour for many years, and who has owned and blessed your efforts, will not lose you,—no, Louis, he *will not* lose you in that day."

A gleam of hope lit up Louis Thayer's face at these confident words, but instantly faded away.

" The thought of the little good I have accomplished in other days," he answered, sadly,—" for, Allan, it cannot be that God accepts the labours of such an one as I am now,—gives little comfort to my own soul; and what shall I say to my Judge, when, asking for the talents He entrusted to me, He will demand why I did not do more? Why, with such power to rise, I have sunk so low? It will stand me in little stead to remember that ' I have preached to others, being my-self a castaway.' "

" Now, Louis," said Allan Richmond, " must I preach the Gospel to you? How many times have I heard you tell a convicted sinner—ah, Louis, do you remember those noon prayer-meetings in the college chapel, when you and I laboured together ?—to cast all the burden of his past sins upon the Saviour; that if a sinner perishes, he perishes not because the merits of Christ are insufficient for his guilt, but because he will not repent and believe. Don't you believe that, my dear friend? Now, leave all this wreck and ruin behind you. Forget that it has ever been. Leave it like a dead corpse in its grave, and do you wake to a new life. There is work for you to do. There are souls to save. God has owned and blessed your labours; He will own and bless them again. Your people reverence and love you—."

"And do you. think *that* is any comfort to me?" he said, almost fiercely. "Would they reverence and love me if they saw me as I am? Is it not an awful increase of my guilt that I am continually acting a lie? I have longed, sometimes, to stand up in my pulpit and tell the shameful story. Shall I do it, Allan? Will it bring me any peace of mind?"

"Your sin is between your own soul and your God, Louis. Its very secrecy has prevented it from injuring your fellow-men. To proclaim it would be to bring dishonour upon the church of God, and affect your influence in the future. I have felt that the hand of Providence was in this; that God has guarded you, and held you back, else in your recklessness you would long ago have betrayed yourself. Your way is not hedged up. It is open before you. Ask forgiveness of God, and His help in the future. Bind yourself by a solemn vow to touch not the unclean thing."

"And if I break the vow? I tell you, Allan, my resolutions are as flax in the fire."

"Then you break it."

"And debauch my conscience, and fall ten times lower than before. With all my humiliation, I have been spared this."

"But I believe, Louis, that had you fortified yourself by a written pledge, you would have kept it. There is something in a man's nature,—call it obstinacy, or firmness or self-will, or what you please; but there is a power within him,—that forces him to stand by a recorded public vow. But, even if you break it, Louis, there is many a man strong in Christian liberty to-day, who was once bound hand and foot by this tyrant that holds you in his grasp, who, struggling to rise, has been beaten down again and again by his fierce foe, but has gained strength at last to wound him even unto death. Have you not men in your church, who have fallen away through some besetting sin of the flesh? You believe they are Christians; that they have the root of the matter in them, and that they will return to their first love; receive pardon for this and other sins, and be saved at last.

" And, Louis, who knows but God is preparing you by this terrible ordeal of sin and suffering for a peculiar work? I think, my dear brother, that, fallen and sore hurt as you are, if by the grace of God you are permitted to rise again, you will be brought into such keen sympathy with the weak, and the tempted, and the fallen, that you can take their pain into your own heart; that, knowing all their weakness, and their grievous temptations, as only one can know them who has borne them in his own flesh, you will go among them, on a level with the lowest, feeling in your inmost soul that the vilest of them all is your brother; and you can speak, oh, how earnestly, how believingly, of that blood of sprinkling that availed even for you. Will you do this, Louis, or will you lie down and die for very weakness?—there is no other reason. Will you do this work for your Master? Will you lift up the hands that hang down, and the feeble knees? Will you strengthen the diseased, heal the sick, bind up that which was broken, bring in that which was driven away, seek that which was lost, and in the last day hear those words of commendation, ' Inasmuch as ye did it unto one of the least of these, ye have done it unto me?' Louis, John Newton was a drunkard, and Bunyan, and Gardiner, and Headley Vicars, and Vine Hall. But they ' are washed,' they ' are sanctified,' they ' are justified in the name of the Lord Jesus.'"

Before he finished, the tears stood in Louis Thayer's eyes, and his friend felt, as he grasped the hand extended to him, that an earnest vow from a deeply repentant heart was registered at that moment in heaven.

They shared the same room, for it was a part of Allan Richmond's plan to keep his friend constantly with him; and long after one of them was sleeping as peacefully as a child, who, confessing his fault, has wept his heart out on his mother's bosom, the other, with hardly less tenderness than that mother might feel for her erring but repentant son, kept loving watch. During the few days the friends were to-gether,—and by reason of what followed, one of them will remember that visit to the day of his death,—the same loving relationship existed between them. With almost a child's dependence upon the brave heart that sustained him in his weakness, Louis Thayer trusted and clung to his friend; and the other, all the sterner traits of his character overborne by as constant and warm a friendship as ever man felt, returned the confidence with the watchful care and brooding tenderness of a mother for her ailing child.

"There is a meeting of the 'Iron Club' to-night," he said one evening to his friend. "Shall we go in for a few moments, and see what they are doing?"

They climbed a flight of stairs to an unfinished room in the foundry. It was lighted by tallow candles, and a couple of lamps on a packing box which served for a table. A dozen rough-looking men, in their working clothes, some of them with unwashed, smutty faces, stood talking together in groups as the friends entered. They crowded round their minister, greeting him with a noisy and rude familiarity that jarred a little upon Louis Thayer's refined ear; but Allan seemed well accustomed to it, and responded with hearty good-will. They appeared eager to communicate something, and Louis withdrew himself a little from the circle, but could hear all they said.

"We have got Bart Tyler," one said; and that this was good news all testified by look and gesture. "Sawyer's done it, and there ain't another man in the club could have fetched it about."

"Sawyer's a little feller, but he's a keen one," said

another. "He followed Bart over to Wakefield Monday night, where he'd gone to get his liquor. (He can't get a dram in Grantley, thank God!) It beats all, the way he's followed that man round lately. They say he's kept after him for a week, out of work hours; and last night he got him to promise he'd swear off. Hollo! there he is now. Be quiet, all of you."

There were steps on the stairs, and two men entered the room, the one slender and undersized, but with a firm step, and a strong, resolute face; the other tall, ungainly, his ragged, ill-fitting clothes hanging loosely about him, and a look of shame and hesitation on his haggard face. He lingered, and seemed inclined to draw back; but his companion held him firmly by the arm, and called out, in a cheery voice, "Here we come, boys!" The two walked the length of the room, and took seats near the table. Then every one else sat down; and, after a short introductory exercise, a paper was produced. The man they called Sawyer, still holding his companion by the arm, as if fearful of losing him, whispered a few earnest words in his ear.

"I dursn't do it," said Bart Tyler, aloud. Then rising slowly and hesitatingly to his feet, he said again, in a harsh, broken voice, "Boys, I tell you I dursn't do it. I'm afeard I shan't hold out. I ain't got no more resolution than a rag. My head and my heart say No; somethin' inside of me says Yes, yes; and the

Yes always carries it. Boys, I guess I'd better not."

He was interrupted by cries of "We'll help you, Bart!" "We'll stand by you!" "Bart Tyler, you are not the man to go back on your word now," &c.

He looked from one to another of the eager, honest faces of his fellow-workmen, and then into the strong, resolute eyes of the friend close beside him.

"I'll sign," said he; "and the Lord help me to keep it."

There was a shout of triumph; and above it all rose Sawyer's cheery voice. "Hurrah, boys! we've hit King Alcohol a hard knock with the 'Iron Club' to-night." Then there was sudden silence, for where Bart Tyler stood a moment before, the members of the "Iron Club" saw the pale stranger who had come in with their minister.

"Friends," said he, and the voice to which admiring crowds had listened was never sweeter in its tones, "friends, will you give me leave to add my name to this paper? I want to go with this brother (he laid his hand upon Bart Tyler's shoulder). I know what he means when he calls himself weak. If ever men needed the help of God, and of their fellow-men, Bart Tyler and I need it. Friends, may I join your 'Iron Club' to-night?"

They heard him with serious, attentive faces, and when he finished there was a faint murmur of applause; but only Allan Richmond understood the import of his words. He came and stood by his friend's side, as Sawyer had stood by Bart Tyler, saw him write that name, honoured and beloved as it was, close beside that of the drunkard, acknowledging the same weakness, the same necessity, and imploring the same aid.

CHAPTER XXI.

THE DELIVERER.

"As the Lord liveth, and as thy soul liveth, this man shall
surely die."

RACE was returning the next Monday even
ing from her farewell visit to Nurse Bidwell, an old lady who claimed the particular
regard of our heroine, inasmuch as, twenty years
before, her eyes were the first that had looked upon
the baby face, and her motherly hands the first that
had administered to the necessities of the new-comer.
A warm affection existed between the two, Nurse
Bidwell interesting herself in all that concerned the
young lady's welfare, and Grace repaying her regard
by attentions that were exceedingly grateful to the old
woman.

And this Monday afternoon, though the bride elect
was somewhat weary—for, under her sister's direction
that morning, she had wreathed the walls of Dr.
Willoughby's old-fashioned parlour with myrtle and
evergreen—she would not neglect this last piece of
attention to her old friend. Seated close to Nurse
Bidwell's chair, and raising her voice to an uncomfortable pitch, to favour her listener's infirmity, Grace had

spent the afternoon in answering eager questions, and volunteering such information about the "pretty things," all ready now, and laid away for the bride's use, as she knew would gratify the old lady's curiosity. Then she must drink a cup of tea from Nurse Bidwell's "chany cup;" and so the hours slipped away, and when at last the withered hand was laid upon the bright, young head, and the tremulous voice said, "Good-bye, dearie, and God bless you," the short December day was gone.

But Grace was not a timid girl, and she had many a time walked a longer distance alone after dark than the mile between her father's house and Nurse Bidwell's cottage. It was bright moonlight. The air was cold and still, and her footsteps rang upon the frozen ground. She walked rapidly, enjoying the keen, bracing air, until she came opposite Crazy Joe's cottage. A bright light shone from the uncurtained window, and, with what her sister would have called very unladylike curiosity, Grace stole up softly, and looked upon the scene within. The room was in perfect order, the uncarpeted floor swept clean, and the bed in the corner neatly made. There were pictures on the walls, and dried everlasting, and gay, red coxcomb, in a vase on the mantel-piece. On the table were Joe's Bible and hymn-book. An immense yellow cat, the only living occupant of the room besides Joe, was dozing in an arm-chair close to the fire.

Joe sat a this instrument—a cracked melodeon,
which, after long years of service in Dr. Willoughby's
lecture-room, had, at Grace's earnest solicitation, been
given to him. It was bright with paint and varnish,
and to-night, under his touch (he had acquired in his
wanderings, no one knew how, some knowledge of
instrumental music), it gave out more melodious sounds
than Grace supposed it contained. He was playing
softly, now and then singing a verse or two of a hymn
or ballad. His peculiar voice, and the words he sang;
possessed a charm for the young girl, and, quite re-
gardless of the cold, she crouched under his window
and listened attentively. He played a lively prelude,
and then, in his high, clear voice, sang these words:—

> " King Jesus He was so strong, my Lord,
>   That He jarred down the gates of hell.
>   Oh, I could not stay in hell one day—one day ;
>   For heaven it is my home.
>   Hark what the chariot wheels do say—do say—
>   The fore wheels run by the grace of God,
>   And the hind wheels run by faith."

Here the cat jumped down from his chair, and
crossing the room, put his fore paws upon the
musician's knee. Joe stopped short in the interlude
he was playing, lifted the creature to his lap, smoothed
and caressed him, laying his cheek more than once
against the soft yellow fur, until, apparently satisfied
with the notice bestowed, the cat returned to his
cushion. Then Joe resumed his music. His fingers

wandered aimlessly over the keys for a few moments,
then he struck a strain that seemed to please him, for
he smiled, put his hand to his forehead, and, after
playing a simple air, sang the following ballad, not
one word of which Grace lost, so distinct was his
utterance:—

> "The wicked, wicked wife of Bath,
> She at the length did die;
> Straightway her soul at heaven's gate
> Did knock most mightily.
>
> "Then down came Adam to the door,
> 'Who knocketh there?' quoth he.
> 'I am the wicked wife of Bath,
> And fain would come to thee.'
>
> "'Thou art a sinner,' Adam said,
> And here shall have no place.'
> 'Old Adam, hast thou done no wrong,
> That thou shouldst judge my case?'
>
> "'I will come in, in spite,' she said,
> 'Of all such churls as thee;
> Thou wast the causer of our woe,
> Our pain and misery.
>
> "'For thou didst eat forbidden fruit,
> To please thy naughty wife.'
> When Adam heard her tell this tale,
> He ran away for life.
>
> "'Begone, thou sinner!' Noah cried,
> 'Thou must go down to hell.'
> 'If *drunkards* went to their own place,
> Where, Noah, wouldst thou dwell?

" ' For thou didst plant a vine,' said she,
    'And drank to thine own shame.'
Thereat did Noah blush, and Lot,
    Who likewise came to blame.

" Then Father Abraham looked down,
    'False woman, end this strife.'
  'I call him false who *lied*,' said she,
    'To save his coward life.

" ' And thou too, Jacob, who didst cheat
    Father and brother too.'
Away slunk Jacob sore abashed,
    And made no more ado.

" Quoth David, ' Drive the jade from hence,
    She led a life of sin.'
  'Didst drive Uriah's wife away,
    Most pure and righteous king?

" ' The woman's mad,' said Solomon.
    'And so was he, my lord,
Who kept seven hundred wives,' quoth she,
    'To turn his heart from God.'

" Then rose the great Apostle Paul.
    ' Oh, wretched soul! ' he cried;
  ' Because the chief of sinners thou,
    Thy suit must be denied.'

" ' Paul! Paul ! remember what thou didst
    In thy most mad desire ;
How thou didst persecute God's church
    With wrath as hot as fire.'

" ' Cease, woman,' Peter sternly called,
    'Thou grievest Christ with cries.'

'Methinks one grieves him more,' she said,
  'Who him from shame denies.'

" When as our Saviour Christ heard this,
  With heavenly angels bright,
He came unto this sinful soul,
  Who trembled at his sight.

" 'O Lord, my God !' she did entreat,
  'These saints did sorely sin,
Yet now thy sweetest glory share;
  Then let me, too, come in.'

" To whom with awful majesty,
  'They sinnèd sore,' said he,
'And sorely, too, they did repent;
  Therefore they pardoned be.'

" She cried a great and bitter cry,
  With knocks did shake the gate:
'I, too, repent.'—'For thee,' said he,
  'Repentance comes too late.

" 'Long did I call—thou me refused,
  And put to open shame;
And now, "The door is shut," and thou
  Must dwell in burning flame.'

" The wailings of that damnèd soul
  Made angels quake with fright;
But she, amid her torments, owned
  Her sentence just and right."

The song ended. Joe drew a long sigh, and his head dropped upon his breast, while Grace, hardly released from the spell of the weird melody to which she had listened, still crouched under the window in the moonlight, until she heard the sound of carriage-wheels approaching at an uneven, rapid pace. She drew back in the shadow; and, a moment after, two men in a light open buggy dashed by, at a speed that was frightful to witness. There was a sharp turn in the road, a little way from Joe's cottage. She heard a grating sound as the wheel struck a projecting rock, then a crash, and, directly after, the sound of the horse's feet galloping down the road. Without an instant's hesitation, she ran to the scene of the accident. The carriage-robe, and whip, and some parts of the broken vehicle, were scattered about; and the buggy, with only one occupant, and the horse running at full speed, was almost out of sight.

Close by the sharp, jutting rock that had occasioned the disaster, a man lay face downward upon the ground. She went to him, and tried to rouse him. He was breathing heavily, but gave no other sign of life. Then Grace looked anxiously up and down the road, but not a person was in sight. "I must call Joe," she thought; and running back to his cottage, she pushed open the door and entered.

Though taken entirely by surprise, Joe manifested no confusion or hesitation of manner, but heard her hurried explanation in silence; and comprehending at once the state of things, took his cap from its nail and was ready for action. He lifted the still unconscious man tenderly in his strong arms, and bringing him

into the cottage, laid him upon his own bed. But as
he did so, the lamp shone full upon his face; and Joe
started back with a cry so wild and strange, that Grace
hurried to his side.

"Look! look!" said Joe, seizing her by the arm and
pointing to the bed. "Behold the righteous judgment
of the Almighty!"

With a sudden terror at she knew not what, Grace
bent over the unconscious man. It was Horace Landon. His eyes were closed, his usually sallow face was
flushed, and the thin black hair he kept so sleek and
orderly hung straggling over his forehead. He was
still breathing heavily, but gave no other token of life.

"O Joe, what shall we do?" she said, in great alarm
and distress. Run quick for help, and I will stay
with him till you return."

"Hush, hush! Miss Grace," he said, in a strange,
deep voice. "We need no help—you and I. The
Lord has delivered him into our hands. Twice, yea,
thrice have I besought this thing at the hand of my
God, and He hath hearkened unto my cry. Stand
back, Miss Grace, and see what great things the Lord
will do for you by the hand of His unworthy servant
this day."

He looked with gleaming eyes all around the room,
as though in search of something.

"What do you mean?" said Grace.

His strange manner and wild eyes frightened her
more than his words, to which she attached no impor-

tance. She knew that, for some reason, Joe had conceived in his crazy head a violent dislike to her affianced husband; but since her father's sharp rebuke, the dislike had manifested itself in no open expression; and if she had thought of it at all, it was to consider it passed away and forgotten. But it all came back to her. The bitter hatred and anger his face expressed, when for the first time he saw this man in Grace Willoughby's company, was in every feature now. The veins in his forehead were swollen almost to bursting; his whole face worked and quivered with passion; and the scar on his cheek, turning a deep purple colour, moved itself like a living thing. His usual quiet melancholy was exchanged for the vehemence of gesture and the frenzy of a madman; and, in addition to this, there was a look of fierce triumph and deep, determined purpose in his eyes, that, though she did not comprehend its meaning, made Grace Willoughby's blood run cold.

"I knew the Lord would provide a way of deliverance," said Joe. "I knew he would not suffer the little white lamb to be given over for gold into the hands of this unbelieving Jew, even as our blessed Saviour was sold for thirty pieces of silver; but, O my God! I thank Thee that Thou hast heard my prayer, and that Thou hast brought this mine enemy to my very hearthstone, that I might 'take him by the beard and smite him and slay him.' Ha! ha! Miss Grace, shall I do unto him as did David, the son of Jesse, to

Goliath of Gath? or shall I hew him in pieces, as 'Samuel hewed Agag, king of the Amalekites, in pieces before the Lord in Gilgal'? 'for as the Lord liveth, and as thy soul liveth, this man shall surely die.'"

His fierce, determined eyes sought the corner of the room, where, with a shudder, Grace saw the sharp edge of his axe gleaming in the lamplight.

She tried to speak, but her tongue seemed paralyzed; for, with the sudden conviction of the awful peril to which she had innocently brought the helpless man before her, came the thought that she was powerless to save him—that he was entirely at the mercy of his deadly foe, who would only be satisfied with his life-blood.

Joe watched her with his horrid, gleaming eyes.

"She don't like that way," he muttered. Then he looked all round the room again, as if in search of something. There was a hammer on the shelf under the clock—to her dying day Grace remembered the ticking of that clock in this awful moment of silence and suspense—and when the madman saw it, he darted forward, and, seizing it with an exclamation of pleasure, swung it above his head.

"I have it now," said he; "it'll be sure to please her, for it's a woman's way. See here, Miss Grace, we'll do unto him as Jael, the wife of Heber the Kenite, did unto Sisera, and was 'blessed above all women in the tent. For she put her hand to the nail, and her right hand to the workman's hammer. She smote Sisera, when she had pierced and stricken through his temples.'"

He danced round her, brandishing the horrid weapon, and at every evolution coming nearer to the bed on which his victim lay. The imminence of the peril gave Grace the courage she needed. She placed herself in such a position that a blow from the furious man must first fall upon her, and, looking steadily into the glittering, restless eyes that wandered here and there, and speaking with a calmness and authority at which she was herself surprised, she said,—

"Joe, put down that hammer and listen to me."

He obeyed her, coming close to her side.

"You must not do it, Joe; do you hear me?—you must not do it. It would be mean, and cowardly, and wicked, to kill a helpless man that can offer no resistance."

"Blood for blood," said Joe; "'an eye for an eye, and a tooth for a tooth.' 'Whosoever sheddeth man's blood, by man shall his blood be shed.'"

He stopped, put his hand to the scar upon his cheek, and broke into an ungovernable fit of fury. He ground his teeth, he stamped upon the floor, and uttered inarticulate cries of rage, then, darting into an adjoining room, returned with a monstrous carving-knife, which he brandished aloft.

"Stand back, girl," said he, coming close to her with the murderous weapon in his hand. Stand back, and let me do my appointed work."

"Stop!" said she. "Oh, wait a moment, Joe! See, he is coming out of his swoon. Do you want to kill him, body and soul? Do you want to send him into the presence of an angry God with all his sins unrepented of? Let him offer one prayer for mercy. Look, Joe!"

The man, whose life was hanging by the thread of a madman's whim, stirred and opened his eyes, then, with a deep sigh, relapsed into unconsciousness. But Grace fancied she saw signs of indecision in Joe's face, and she pursued her advantage.

"If you do this cruel thing," she said,—and her father in his pulpit never thundered forth a denunciation in a sterner tone,—"if you do this cruel thing, Joe Martin, I will ask God *never, never* to take the mark of the beast from you, but to let him torment you for ten thousand two hundred and sixty years." And then, without waiting an instant to see the effect produced by this terrific threat, she sprang to the door, for she heard the sound of carriage wheels, threw it wide open, and screamed for help at the top of her voice, and then turned, half expecting to see Joe's deadly weapon buried in her lover's heart.

But the crazy man's mood had changed. The knife had dropped from his hand ; and, sinking into a chair, he said, beseechingly, "Take that back, Miss Grace, take it back! You never will do the dreadful thing you said—?" He stopped, for the door was flung open, and old Dr. Jenks, a physician in a neighbouring town, muffled to the ears in his greatcoat and tippet, bustled into the room.

"Why, what's all this?" he said, in his quick, business way,—"robes, cushions, and whips all along the road, and a woman screaming for help in the door-way! Why, Miss Willoughby, is this you? I want

to know. Have you had an upset? Holloa!—" he saw the prostrate figure, and hurried to the bedside.

Grace stood by him, trembling in every limb, and, now that the great danger was over, quite unable to keep back her tears.

"Do you think he is much hurt, doctor?" she said, anxiously.

"Hurt," said the rough old doctor, speaking very

deliberately,—" well, no, I shouldn't say he was. It would take more than a fall from a buggy to hurt a man in his condition. The fellow's dead drunk. Holloa! where's the girl going?"

" Home," said Grace Willoughby. And home she went.

CHAPTER XXII.

GRACE WILLOUGHBY SPEAKS HER MIND.

" ' Yes,' I answered you last night.
   ' No,' this morning, sir, I say.
Colours seen by candle light
   Will not look the same by day."
MRS. BROWNING.

R. JENKS stood staring at the door through which the young lady had so suddenly departed.

" Well," said he, " that girl has a cool way of getting herself out of a scrape. If she hasn't taken herself off in a hurry, and left me with an ugly job on my hands too. I thought there was murder going on at least, by the way she screamed to me a minute ago, and now she's walked off, and left me to take care of this drunken brute. I have half a mind to follow her example; but no, it will never do to leave him here with poor Joe, for he might wake up ugly. Well, I suppose I'll have to take him to West Union tavern, where it's likely he got his liquor. Here you, Joe, who is he, and how did he come here ?"

Joe, sitting in an attitude of the deepest dejection, his head resting on his hands, muttered something in reply, of which the doctor only heard the word " beast."

"Confound your beasts!" said Dr. Jenks, thoroughly out of patience; "there's a beast yonder that's got to be attended to, unless you want I should leave him on your bed all night. Come, Joe, help me to carry the fellow out to my chaise."

But Joe refused to move, and Dr. Jenks, after vigorously shaking his patient, succeeded in rousing him to partial consciousness, and, half dragging, half carrying him, finally succeeded in getting him into the carriage. He drove to West Union hotel, and, delivering up his charge to the landlord, went about his business.

Mr. Horace Landon was provided with comfortable accommodations for the night, and woke the next morning about ten o'clock, very stiff and sore, with a decided headache, and a confused recollection of a rapid ride over an uneven road, a crash, some loud talking, a rough handling; after which he remembered nothing further. He took a hasty breakfast, hired a livery team, and went back to the city. The landlord watched him as he drove from the door.

"A pretty scrape," said he, "for a man to get into three days before his wedding. Why, in the name of all that's decent, if he wanted a farewell spree, didn't he go a little further from home?"

Grace was sitting alone in the parlour that evening, when Mr. Landon was announced. He entered smiling, deferential, and thoroughly self-possessed. Grace, on the contrary, manifested great embarrassment. She coloured painfully, and then grew very pale, and, after one shy, conscious look in her lover's face, fastened her eyes steadfastly on the carpet. Mr. Landon took his usual seat at her side, smiling at her evident confusion. "She has heard something of this unfortunate affair," he thought, "and expects an explanation. Well, we will have it over with as soon as may be." So, after a few commonplace remarks, to which she hardly responded, he said, playfully, "Are you aware that you have especial cause for thankfulness in my behalf to-night, Grace? A lucky chance, or, as your good father would put it, 'a special providence,' has returned me to you in safety, my dear girl. About this time last evening—he glanced at the clock, whose hand pointed at half-past seven—the life you have so soon promised to make complete was in peril. What! turning pale, dear? when it is all over, and you see I am safe and sound?"

She did, indeed, turn pale at the significance of his words, for the scene in Joe's cottage the previous evening, at that hour, was before her again; the furious gestures, and fierce, murderous eyes of the madman, as he stood over his helpless victim.

"Though your alarm is quite unnecessary," said Mr. Landon, "it is pleasant to know that you feel it. Why, dearest, you will teach me to say with Othello:—

'She loved me for the dangers I had passed;
And I loved her that she did pity me;

but keep your sympathy till you have heard my story.
I attended court, you know, in Barton yesterday, and
when we were through, Dyke and Henderson, and two
or three more of my own cronies, arranged for a
farewell dinner, to commemorate my desertion of their
bachelor ranks. Now, a little unsophisticated country
girl like you, Grace, cannot be supposed to know
much about such gatherings. Dyke and Henderson
are capital fellows, but convivial. They had good
wine, and plenty of it. I have pretty much given up
that sort of thing, as you know, but on such an
occasion it would seem scrubby to refuse. So I
partook with the rest, of course in moderation. Well,
we broke up early, for I had an appointment at my
office,—I am crowding my business into these last
days, that I may uninterruptedly enjoy your sweet
fellowship by and by,—and Winslow drove me home.
He had a spirited horse, and, to tell the truth, was in
no condition to manage him, and about a mile from
West Union he ran over a rock by the side of the
road, broke the buggy, and spilled me out, but
hung to the lines himself, for half a mile or so, till the
concern went to pieces. He was not hurt, but was
obliged to walk into town; and it was an hour or two
before he came to look me up. I suppose the fall
stunned me, for I have no distinct recollection of what
followed. I learned this morning that an old doctor,
who lives somewhere out in the country, picked me
up, and brought me to the hotel, where I found myself

this morning, sound in limb, but very stiff and sore from bruises and exposure. It was a marvel that I was not killed."

Grace was looking him steadily in the face.

"Dr. Jenks said you were not injured by the fall," she replied, very quietly.

"Indeed! it seems I was injured enough to remain unconscious for several hours," he replied.

"He said," she continued, "that it would take more than a fall from a carriage to injure a man in your condition."

Horace Landon bit his lip. "And what else did this learned doctor say?" he inquired, with a supercilious smile. "Tell me all, Grace."

"He said," she answered, looking him full in the face, "that *you were dead drunk.*"

"And I say," said Horace Landon, in sudden passion, "that he lies.' Then, recovering himself instantly,—"I ask your pardon, Grace, for my hasty expression. I was naturally indignant at such a perversion of the truth to my disadvantage. The facts are these :—I had spent five hours in a heated court-room, before breaking my fast, and my head was in a poor condition to bear the little stimulant I took. I do not deny that the few glasses of wine I drank affected me more in my over-wearied state than they would under ordinary circumstances ; that in any degree I approached the condition you have so elegantly described, I emphatically deny."

"The expression was Dr. Jenks's, and not mine," she replied.

"And may I inquire to whom Dr. Jenks imparted this delightful piece of intelligence?"

"To me, Horace."

"To you? Now you surprise me, Grace. Where have you seen him?"

"I saw him," she answered, "in Joe Martin's cottage, where you were taken directly after the accident. I was returning from a visit to a friend last evening, when your upset occurred. It was near Martin's house, and he carried y u i his arms, and laid you on his own bed. I cal ed in Dr. Jenks, who was passing, and who relieved my fears as to any bodily injury you had sustained in the manner I have told you."

She watched him closely while she was speaking; but, well-schooled in self-control, he suffered his face to exhibit no sign of emotion.

"Truly," said he, with his bland smile, "I was well supplied with helpers in my hour of need,—a crack-brained wood-sawyer, a garrulous country doctor, and last, but not least, a fair, wandering damsel in search of moonlight adventures. I shall take better care of my little girl presently, than to suffer her to run about the streets at night, especially in the vicinity of that Bedlamite."

"Will you tell me, Horace," she said, "why Joe Martin hates you with such a bitter hatred?"

He gave her a quick, searching glance.

"I should be glad to gratify your curiosity," he said; "but it takes more logical acumen·than I possess to account for the wild fantasies of a crazy fellow's brain."

"He is gentle and loving toward every other human being," said Grace; "he hates you with a deadly hatred. You acknowledged to me once that his name was familiar to you. I am sure you are in some way connected with the history of his early life. Will you please explain this mystery to me, Horace?"

"My dear girl, you ask impossibilities. What do I know of Joe Martin's likes or dislikes? It strikes me, you spend a great deal of unnecessary sympathy upon that vagrant. I would have had him in a strait-jacket long ago, but for your father's objections."

"You evade my question, Mr. Landon. Who gave him that cut on his cheek?"

The colour flushed into his sallow face.

"How do I know?" said he haughtily. "Grace, we have had enough of this. Am I to sit here and defend myself against the ravings of a madman? 'Tis passing strange, if the lady who has confidence enough in my honour to trust her life's happiness in my hands, cannot take my word against that of a wandering vagrant. Now let us drop this subject. My dear girl, I came to you to-night to talk on pleasanter themes. Will you put away that dignified air of sanctity, which does not in the least become you, and be my own Grace again?

> ' Be a saint, if you will, in the morning,
> But, oh, be a woman to-night.' "

She hastily withdrew the hand he had taken.

" Tell me whether you ever knew him before ? " she said.

" Now, this passes my patience," said Horace Landon. " Grace, you will oblige me to speak very plainly. Whether I have ever known Joe Martin, or not, does not in the least concern *you*. I deny the right of man or woman to interrogate me as you have done to-night. It is perhaps as well for us to come to an understanding on this matter at once. In asking you to share my future, I by no means recognize your right to pry into the past. My wife will have my confidence in time to come, just so far as she proves herself discreet and worthy; but what is past is past, and not even her hand shall withdraw the veil that hides it." Then, in a softer tone,—" Now, Grace, you understand me once for all, and the subject need never be mentioned between us again. What I had to do with this vagrant fellow happened many years ago, and in no way concerns you. That he raves against me speaks loudly in my favour, for it is a well-established fact that crazy people turn against their best friends. And let us have done with this for ever. Whose handiwork is this festive-looking apartment with its wreaths of evergreen ? And is Mother Willoughby at rest, having completed all her arrangements for the wedding?"

"There will be no wedding," said Grace.

She had risen from her seat at his side, and, taking her engagement ring from her finger, stood holding it in her hand. The cluster of diamonds that flashed and sparkled in the lamplight was not brighter than the light that shone from her blue eyes.

"There will be no wedding," she repeated. "You say truly, that it is well to come to a thorough understanding of this matter now. I had no thought of making an unreasonable request. I was so ignorant as to suppose that, as your affianced wife, I had a right to your unreserved confidence, in the past, the present, and the future. I am only a simple girl, 'unsophisticated,' as you say; but if I am to marry, I will not 'dwell in the suburbs of my husband's good pleasure.' I will share his heart, as well as his home. I will be all, or nothing. Take back your ring, Mr. Landon."

"Grace, what folly is this?"

He looked at her with surprise and admiration, for her excitement changed the whole character of her beauty, but with no serious thought that she was in earnest. He had described her to his friend the day before, as they drove over to Barton, as a gentle, affectionate little creature; not particularly brilliant, not the woman to shine in society, but mild and amiable, to be moulded in all respects to her husband's will; 'in short, Winslow, 'a wife to come home to;' just what a *blasé* world-citizen like myself needs." Having formed this opinion of his bride elect, he looked at her with some curiosity in the new character she had assumed; then he rose and stood by her side.

"What folly is this?" he said.

"It is a folly that will never be repeated," she replied. "I thank God it is not yet too late to retrieve it. Take back your ring, Mr. Landon. If I am not fit to share your confidence, I am not fit to be your wife. Release me from this unequal engagement, where one gives all and the other a part."

While she spoke, Mr. Landon was thinking what he had done for this girl,—how, finding her in a country town, with no fortune, no high social standing, only a minister's daughter, with her pretty face alone to recommend her, he, Horace Landon, possessed of money, position, and a name, all that in his estimation made life desirable, had offered to share these gifts with her, asking nothing in return but her love and gratitude. *She* to talk in that high-flown strain about her rights to his unreserved confidence, her claims to be taken into his secret counsels! It was preposterous! Her future life ought to be one expression of gratitude for what he had done for her. Even yet he could not understand that she was in earnest in what she said, and his face expressed a little of the angry surprise he felt that she dared to trifle with him.

"Grace," he said, "I have never seen a trace of coquetry about you before. It is late to practise it upon me now; yet it is impossible that you can mean what you say."

"I am so much in earnest, Mr. Landon," she said, "that I feel my engagement to be an intolerable burden, from which, as an honourable man, you cannot refuse to release me."

His face was pale with anger, but he said, very calmly, "May I inquire the cause of this sudden change in your feelings?"

"Must I tell you?" she answered. "Last night, Mr. Landon, I saw the man whom in my heart I had promised to *honour*, whom if I am to live happily with I must *reverence*, in a condition so low and beastly that for very shame I hurried out of his sight. Isn't that cause enough? Just now I heard, from his own lips, that his wife will share his conveniences, but not his confidence—his hearth and his home, not his heart. I vowed last night I would never call that man husband, and I have just vowed it again. I owe a debt of gratitude to this poor fellow whom you have wronged, and refuse to tell me how, since indirectly he is my deliverer."

There was no anger in her voice. She spoke with quiet determination, and met his stern look unwaveringly. Her answer stung him, and he seemed to be trying to control himself before he spoke.

"I am sure we need not prolong this interview," she said, after waiting a moment for his reply. "Release me from my promise, Mr. Landon, and let me go."

He looked upon her with as black a frown as ever darkened a man's face.

"Let you go?" he said; "yes, certainly, since your reasons are so good and sufficient;" then, bending down to look in her face, with a peculiar and sinister expression he said, "Miss Willoughby will find the sight that shocked her last night repeated *very near home.* Will you give my parting regards to your sister, and ask her if she remembers *the night of the fifteenth of last September* at Congress Hall?"

He took up the ring she had laid upon the table, and left the house.

Grace went immediately to her father. The Doctor looked up from his sermon-writing in surprise.

"Has Mr. Landon gone so soon?" he inquired.

"Father, he has gone, never to come back again," said Grace. "I belong only to you and mother now." Then she told her last night's adventure and its consequences. "And, father," she said, "when I heard Dr. Jenks's words, and saw him lying there, such a loathing and detestation of that man came over me, that I could not stay in the room with him another minute, and I said again and again to myself walking home, 'I will never call him husband;' and I thought about it all night, and to-day, and now I am free. This hateful engagement is at an end. You are not sorry, father? You are not tired of your little girl?'

"This is very sudden, Grace. I am afraid you have acted hastily, my child."

"No, father, it is not sudden. From the first day of my engagement I have had doubts and fears, but have stifled them as best I could, and till last night there was no way of release opened to me. And now there is only room in my heart for one thought, and that is, I am free."

Dr. Willoughby looked at his daughter in surprise.

"What is there in Mr. Landon," he said, "that leads you to conclude your life with him would not be happy? He has every outward advantage,—wealth, position, and professional talent. He is not unprepossessing in appearance. He is polished in his manners, and devotedly attached to you."

"Do you think he is a good man, father?"

"I could wish, my child, that he was more settled in his religious belief; but the road to the understanding is through the heart, and I have hoped his love for you might, under God, be the means of his conversion."

"Never, father; he has not a particle of sympathy with my religious feelings. Weak and imperfect as I am, I should be far more likely to expose my faith to his contempt than to gain for it his love and reverence. If there were no other reason, the different views we entertain on religion would prevent any real union of soul between us; but there *are* other reasons. I detest him. I despise him. I hate—no, I don't mean that, because it is wicked to hate—but, father, I would rather die this minute than marry him."

After this feminine outbreak, there was nothing to be said on the other side, and Dr. Willoughby was easily reconciled to the prospect of keeping his child with him.

"But have you considered, my dear," he said, "that in all probability you will never again have the opportunity to make so eligible a match?"

"Father," said this young lady of twenty, "I shall never marry. I see it plainly my duty to stay with you and mother as long as you live."

The disappointment and indignation of Mrs. Willoughby and her eldest daughter, when they were informed of the step Grace had taken, can be imagined. Mrs. Thayer wrote to her husband, "that in consequence of a lover's quarrel there would be no wedding on Thursday; that Grace had behaved very foolishly, but she hoped all would yet be well." She also wrote, that Mr. Barstow had kindly offered to see that the pulpit was supplied the coming Sabbath, if he desired to remain longer with his friend.

"And what, I should like to know," said Mrs. Willoughby, after a somewhat stormy interview with her youngest daughter,—"what, I should like to know, is going to be done with all those elegant dresses,— the pearl satin, and the *gros grain*, and the *moire antique*, and all that point lace?"

"Why, mother!" said Grace, "we can sell them, *and send the money to the missionaries.*"

Dr. Willoughby was sent for one day, to visit a sick person in the city. He grumbled a little as he climbed the long flights of stairs in the tenement house to which he had been directed. "There are plenty of ministers in town," he thought, "to do this missionary work, without sending three miles out for an old man like me." He found the object of his search, a decent, middle-aged man, far gone with consumption.

"I have sent for you, Dr. Willoughby," he said, "to tell you some facts I ought to have told in the time of them, and that was a good many years ago. I've been an honest, hard-working man, sir, all my life, and tried to do about right; but there's an underhanded piece of business I was knowing to, that it troubles me to think of, lying on this bed; and it concerned a person that you made a good many inquiries about sixteen or seventeen years ago. I mean the boy, Joseph Martin."

"What of him?" said Dr. Willoughby, quickly.

"I'm going to tell you, sir. When his mother got him in at Grimes and Blodgett's, I was porter to the house. The head clerk's name was Landon. Perhaps you know him, sir? He went to college afterward, and now he's got to be a rich lawyer in the city. Well, he was a high blade then, and he and another clerk by the name of Winslow used to drink, and carouse, and play cards in the store all night sometimes. I knew about it, you see, for somebody must clean up the muss they made, and they paid me well to keep dark. They drew that boy into it. You know what he was, sir,—a high-strung little fellow, as handsome as a picture, and as smart as a steel trap. Well, they used to coax him to drink, though he'd promised his dead mother he wouldn't; and when he was half tipsy he'd sing his songs, and spout Shakespeare, and make lots of fun for them.

"One night I went down late, to see about some goods that were to be shipped early in the morning, and there they were at it, drinking and carousing, and Joe Martin on the table, so drunk he couldn't stand straight, singing his songs, and making his speeches. I was at work in the next room, when I heard a noise like a scuffle, and I got to the door just in time to see. Landon give that boy an awful cut, right across the jaw, with a bowie-knife, and then fling him backward with all his strength. His head struck a corner of the iron safe, and he lay as if he was dead. 'What do you want to use the boy like that for?' said Winslow. 'Because he meant mischief,' said Landon; 'he came at me like a young tiger-cat.'—'And you could have mastered him with one hand,' said the other. 'I believe you've done for him, Landon.'—'No, I haven't,' says he, kind of jeering like; 'but I've spoiled his beauty.' Then he saw me in the doorway. 'Here, Carter,' said he, 'if you'll run for a carriage, and take this fellow to the hospital, I'll give you ten dollars.' —'I wouldn't do it for twenty,' said I. 'You may take him yourself.'

"Well, sir, I'm making a long story. I needn't tell all that was said, but the upshot of it was, I got the carriage, and he and I took the boy to the hospital; and there he lay all those weeks when you were hunting for him; and nobody thought of looking there. And Laudon never went near him, and he paid me hush-money, and I kept still; but twice I went on the

sly to the hospital, to find out about him, and they said he would get well, but had better have died, for he would never find his mind again. The next time I went he had gone, no one knew where. And I have never seen or heard of him since, sir."

Dr. Willoughby narrated this story to his wife and daughter in burning indignation.

"Thank God on your knees, Grace," said he, "for your deliverance. The man who committed that dastardly deed is not fit to live, and hanging is too good for him."

Grace looked up with a pale face.

"I should be his wife to-day, father," she said, "but for Crazy Joe. The poor fellow's prayer is answered, for he is indeed my *deliverer*."

CHAPTER XXIII.

DAVID AND JONATHAN.

" The path by which we twain did go,
    Which led by tracks that pleased us well,
    Through four sweet years arose and fell,
From flower to flower, from snow to snow.

" But where the path we walked began
    To slant the fifth autumnal slope,
    As we descended, following hope,
There sat the shadow feared by man."—TENNYSON.

" O see them two together," said Mr. Richmond's landlady one day, as she watched her minister and his friend walk arm in arm down Grantley Street,—" to see them two together makes me think for all the world of David and Jonathan, they do seem so mightily taken up with each other. There's David (that's Mr. Richmond, you know, and I'm sure the real David couldn't have been any more 'ruddy' nor 'goodly to look to' than our minister); he tends right up to Jonathan (that's Mr. Thayer), and don't hardly let him out of his sight. It does beat all, the fuss he makes over that man. Why, he slipped a ten-dollar bill into my hand t'other day, and says he, 'Miss Bigley,'—he, that in all the year and a half he's boarded with me never opened

his mouth about his victuals afore; he's a dreadful
easy man to get along with; I tell him he's jest like
the apostle Paul, for he eats what's sot afore him, and
don't ask no questions for conscience' sake. Well, as
I was tellin', he slipped that ar' ten-dollar bill into my
hand, and says he, ' Miss Bigley, I'll be much obleeged
to yer,' says he, ' if while my friend's here, you'll buy
the best beef you can find in the market;' and what
does he do one night but come slyin' round to the
kitchen door, with a keg of oysters, and half-a-dozen
pounds of Java coffee,—coffee," said Mrs. Biglow,
" that you can smell all over the house while you are
bilin' of it,—for peas is peas, and coffee is coffee. And
t'other day, when they came in from their walk, and
Mr. Thayer, he was too tired to go upstairs, but lopped
right down onto the keepin'-room sofy, and was fast
asleep in a minit; our minister, he went a-steppin'
round on tiptoe, and fetched a pillow for his head, and
a shawl to kiver him, and tucked him in all snug and
comfortable, and he shet to the door, for fear a breath
o' wind should tech him. Then he sot right down by
him, and never stirred, nor hardly took his eyes off
him; but kep' a-lookin' at him so kind of tender and
pitiful like, it eeuermost made me cry. And I thought
as I sot there a-watchin' of 'em, what David says
about Jonathan :—' I am distressed for thee, my
brother Jonathan. Very pleasant hast thou been
unto me; thy love to me was wonderful, passing the
love of women.'

"Well," said the old lady, "that ar's a kind of love our minister don't know 'bout yet by experience, though to my sartin knowledge there's more'n one girl in Grantley village would like to hev the teachin' of him, if he'd gin her the chance."

It was the evening of the preparatory lecture in Mr. Richmond's church, and Louis Thayer, who had passed a day of more than usual suffering (the fight he was carrying on with his demon appetite was a fearful one), seemed so weary, that his friend advised his remaining at home. So the fire was replenished, the study-lamp lighted, and Allan left the invalid with books and papers to amuse him, and went to his hour's service in the chapel.

The last stroke of the church-bell vibrated on the keen winter air. The house was very still, for Mrs. Bigley had also gone to the lecture, taking with her her little maid-of-all-work, so that the visitor was quite alone.

"If you'll be so kind, sir," Mrs. Bigley had said, putting her head in at the study door, "jest to turn the key in the front door after we are gone, 'caus' somebody might get in. Miss Williams had two bran-new sheets stole off her line last summer. It was dretful kerless in her leavin' of 'em out. A body can't be too kerful, when there's so many old trampers round."

As Mr. Thayer descended the stairs to do her

bidding, the door-bell rang, and when he answered the summons there stood before him a respectable-looking, gray-haired man, with a stone jug in his hand. Louis recognized him at once as one of the deacons in his friend's church.

"Any the folks 'bout hum?" he inquired.

"All at church, deacon."

"Wal, I reckoned they would be; but I s'pose I can leave this ere with you jest as well. You see, I stopped down below to have the communion jug filled for next Sunday, calkerlatin' to get to the meetin'-house afore the sexton was through tollin'; but I got belated somehow, and it's shut. I don't care to take it inter meetin' with me, and I'm afeard to leave it in the waggin, for we've got some dreadful sassy boys in Grantley, an' they might meddle, you know. So, thinks I, I'll fetch it inter Miss Bigley's, an' she'll take care on't till Sabbath day. I'll set it right down here in the entry, an' tell her 'bout it arter meetin'."

Mr. Richmond was detained a moment after service, and Mrs. Bigley, returning to her home, found the door securely fastened against her. There was a bright light burning in the study, but her repeated summons elicited no response, and while the good lady stood shivering on her door-step the minister joined her. .

"He must have fallen asleep in his chair, Mrs. Bigley," said Allan Richmond, after his efforts met with no better success than those of his landlady. "I can climb up by the porch, and get in at the front window;" which he accordingly did. When, a moment after, he opened the door to Mrs. Bigley, his face wore so grave and anxious an expression that she quite forgot her impatience at being kept waiting in the cold, till, as she told her little maid, "all her bones were in a shiver," but eagerly inquired what was amiss.

"Mr. Thayer is not well," Allan replied; but he declined all her offers of assistance, and hurried to his friend.

"I shouldn't wonder," said Mrs. Bigley to her maid, Betsy Jane, "if that poor creetur had fainted dead away in his cheer. He told me, when I was a-questionin' of him about his ailments, that he had a dretful faint feelin' the biggest part o' the time. 'Now, Mr. Thayer,' says I, 'if you'd git a bottle of Hostetter's Bitters, an' whenever you feel that sense o' goneness at the pit of yer stummick, jest take a large spunful,— 'twould cherk yer up wonderful.' But he shook his head and smiled that kinder mournful smile o' hisn, that allus makes me think of our little Susan Ann jest afore she died. I'm afeard he's got some in'ard disease a-preyin' on his vitals. Why, where's the deacon's communion jug? He told me he sot it down jest inside the door, and wanted I should put it on the cellar bottom till he called for't. Now he's put it somewhere else, and forgot it. The deacon's gettin' dretful forgetful 'bout little things."

The minister locked his study door, and taking in

his strong arms the senseless form that was half
sitting, half lying in his chair, carried it into the
adjoining sleeping apartment. Allan Richmond looked
grave and sorry, but not discouraged.

"It must have come sooner or later," he thought.
"I hardly dared to hope he would conquer the foe at
one struggle. This devil must needs tear him before
he comes out of him. But in the name of Jesus
Christ of Nazareth, whose servant he is, it shall be
cast out. It is not the Saviour's will to lose this dear
disciple."

Then he looked at the jug of communion wine
which he had found at his friend's side. If he had
not overheard Deacon Alden's whispered communication to his landlady, the minister would have known
this jug, for on communion Sabbaths it used to stand
in a recess under his pulpit, and had become familiar
to his eye. It may seem strangely inconsistent in so
staunch a temperance man as Allan Richmond, that
he had hitherto put into the hands of his church-
members, when commemorating their Saviour's death,
that which he elsewhere denominated a curse, and
under all other circumstances adjured them in the
most solemn manner not to touch. Whether this was
through culpable ignorance of the fact, that the
unfermented juice of the grape, pure and unintoxicating,
is an article of commerce, and can easily be procured,
or through a superstitious reverence and fear of an
unhallowed innovation in the manner of performing a

sacred rite which has been practised for ages by the church of God, we know not; but it is a sin that can no longer be laid at his door.

Sitting by the bedside of his friend, to whom the cup of salvation had proved the cup of devils, the young minister resolved that night, before God, that never again, in the administration of the sacrament of the Lord's Supper, would he touch the unclean thing.

He felt no disposition to sleep, with this and other thoughts crowding upon his mind, and it was nearly morning before he laid himself down by his friend's side. Then he must have slept heavily, for the first sound he heard was the breakfast bell rung sharply by Betsy Jane, very near his door. His first waking thought was of his friend, and, turning quickly, he was not a little startled and agitated to find his place vacant. He tried to reassure himself while hastily dressing. " He has gone for a walk before breakfast," he thought; but the explanation was not satisfactory, and he hurried downstairs. Mrs. Bigley's little maid met him in the hall.

" If you please, sir," said Betsy Jane, " I was to tell you that Mr. Thayer he'd gone home this morning by the first train, and I was to say good-bye to you, and you was never to trouble yourself any more about him. I was to tell you that last *peticelar*."

" When did you last see Mr. Thayer, Betsy?"

" If you please, sir, I was a-makin' up the kitchen fire about six o'clock. And he come right out there, he did, with his overcoat on, and his carpet-bag, sir, and he scar't me at first, for he looked so pale, and his eyes kinder wild like. But he spoke as pleasant as ever, and he gave me a whole dollar to remember him by, and—."

"Now, Mr. Richmond," said Mrs. Bigley, appearing in the doorway, her motherly face all red and perspiring from the kitchen fire, "I feel hurt—I reelly do feel hurt. To think he should have gone off in that way, so sudding, and on an empty stummich. I could have made him a cup of tea in five minutes if I'd knowed he was a-goin'. Why, I never was so beat in my life, as when Betsy Jane told me. I feel hurt, Mr. Richmond, I reelly do feel hurt."

" So do I, Mrs. Bigley. He has stolen the march upon us both, and I shall take the noon train and bring him back; you may depend upon seeing him again this evening. You and I were in a fair way to make a well man of him, Mrs. Bigley. We can't give it up in this way."

He spoke cheerfully, but his heart sank within him. Louis had gone off desperate; his dearest friend was "to trouble himself no more about him." The hours were long till twelve o'clock.

"Be sure you bring him back," Mrs. Bigley called after him from the porch. "I'll have a hot supper all ready for you against you come."

At the depot he found a group of discontented travellers, and the news that greeted him was not encouraging. " A freight train smashed up the other side of Long Bridge; engine right across the track; no down train for three or four hours at least."

He employed the tedious hours of waiting in driving two miles, over the hills, to Deacon Alden's farm-house. He found the good man arrayed in blue cotton overalls, and a beaver hat that defies description, in his barn-yard, cutting up pumpkins for his cow. Mr. Richmond stated to him his change of views in regard to using intoxicating wine at the communion-table; "for, deacon," said he, " a mixture that can stimulate into convulsive cravings an appetite as strong as death, in the presence of which reason, conscience, and religion are all swept aside, is no fit emblem of that precious cleansing blood which flowed for the salvation of mankind. The cup of the Lord shall never again in my church be filled with intoxicating drink, and never again will I put it to the lips of believers, saying, ' Drink ye all of it;' and, deacon, you must find something between now and Sunday for a substitute, for I cannot in conscience put the cup of intoxication into your hand to be again distributed to my people. Before another communion season, I will see to it that the cup we offer contains no alcohol, and no intoxicating qualities, and yet is that symbol of the blood of Christ, the fruit of the vine."

Deacon Alden, resting his spade upon a great yellow pumpkin, smiled at his young pastor's impetuosity. Allan Richmond was quick in coming to a conclusion;

impressible, demonstrative, and eager, pounding down his ideas with his fists as well as his voice.

"Wal, now, Mr. Richmond," said the good old man, very deliberately, "you've expressed my idees exactly. I've been a-comin' to that way o' thinkin' for quite a spell. It goes ag'in the grain every time I put that jug inter my waggin. I tell yer it ain't the thing to go an' buy for Christian folks to use, on sich a solemn occasion,—the very stuff that makes men drunk. I feel streeked every time I do it. An' if you'd passed the cup 'forty year, as I have, Mr. Richmond, and seen some on 'em take a long, deep swaller, as though they loved it, you'd call it dangerous, to say the least. Why, 'twas only the other day, Sawyer,—he's one of your 'iron men,' you know, jined the church in the revival,—says he, 'Deacon, I don't know what I'm a-goin' to do communion days. I can't trust myself,' says he, 'to smell a glass o' spirits, and jest the taste o' that wine the other Sunday,' says he, 'made me mad for drink.' An' there's another thing. If we are a-goin' to give our testimony, as a church, ag'in the use of intoxicatin' drink, it seems a mighty poor way to do it, to buy an' use it for *any* purpose, an' what's to hinder our bein' reproached by them moderate drinkers; for, say they, 'they call it a curse, an' they go an' use it in their most solemn act of worship.'

"Wal, now, don't you fret, Mr. Richmond, 'bout next Sunday. Miss Alden, she did up a lot of grape jel last fall, an' I'll put some water to it, and that won't tempt nobody."

There was no train that night to the city. The next day was Saturday, and there were preparations that must be made for the Sabbath; and so, though

very reluctantly, Allan deferred his visit to his friend until the following Monday. He quieted himself by thinking that, despairing and almost desperate as he knew Louis to be, he was yet at home, and was therefore comparatively safe. But, busy and hurried as he was that Saturday, every now and then a pale, haggard face came to his remembrance, and the little girl's message,—

"I was to say good-bye for him, and you was never to trouble yourself any more about him."

CHAPTER XXIV.

DESERTED.

" I'll gang awa' to my fayther's ha',
   I and my bairnies three,
    An' thou may'st woo thee anither wife,
     For I winna bide wi' thee."—*Old Ballad.*

MRS. THAYER was sitting in her nursery with her children. It was a pretty domestic scene. The plump, rosy boy she held in her arms was laughing and crowing, and clutching at his mother's hair, while his older brother, seated on the carpet with books and playthings about him, now and then looked up with his large dark eyes, his father's own, to chirp to the baby, or say something in his pretty, childish way to his mother. Mrs. Thayer was a handsome woman, and her beauty was as noticeable in the retirement of her own home as when set off by dress, and seen under the gas-lights, at an evening party. She had risen from her seat, the child still in her arms, when she heard a stumbling, unequal step in the hall. The door opened, and her husband entered the room. The little boy on the floor sprang to his feet with a glad cry of recognition, but stopped, half afraid, before he reached his father's side.

It needed but one glance to tell Frances Thayer her husband's condition. His disordered dress, his uncertain step, his flushed face,—all proclaimed the sad story. He came across the room to where his wife stood, and would have taken her in his arms, but she repelled him with quiet dignity, and held the child close to her bosom.

"Oh, Louis! Oh, my husband!" she said.

He took no notice of her repulse, or of the tone of distress in which her words were spoken.

"I have taken you by surprise," he said, trying to hide the thickness of his speech by a slow enunciation. "I am sick, Fanny, in mind and in body, and I wanted my wife and my children. But it don't seem right! What's the matter? Aren't you glad to see me home again, Fanny?"

"Home!" she repeated, bitterly.

The baby knew his father's voice, and stretched out his arms to be taken.

"Ah, Louie is glad to see papa. Come to papa, darling."

"You shall not take the child," said his wife, holding the boy closely to her bosom. "You shall not pollute my innocent baby with your drunken touch."

He lifted his heavy eyes to her face, as though but half comprehending what she said.

"I told you I was sick, Fanny," he replied, "and I have taken a little of your father's medicine this morning,—'Good Father Paul,' you know,"—he smiled idiotically; then, in a half-whimper,—"It's very hard to be treated like this, when I have come home to you like the prodigal son."

"Like the prodigal son!" said Frances Thayer, with scorn and anger in her face. "I, too, will be like the prodigal son, for 'I will arise and go to my father.' I have borne this long enough, Louis. If it is to go on, you and I must part; for no power in heaven or earth shall compel me to live with a drunkard. Take your choice, my husband. Give up your cups, or give up your wife and children. Look at that boy. Oh, shame! shame! that he should see his father like this! He shall *not* see him another moment. Everett, come with me. I am going home, Louis. I have no home, no husband, here. I will come back to you when you prove yourself worthy to receive me."

With her infant in her arms, and the little boy clinging to her dress, she hurried from the room. Her husband followed her to the door. He called to her in tones of entreaty, but she did not stay her steps, or turn her head. She put up a change of clothing for the children, sent the nurse girl to a livery stable close at hand, to order a horse and carriage, and a man to drive her over to West Union, and in less than an hour was under her father's roof.

Her excitement and indignation made her very strong and resolute, and she told her story with flushed cheeks, and eyes that yet sparkled with anger; but her father's grave face, and her mother's exclamations of surprise and grief—Grace was not present—disturbed her.

" Father, you will not send me back? You are not going to chide me," she said. " Mother, what could I do? Only think of it! It was hardly nine o'clock in the forenoon, and he walked from the depot in that condition. He must have met people who knew him, and wondered at his appearance. It is impossible, if this goes on, to keep the secret much longer. It will become town-talk. Oh, the shame! the disgrace! I never can bear it!" and the proud woman burst into tears.

Dr. Willoughby looked at his favourite daughter, humiliated and crushed to the earth as she was, in all the pride of her womanhood, and his anger was kindled against the man whose weakness and sin had brought this great sorrow upon her.

" No, my child," he said, " I have no disposition to chide you. I should not have counselled you to take this step. In all my ministerial experience, though frequently appealed to, I have never yet advised the separation of husband and wife; but it may be you have acted for the best; desperate diseases sometimes require desperate remedies; and since you have taken this step, and have come to me for protection, you shall not be refused. My doors will never be closed against my children. Frances, you have the shelter of your father's roof for yourself and your children as long as you desire it."

"Oh, thank you, father; I knew you would say so. I am sure it will not be long. If anything can rouse Louis to make the effort, it will be this. You think it will come out right in the end, father? He is my husband. I love him dearly, though he has tried me so by this dreadful habit."

"Come out right!" said Mrs. Willoughby; "of course it will. People who have been married as long

as you have, with children too, talking of being separated! Why, it's awful!"

"Mother, I don't want to be separated from my husband, but I cannot live with him if he drinks. Father, I know I have done right. It will work this way. He will feel very lonely and desolate, now that I am gone, and will sit down and think it all over. He knows I am thoroughly in earnest, and he will see as he has never seen before, the consequences of his course. I will write to him, father, if you think best, a very kind and decided letter, telling him how gladly I will come back to him if he will reform. And this need never be known. I told the cook I was coming for a visit, and gave her directions how to manage while I am absent. Say nothing to Grace about it. She has trouble enough of her own at present, without sympathizing in my sorrows. Oh, thank you, father, for making me welcome!" .

CHAPTER XXV.

THAT SCANDALOUS STORY.

> " A lie that is half a lie
>   Is ever the blackest of lies ;
> A lie that is all a lie
>   May be met with and fought with outright;
> But a lie that is half a truth
>   Is a harder matter to fight."—TENNYSON.

>   " This man so complete,
> Who was enrolled 'mongst wonders, and when we
> Almost with ravished list'ning could not find
> His hour of speech a minute ; *he*
> Hath into monstrous habits put the graces
> That once were his, and is become as black
> As if besmeared in hell."—SHAKESPEARE.

A WORD with you, Barstow," said Mr. Coleman, as the two gentlemen met on Broad Street the day after Mrs. Thayer's sudden removal to her father's house. " Step into the store a moment; we can't stand here in the storm."

" Now, I want to know," said Mr. Coleman, very emphatically, as the two sat warming themselves by the register,—it was a bitter day, a keen north-east wind blowing, and snow falling,—" I want to know what is to be done with this scandalous story that is going the rounds about our minister? I paid no attention to it at first, supposing from its very absurdity that no sensible person would credit it, and that it would die a natural death; but it comes back to me again and again. I have denied it out and out a dozen times, and the next person I meet is sure to put it to me in some form. You have heard of it, of course?"

"You mean the Saratoga scandal," he replied. "Yes, twenty times at least. The Broad Street people seem wonderfully pleased to get hold of something to annoy us. Hawley was in my office not five minutes since, and must needs speak of it. I believe he came in on purpose."

"Yes, and Richards, and Townsend, and three or four others of the same clique," said Mr. Coleman; "and my Charley says the young men were joking about it after dinner yesterday, on the steps of the Truman House. I tell you, Barstow, it's got to be stopped right off somehow. If we could trace it to its source, we might cure the mischief; but no one seems to know how it started."

"Why, as to that," said Mr. Barstow, "Hawley said it came to him very direct. Tom Winslow, who is in Landon's law office,— the Landon who is to marry Mrs. Thayer's sister, you know,—was in Saratoga at the time wife and I went with the minister. I don't remember seeing him; but he says he was there, and he declares the story is true."

"Then he shall eat his own words," said Mr. Coleman, "before he is twelve hours older. Come, Barstow, you and I must settle this matter. Let's go to head-quarters, and get authority to give it the lie publicly. We needn't mention any names, but we can put a card in the evening paper that all concerned will understand."

"I don't like to trouble Mr. Thayer with it," said tender-hearted Mr. Barstow.

"Nonsense! he's not going to be troubled at such a trifle. He has only to deny the story point-blank to you and me, and we will see that the talk is stopped. Come, Barstow, let's go and have it over with. He is at home, for I met him last evening in the post-office. I'll do the talking."

The two gentlemen walked through the storm to the parsonage. They were shown directly to the study, and both noticed, as their minister rose to receive them, his nervous agitation of manner, and that his face was pale even to ghastliness.

Mr. Thayer's parishioner found it more difficult than he had anticipated to deliver himself of his errand. To inform this saintly, spiritual-looking man of a shameful story concerning him, that was banded about from mouth to mouth in the street, and stores, and on the hotel steps of the city, was a task that even Mr. Peter Coleman lacked confidence to perform. He coughed and cleared his throat more than once, looked toward Mr. Barstow for assistance; but that gentleman took no notice of his appeal. Then Mr. Coleman, with a desperate effort, plunged into his subject.

"Sorry to interrupt you, Mr. Thayer. We know Saturday is a busy day with ministers. We won't detain you three minutes, sir. We want one word, and then we are off. The fact is, Mr. Thayer, there's an unpleasant report going about, that's got to be stopped. It shows what fools people are, that they will credit such a story; but we find it will not answer to let it alone. A word of denial, sir, from you, with permission to make it public, will stop it directly."

Mr. Barstow, watching his minister closely, saw that he was strangely agitated. He looked with terrified eyes at Mr. Coleman while he was speaking. His mouth was forcibly compressed, but the hand that rested upon the table trembled visibly. When Mr. Coleman paused, he motioned to him to continue, but did not speak.

"One word, Coleman," said Mr. Barstow. "Before you repeat this piece of scandal, I wish to say to our pastor, though it seems quite superfluous, that his friends have not entertained the thought that there could be the shadow of a foundation for such a tale. It has doubtless been manufactured by an enemy, who has taken pains to circulate it where it would do the most harm. It has been greedily seized upon, Mr. Thayer, by members of a rival church, who are envious of our growing prosperity and the popularity of our pastor."

Again that eager gesture of the hand, but no words,

This strange silence embarrassed Mr. Coleman, and he blurted out his communication awkwardly enough.

"They say, sir, that when you were in Saratoga, last fall, you drank brandy in the bar-room of Congress Hall, and was carried to your room after midnight between two of the waiters. Now, give us leave to say, sir, that it is as black a lie as was ever manufactured by spite and malignity. Just deny it, Mr. Thayer, in as few words as you please,—that's what we've come for."

Mr. Barstow, still watching his minister's face, marked that strange agitation. Great drops of perspiration stood on his forehead, and his frightened eyes never left Mr. Coleman's face. There was a moment's silence, and then he said, very calmly,—

"I cannot deny it."

"Cannot deny it!" said Peter Coleman, springing to his feet; "and why not?"

"*Because it is true*," said the minister.

Then he rose and stood before the astonished men.

"Brethren," he said, "you have loved me, have confided in me as your pastor, before whom I have walked in a solemn show of sanctity, whose prayers I have dared to offer to heaven with my polluted lips, look at me, behold me as I am. I am a drunkard and a hypocrite. I have wronged you sorely, beyond all reparation. I have brought dishonour upon the church you love. I have 'trodden under foot the Son of God, and have done despite unto the Spirit of grace;'

but in pity to a lost soul, whom Heaven may no longer pity, forgive me!"

He covered his face with his hands, and they heard him sob. The two men looked at each other in bewilderment and horror. Then Mr. Barstow came, and laid a trembling hand upon his minister's shoulder. There were tears in the kind old man's eyes.

"My pastor," said he, "my dear pastor, confess your sins, and ask pardon of God, not of poor erring fellow-creatures, such as we are. The mercy you have recommended to others you may abundantly claim for yourself."

He answered, in those tremulous, thrilling tones to which none could listen without emotion,—

"'For if we sin wilfully, after that we have received the knowledge of the truth, there remaineth no more sacrifice for sin, but a certain fearful looking-for of judgment and fiery indignation.' Brethren, it is meet that I should confess my sin to you now, and to-morrow I will take my public dishonour upon me; for my Lord has commanded me to 'give an account of my stewardship, for I may no longer be steward.'"

He turned to Mr. Coleman with a kind of fierceness, so eager was he to tell the whole.

"There is a dear saint in heaven," said he, "whose last hours were full of gloom because of the unfaithfulness of her spiritual guide. Brother, brother, can you forgive me for the cruel wrong I did your dying child?"

"Indeed, sir," said Mr. Coleman, earnestly, "we never blamed you for that. We knew you would have come if you could."

"It is required in stewards," said Louis Thayer, "that a man be found faithful. 'But and if that servant say in his heart, My Lord delayeth his coming, and shall begin to eat, and to drink, and be drunken'—."

He did not finish the sentence of condemnation, but sank into his chair again, as if overcome by bodily weakness. His listeners, thoroughly appalled by the drama of sin and sorrow laid open to their view, knew not what to say.

"If Gabriel himself had fallen out of heaven," Mr. Barstow said, as they walked homeward, "I could not wonder more. In my reverence, I already counted this man a saint and an angel."

Shut up in his private office, he was yet meditating upon the scene he had witnessed, when a clerk announced a lady on urgent business, and, directly after, Bethiah Emmersly, with snow-flakes clinging to her shawl and bonnet,—for the storm was raging violently, —entered the room. She walked directly up to the old gentleman's desk in great agitation.

"This story about our dear minister," she said, —"it isn't true, Mr. Barstow? Oh, tell me it isn't true!"

He was in no mood to evade the question.

"I am afraid it is quite true, Bethiah," he said, gravely.

She threw up her hands with a gesture of despair.

"The Lord forgive me!" she said. "Mr. Barstow, I have done an awful wicked thing; but I didn't go to do it. I knew 'twas dreadful alluring stuff; but I never once thought it was a-going to tempt *him*. Oh, my poor dear minister! To think that I should have gone and acted the part of Satan to him! The Lord knows I didn't go to do it."

Bethiah's feelings overcame her, and she turned away that Mr. Barstow might not see her weep. He looked at her in astonishment.

"What is it that troubles you, Bethiah? What have *you* to do with this sad business?" he said, when she grew more composed.

"I have put the bottle to my neighbour's lips," she replied. "Oh, Mr. Barstow, these hands have ministered to his destruction. I made him some of mother's spiced wine. I put in everything that was good, and it was so alluring! Only the taste of it made my mouth water. I took it to him with my own hands, Mr. Barstow, and it's led him astray; good man as he was, that alluring stuff has led him astray;" and Bethiah wept again.

"Hush! hush!" said Mr. Barstow, quickly, a shade of self-consciousness crossing his face. "You are not to blame, my good woman; you had no means of knowing his weakness. You did it for the best. I have sent him wine from my own cellar more than once."

"It wasn't like mine, Mr. Barstow," she said, in the midst of her grief, indignant at the comparison.

"Mother's spiced wine would seduce the very elect. Oh, Mr. Barstow! that wine has been to that good man

‘ the poison of dragons, and the cruel venom of asps.’ I can’t find any comfort only in what St. Paul says, ‘In that I did it ignorantly I obtained mercy.’ I didn’t go to do it, Mr. Barstow. I was a poor mis-guided creetur; but I didn’t go to do it.”

It was perhaps partly in consequence of Bethiah’s visit, that Mr. Barstow, after thinking awhile, resolved to see his minister again that night. “ I will persuade him,” thought this good man, “ to spare himself the shame of a public confession. If he must resign his charge,—and indeed I think I could not hear him preach again, after what has happened,—his failing health is a sufficient reason.” So the old gentleman wrapped himself up thoroughly, and once more went out into the storm. But his journey was a fruitless one. Mr. Thayer, the girl told him, had gone out, leaving no word when he would return. Then Mr. Barstow inquired for Mrs. Thayer, who, as we already know, was in West Union.

“ I will call again in the morning,” Mr. Barstow said, as he turned away disappointed. “ Well, well, what a storm this is !”

CHAPTER XXVI.

THE OUTCAST.

" Found dead! dead and alone!
   There was nobody near, nobody near
When the outcast died on his pillow of stone,—
   No wife, no mother, no sister dear,
Not a friendly voice to soothe and cheer,
   Not a watching eye, or a pitying tear.
Oh! the city slept when he died alone,
   In a roofless street, on a pillow of stone."—LAIGHTON.

" And when they talk of him they shake their heads,
   And whisper one another in the ear."—SHAKESPEARE.

DR. WILLOUGHBY sat in his pleasant home that Saturday evening, reading his paper. He was alone, for Mrs. Willoughby had gone with her daughter to the nursery to assist in putting the little ones to bed, and Grace was in her own room. With a comfortable sense of security from the storm that was beating against the windows, the Doctor put his slippered feet to the fire, and had fallen into a half doze, from which he was awakened by the opening of the door. He started, rubbed his eyes, and uttered an exclamation of surprise.

Louis Thayer stood before him. His hair and beard were white with sleet and snow. His face was dreadfully pale and haggard, and his dark eyes, unnaturally large and bright, searched the room with a wild and anxious look. He tried to speak, and stretched out his hand with an imploring gesture, then, staggering back to the wall, leaned against it for support.

Shocked and displeased—for, judging by his appearance, Dr. Willoughby at once concluded that his son-in-law was under the influence of liquor—he spoke sternly.

"Louis," said he, "why do you come here to-night?"

"You have taken away my wife," he cried. "Give me back my wife."

"Your wife came to me of her own free will," said Dr. Willoughby. "She sought the protection of her father's roof, because he who promised to cherish and protect her, proved false to his trust. She says she has no longer a husband or a home."

He paid no attention to the words. He did not seem even to hear them. His eyes went wandering all over the room, and he repeated in pitiful tones:—

"You have taken away my wife. Give me back my wife."

"I have *not* taken away your wife," said the Doctor, impatiently. "She can return to you when she pleases, and that will be as soon as you prove yourself worthy to receive her. For shame, Louis Thayer! How dare you present yourself before me in such a disgraceful condition? Don't deny it, sir! Don't add falsehood and perjury to your other sins. Oh! my son, you have fallen low indeed!" To these reproaches the wretched man made no other answer than to repeat the words he had twice spoken,—

"Give me back my wife."

"You have forfeited all right to call her wife," said Dr. Willoughby. "It would serve you justly if she never returned to you; but she loves you, Louis, notwithstanding all the grief and anxiety you have caused her in the past, and the mortification and disgrace you will bring upon her in the future, if this continues. She loves you. Even now she was talking to me hopefully about you. She will return to you at the first proof you give her that you have entered upon a new life. You have everything to gain if you do this. You have everything to lose if you continue the mad course upon which you have entered. But there," said Dr. Willoughby, "why do I waste my words upon him? He does not even hear what I say."

It was quite true. Perhaps Louis Thayer had borne all that day his nature could endure. His arms dropped. He no longer looked eagerly about the room, but, with glazed eyes and with an air of weary indifference, stood leaning against the wall. When Dr. Willoughby ceased speaking, he moved slowly toward the door,—slowly, aimlessly, as if no further object in life remained to him, and he saw no reason for taking another step, but would gladly lie down and die. He turned as he reached the door, to say in his sweetest tone :—

"Good-night, father. Say good-night to Fanny and the children, and God bless you all!"

A moment after, Mrs. Willoughby bustled in.

"Doctor," she said, "would you mind stepping over to the drug-store? We are out of 'soothing syrup,' and Louie's gums worry him so, Fanny cannot get him quiet. Dan is down to Briggs's, of course; and I don't like to send Katie out in such a deep snow. By the way, whom have you had here? I heard you talking very loud."

Then Dr. Willoughby related the interview.

"It looks dark for Fanny, my dear, and for all of us," he said. "He was so intoxicated that he was obliged to lean against the wall for support; did not know what he was saying, but repeated the same thing over and over; and when I talked to him, appeared to be half asleep. Poor Fanny! I am glad she was upstairs. I would not have had her see him for any-thing."

Mrs. Willoughby looked disturbed and anxious.

"How could he drive out here in such a storm?" she said; "and think of his going back in the condi-tion you describe. Doctor, I am afraid you did wrong to let him go."

"He can return as well as he came," said Dr. Wil-loughby. "The horse he always drives knows every step of the way, and will take him back in half an honr. There is no occasion for anxiety, dear. He could not stay here, of course, for to-morrow is Sunday, and it would undo all Fanny is trying to accomplish if I had made him welcome and allowed him to see her. No, wife, I have acted for the best; let him return to his lonely home; let him learn by painful experience that 'the way of transgressors is hard.'"

The Doctor put on his heaviest overcoat, lit his lantern, and went through the snow-drifts to the drug-store. The sharp sleet pricked his face like needles, and the wind chilled him to the bone. He looked for sleigh-tracks by the hitching-post near his gate. The surface of the snow was unbroken. "It is impossible that it has filled in," thought the Doctor, "so soon. He must have put his horse under shelter at the hotel."

The snow stopped falling about ten o'clock. The clouds passed away, and the stars came out, but the wind changed and blew a gale all night. The oldest inhabitants had never known, in the winter season, so high a wind. Trees were blown down, old buildings capsized, and great damage done in the region. The great trees near Dr. Willoughby's house tossed their bare branches, and creaked and groaned dismally all night, and the pines trembled, and bent toward each other, murmuring hoarsely, as though whispering some horrid secret.

In the city the tumult was frightful. Chimneys fell, roofs were lifted, or their tin sheeting torn partly off, and left to swing clattering in the breeze. The bell-tower of the Wilmot Street Church terminated in a long slender spire, and the whole structure had more than once been pronounced unsafe by those competent to judge. To-night it rocked fearfully; and every now and then, heard plainly above the roar of the tempest, and the clatter, and din, and tumult all around, the great bell tolled a mournful peal.

"I shouldn't wonder if the crazy concern came down with a crash," said a member of the rival church, as he turned himself in his bed. "I told them, when that steeple was building, they were carrying it nearer heaven than any of them would ever get. Well, they need a downfal over there of some sort."

"Mother," said a child wakened by the tumult,— "mother, I hear the church-bell toll. Is there a funeral? Take me into your bed, mother, for I am afraid."

At daybreak the wind lulled, and the Sabbath morning dawned clear and still. The sexton of the Wilmot Street Church came early with his boy, to clear away the snow.

"Father," the lad called out from the porch, "see how it's drifted in here before the middle door. It looks just like a grave."

"Set to work, boy, set to work," he answered, gruffly. "There's no time for fooling, and all this snow to clear away. I haven't seen such a bed these ten years."

A moment after, the boy uttered a shrill cry.

"Father! father! it *is* a grave."

The sexton threw down his shovel, and hurried up the steps. Wrapped in a soft white mantle, spotless in its purity, but oh, how deathly cold! they found the body of a man. He was lying upon his face, and "his hands were upon the threshold of the door of the house." The sexton got down upon his knees, and carefully scraped away the snow from the prostrate form. Then he gently lifted the head, and looked into the dead man's face.

"Great God!" said the sexton. "It's the minister!"

CHAPTER XXVII.

TOO LATE.

"Oh, my lost love, and my own, own love,
And my love that loved me so!
Is there never a chink in the world above
Where they listen for words from below?
Nay, I spoke once, and I grieved thee sore,
I remember all that I said,
And now thou wilt hear me no more,—no more,
Till the sea gives up her dead."—JOHN INGELOW.

"The eyes that cannot weep are the saddest eyes of all."—
MACKAY.

HOW pleasant Dr. Willoughby's breakfast-room looked that Sabbath morning! The sun shone in at the east windows upon the bountifully-spread table, and upon the family group gathered around. Dr. Willoughby gave devout thanks that his dear ones had been sheltered and protected from the dangers of the past night, and brought to see the light of this beautiful Sabbath morning. Then, with the dignity and grace that characterized his simplest act, he dispensed the good things before him, nodded to the baby across the table, or answered the grave questions of his little namesake.

"It was a fearful night," said Grace Willoughby.

"I could not sleep, the wind blew so, and I thought of the sailors, and of the many poor people in the city who were not comfortably sheltered. I suppose I was very nervous. I kept picturing to myself some poor wretch, a beggar or an outcast, struggling through the storm, that bitter wind chilling him through and through, until, faint and exhausted, he sank down to die. I don't know how many times I pictured that all out. Oh, father, what a terrible death it must be!"

"I slept quietly," said Frances Thayer. "Louie kept me awake till eleven o'clock, then I dropped asleep; and though I knew the wind was high,—for I partially woke several times,—it was pleasant to find myself snug and warm in my bed. The consciousness of the discomfort without made the security within the sweeter."

"A man to spake wid his riverence," said Katie at the door; and the visitor following her through the hall, entered the breakfast-room. He was a rough-looking person, a stranger to all, dressed in a shaggy overcoat, with a whip in his hand, and his hair and whiskers were white with the morning frost.

"You are wanted right off, Dr. Willoughby," he said. "They've found your son-in-law dead,—froze to death on his own church-steps."

Shriek after shriek echoed through the room, and her mother and sister, hastening to her side, found Frances Thayer with clenched hands, a face as pale as death, and wide, staring eyes, from which no tears were falling. Every word they spoke to her was followed by a fresh burst of agony. Before starting on his dreadful errand, her father came, and, bending over her very tenderly, spoke her name. At the sound of his voice she gave an awful scream, pushed him from her with all her strength, then, shuddering, hid her face.

Over the road Louis Thayer had twice trodden, oh, so wearily! the night before—the wretched man had walked the distance back and forth—they brought him to his father's door. The wife, sternly denied to him then, bent over him now with bitter wailing, and piteous appeals that came *too late.* His heart was breaking then for the words of affection she lavished upon him now. Those vain words and vainer tears fell all unheeded upon the senseless ear, upon the. marble face. How instantly last night would he have accorded the forgiveness for which she pleaded so fruitlessly to-day! Until she looked upon that dead face, no tears fell from her eyes; then they burst forth in a flood. "Let her go to him," Dr. Willoughby had said, when the mother feared she could not bear the terrible sight. "Let her look upon him; it must needs do her good; for, whatever he was in life, in death his face is 'as the face of an angel.'"

Yes, to that sinning and sore-stricken man, deserted by his dearest earthly friend, lost and despairing, struggling through the cruel storm, and fighting back his earthly faintness, that at last he might sink down and die an outcast's death, " between the porch and the altar,"—to him was given a dying experience that left a smile of rapture upon his face. Did One come to him that night " whose footsteps leave no print across the snow?" When the devil left him, did angels come and minister to him?

It was a quiet funeral. He who, in right of the talents God had given him, his present success, and great promise of future usefulness, should have been followed to his grave by a mourning multitude, and borne to rest with words of Christian hope and consolation, was laid away in silence and in gloom.

A group of sorrowing friends " beheld the sepulchre, and how the body was laid." His aged father was there,—thank God, his mother was dead!—and the poor old man, bent with years and infirmity, standing over the grave, remembered how he had toiled and struggled for many years to enable this only son to prepare for the work of the ministry, and marvelled at the strange providence that had permitted a life so bright with promise and hope to become thus overclouded and go out suddenly in darkness and dishonour.

And Allan Richmond, mourning over his friend with a great and bitter mourning, took up David's lamentation :—

" The beauty of Israel is slain upon thy high places; how are the mighty fallen!

"Tell it not in Gath, publish it not in the streets of Askelon, lest the Philistines rejoice, lest the uncircumcised triumph.

"I am distressed for thee, my brother Jonathan; very pleasant hast thou been unto me; thy love to me was wonderful, passing the love of women.

"How are the mighty fallen!"

There was found lying beside his unfinished sermon a folded paper. It was his resignation of the pastorate of the Wilmot Street Church. It was dated the Saturday night he died; and before the story of sin, and anguish, and deep repentance it contained was to have been proclaimed to his astonished people, their pastor had gone to plead guilty before a higher tribunal.

Those who best knew this man, whose downward path it has been a sad task for the writer to trace, bear unqualified testimony to the loveliness of his private character,—to his intellectual gifts and graces, to his keen moral perceptions, and to a something about him, which can only be described as magnetism, by which he secured and held the sympathy and attention of those whom he addressed. That he would have achieved a brilliant popularity in his sacred office, and have become a bright and shining light in the church of God, living a long and useful life, or wearing himself out early in his Master's work, —in either case leaving behind him precious memories, and the lasting fruit of his labours,—that he would have done all this we cannot doubt, but for the deadly enemy before whose power he fell.

That he died a miserable death, and, if he found mercy at all, was saved as if by fire; that good men speak his dishonoured name below their breath, and bad men use it as an occasion to scoff and blaspheme, let us thank a social custom that some Christian men uphold, some ministers defend from their Bible, and quote the example of the Saviour in its countenance and defence.

O earth! earth! earth! hide not this blood!

CHAPTER XXVIII.

FATHER AND DAUGHTER.

"She speaks poignards, and every word stabs."— SHAKESPEARE.

RS. WILLOUGHBY came to her husband in his study the day after the funeral.

"Doctor, will you go to Fanny," she said, "and try and say something to comfort her? I am afraid she will be crazy."

Dr. Willoughby found his daughter in her darkened chamber, walking the floor, moaning, and wringing her hands.

"My dear child," he said, "will you not try to compose yourself? This is a grievous blow. I know how utterly vain all human sympathy must seem to you. But you are a Christian, Frances, and He who sent this great sorrow can give you strength to bear it."

"Who sent it, father?" she said, stopping short in her rapid walk, and confronting him.

"How can you ask, my daughter? He who 'doth not afflict willingly, nor grieve the children of men,' has, for some wise, though mysterious purpose, given you this trial to bear."

" How dare you say that to me, father? How dare you charge such a deed to such a source? God ' tempteth no man.' "

He looked at her in doubt and dread, for he thought her mother's fears were just. She resumed her agitated walk, but presently coming to him, laid her hand upon his arm, and looked steadily in his face.

" You love me, father," she said. " I have heard people say that I was your favourite child."

" My daughter, I love you with all my heart."

" And you have trained me from my infancy, and taught me to think as you think, and believe as you believe, and I have grown up like you in many things."

" I have been proud to think so, Frances."

" Father, I curse the hour I was born. I wish you had strangled me in my cradle, rather than taught me such a creed, and trained me to such a destiny. It is *you* who have brought me to this hour. It is *you* who have given me this trial to bear. Now, help me to bear it if you can."

Her face, haggard with grief, and shaded by masses of dark dishevelled hair, yet strikingly resembled her father's, and the black eyes he had loved to hear people call so like his own, looked steadfastly into his.

" Do you remember, father, how one morning, five years ago, we stood together in the room underneath, you and I, and the dear one I have lost for ever, and how you put my hand in his, and, in the presence of God, made me promise to be to him a loving and faithful wife?"

"I remember, Fanny."

"Do you remember what he was that day, father?—so good, so noble, so true."

"Oh, hush, my child!—Yes, I remember."

"And do you remember how in those early days of our married life, spent under *this* roof, father, you used all the influence over him you possessed—and he loved and reverenced you above all others—to change his 'narrow views' and the 'crude notions of his college life,' as you called them, and bring him into your own state of liberty, and how you taught me to do the same? I was an apt scholar. I had profited well by my training. And do you remember how we triumphed when he drank his first glass of wine at your table? For it was a struggle, you know. He was loath to give up his principles ; but we are so strong, father, you and I, we succeed in almost everything we undertake. Father! father! there's a grave in the churchyard that shows how we succeeded in this."

"Hush, Fanny, for God's sake! We could not foresee the dreadful consequences. I will not hear you talk so. I cannot bear it."

"Cannot bear it!" she repeated. "Can I bear it, father? Can I bear to remember how the gentlest, dearest, truest heart that ever beat in a man's bosom lies crushed and broken ; how my lover and husband, and the father of my children, sank down, faint and despairing, to die alone? Can I bear to think of that lonely grave all covered with snow? Oh, my darling! my darling! I would buy with my blood one hour, one moment, to kneel at his feet, to cover the poor frozen hands with kisses, to hear from those dumb lips one word of forgiveness, to tell him I loved him in spite of all. Oh, me! Oh me!"

She broke into loud weeping, and piteous appeal to the dead. Her father did not interrupt her, but sat silent and subdued till the paroxysm of grief was over.

"I know how vain it is," she said, at length, "this tardy grief. I can no more atone for the past than I can wound him again in the future; and I shall carry the memory of that disappointed look, the backward shadow on that dear, dead face, with me to my grave. I know the memory of my reproaches rose cold between his parting soul and heaven. Father, pity me! Every hope of my youth is blighted. I am young to carry such a burden of remorse and sorrow all my life. It is such a little while since I was a proud, happy wife, and now I am a desolate, heart-broken widow."

"Fanny," said her father, tenderly, "you have your children to live for, a very precious charge in these dear boys; and let me say to you, my daughter, in receiving you back under this roof in your afflicted and desolate condition, your parents look upon your children as their own. We will share everything together, my dear, and when I am gone there will be enough left for all. It has been a source of grief to me, Fanny, that I have no son to bear my name. Shall I be a father to your boys?"

"They cannot stay here," she said quickly.

He looked at her in silent astonishment.

"They cannot stay here," she repeated vehemently. "Father, I dare not bring them up under this roof. If there is one thing I mean to teach those boys, it is to hate with a deadly hatred the poison that murdered their father. Can I do that here? No. I will beg their bread from door to door, rather than expose them to the teaching and example that proved his ruin."

Of all the sharp, bitter words Frances Thayer ever uttered, none struck deeper than these. Her father's face flushed to his gray hair, and he left her without speaking. But in the twilight of the evening he came to her again, and, sitting by her bedside—for, utterly worn and exhausted by grief, she had thrown herself down to rest—he took her hand in his, looking earnestly in her face.

"Frances," he said, "my poor child!"—and his voice, usually so firm, trembled a little;—"if I could make you understand how the words forced from you in your despair this morning have wrung my heart with anguish—how overwhelmed I was, and still am at what you then revealed to me of the workings of your mind—you would not wonder at what I have to say to you now. My child, the ground that seemed so firm under my feet has all at once given way. For almost the first time in my life, I mistrust myself."

Was this Dr. Willoughby?—the proud, self-sustained man, so strong, so unerring in judgment, admitting no failure or defeat. His daughter lay with her head resting on her arm, and her long hair scattered about the pillow. She looked earnestly in his face, but she did not speak.

"I have painfully pondered your words, Frances," he continued. "If I admit to any extent the truth of the dreadful accusation you brought against me, I am a guilty man, and I cannot blame you for committing to strangers the trust your father has betrayed. But, let me say this, my daughter: if, after all that has passed, your heart still clings to your home, and this danger to your children, of which you have spoken, is the only barrier against your remaining, that barrier shall be removed. Neither by precept nor example will I hinder you in the education of your boys. I *shall drink no more wine, Frances. Your words have poisoned the cup for me.*"

Mrs. Thayer's baby boy, toddling about the room, came, and, leaning against his grandfather's knee, reached his little hands to be taken. Dr. Willoughby lifted him in his arms, and, bending his head till his gray hair mingled with the child's sunny curls, he called him very tenderly by his dead father's name. Then Frances Thayer saw, what she never remembered to have seen before, tears in her father's eyes. The sight melted the proud woman's heart.

"Father, dear father," she said, "I *do* trust you. Forgive me; take me back. I have no home but yours. You will help me to train his children up for God."

CHAPTER XXIX.

DAN TAYLOR'S BROKEN PROMISE.

> " If men of good lives,
> Who by their virtuous actions stir up others
> To noble and religious imitation,
> Receive the greater glory after death,
> As sin must needs confess; what may they feel
> In height of torment, and in weight of vengeance,
> Not only they themselves not doing well,
> But *set a light up to show men to hell?*"—MIDDLETON.

" DEW without speerit, Dr. Willoughby!" said Dan Taylor; " a blessin' put alongside o' corn an' ile in the Bible! one o' the meats tew be received with thanksgivin'! Did yeou ax me if I cud dew without speerit, Dr. Willoughby? I hope I know my dooty an' privilege better'n that. Yer needn't go ter tryin' of me in that way, Doctor. I shall allers stick ter my principles, an' I've got good sound scriptur' reasonin' to gin when I'm tacted. No, Dr. Willoughby, I shan't never consent tew dew without speerit."

" I did not suppose you would, Daniel," the minister replied; " and so it only remains for me to say that I shall not need your services after this month. I am sorry to part with you. You have proved yourself very faithful to my interests during the years you have been in my service; but I shall be obliged to make a change."

The old harness Dan was mending dropped from his hands, with a loud clang, to the kitchen floor, and he looked at Dr. Willoughby in open-mouthed astonishment.

"Yer don't mean it, Doctor," he said. "Why, yer strike me all of a heap. 'Obleeged ter make a change!' An' what kind of a change will yer make, with one o' them raw Irish critters jest over, pokin' his head inter the study door every ten minutes ter ax questions, an' me on the place goin' on eight years, gettin' the hang o' things, so as ter go right along without pesterin' yeou, sir? An' heow abeout yer celery bed, Doctor, that needs sich particilar care? an' that little patch o' seedlin's, Doctor, the puttiest strawberry that ever growed, an' jest a-comin' on ter bear next summer, an' wants as much nussin' an' tendin' as babies? There ain't an Irishman in the country, but what'll kill 'em in a month with their rough handlin'. An' the bay horse, Doctor; why, law, sir, if dumb critters ever speak, Charley talks tew me soon's ever I put my foot on the barn floor; an' the ceow; an' the litter o' pigs; an'—."

"I shall miss you very much, Daniel," interrupted the minister. "I do not expect to find a person to fill your place; but there is no help for it, and you must go."

Dan wriggled in his seat, and looked very un-comfortable.

"Neow, Doctor," said he, "I ain't a blind mole, that I can't see above greound. Yeou've been a sight tew good tew me. I ain't got no complaint tew make agin yer. I don't blame yer, Doctor, for gettin' clear worn eout with my tantrums. I'm willin' tew confess my shortcomin's. I allow I've gone tew far in speerits; but look here neow,—I'm a-goin' tew turn over a new leaf. I ain't a-goin' tew make no more use o' speerit, only as a medicine. I'll be on the safe side arter this. I'll keep a leetle on hand, Doctor, 'caus' when I feel one o' my colicy spells comin' on, there don't nothin' keep 'em off like a stiff glass o' Jamaicy rum; an' for the phthisic—why, I've seen my grandmother so dis-trest, seems though every breath she drawed would be her last, an' mother used ter keep skoke berries an' rum on hand, an' she'd gin the old woman a wine glass full, an' she'd git easy in no time. Wal, whether 'twas constitutional, or from tastin' of what was left in the bottom o' grandma's glass, I couldn't say; but arter a while *I* got ter havin' the phthisic eenermost as bad as the old woman, an' I've kep' it up by spells ever sence, an' I don't find nothin' helps it so quick as raw speerit. So I'll jes' let speerit alone, Doctor, only when I need it for a medicine."

"And your 'sick spells' would come often, I am afraid," said Dr. Willoughby. "No, Dan, it will not do. If you remain in my service you must give up drinking entirely, and in making this a condition I ask no more of you than I expect to do myself."

Dan's astonishment seemed too great for words.

"Yeou don't mean tew say, Doctor, that yeou are a-goin' ter make sich a change at yeour time o' life?" he said at last. "Ain't yer never goin' ter take a glass o' wine at a weddin', nor a leetle hot brandy sling afore yer ride over ter Brighton deestrict ter hold a meetin'? Why, Doctor! *yeou* ain't a-goin' tew jine the teetotalers?"

Dr. Willoughby winced at the word.

"It is not necessary for me to explain my position further to you," he said. "I have no time to answer your questions. I am sorry you cannot make up your mind to comply with my condition, and remain with me; but since you refuse, I must find some one to supply your place, for no person under my roof shall, with my knowledge, use intoxicating drink. Look about for a situation, Dan, and I will give you as good a recommendation as I can."

He was leaving the room when Dan, confused and agitated, rose from his seat.

"Doctor," said he, "I don't mean ter be sassy, an when a man tells me he ain't no time tew answer my questions, I ginerally gin over axin' any more; but, Doctor, yeou must tell me one thing: is speerits a blessin' or a cuss? Does the Bible go agin' the use on 'em, or don't it? When it says, *Look* not on the wine,' does it mean jest that, or may I twist it reound an' get some other meaniu' eout on't? Tell me the sollum truth, Doctor, as it lays in yer mind. I dew think I'm some sort of right ter ax, 'caus', livin' so long under the same ruff, I've got inter yeour notions. I've larned ter believe as yeou dew, sir, an' if yeou've shifted round I want ter know it."

Thus solemnly appealed to—the man was in no joking mood, but with a look of earnest attention on his strongly marked Yankee face, awaited his employer's reply—Dr. Willoughby hesitated.

"You ask me questions, Daniel," he said, " which I find it hard to answer. I cannot readily give up the theory of a lifetime. I have been very sincere in my belief; but the support on which I rested, and the strength of which it seemed impossible, and still seems impossible, to doubt, has all at once given way. I hardly know where I stand; but I am afraid, Daniel, that my theory and my practice have both been wrong."

That Dr. Willoughby made this confession with an effort, a duller man than his listener might have seen. Dan's face was working with emotion before the minister finished speaking.

"I'm goin' ter tell yer somethin', Doctor," said he. " I never spoke on it afore to anybody, but it 's lay on my mind jest like a dead weight these five years. I promised my old mother, when she lay a-dyin', that I'd quit drinkin'. She made me swear it, Doctor. I couldn't pacify her no way till I done it,—on my knees, with the Bible afore me. She said I cud do it easy, 'caus' I was in a minister's family; for, yer see, I never let on tew her that yeou wan't one o' the teetotal kind. Wal, I kep' my promise a spell; but I used to hear yeou talk considerable when I was reound tew work, an' sez I, 'The minister don't think it's wicked tew take a leetle now an' then, an' he knows a sight more 'bout sich things than an old woman like mother.' Yer see, mother got dretful sot agin drinkin', an' no wonder, for father fell eout of his waggin one day, when he was drunk, an' got ketched in the lines somehow, an' dragged hum three miles over a rough piece o' road. I was a leetle shaver, Doctor, but I never shall forgit tew my dyin' day heow he looked with his clothes all tore tew rags, an' kivered with blood where he'd hit agin the sharp rocks, an' mother she screamed till they heerd her half a mile off.

"Wal, as I was sayin', I heerd you talk, an' I went back on my word, an', sir, I was dredful tickled when you made it so clear from the Bible that it was all right tew drink wine. It kinder bolstered me right up, yer see; but somehow when I talked the loudest I didn't feel good inside, for 'twasn't doin' the fair thing by the old woman; neow was it, Doctor? But I kep' a-sayin' tew myself that if I follered ycour example, an' done as yeou done, I should come eout all right in the eend. An' neow, yer see, Doctor, yeou've knocked me all of a heap. If yeou quit, I dursn't go on.   If yeou are afeard yeou are wrong, I *know* I am wrong; an' if yeou dursn't drink wine, I dursn't drink whisky.   Don't turn me adrift, Doctor. Le' me stay with yer, an' see if I can't keep that promise I made my old mother, five years ago."

And Dan stayed.

CHAPTER XXX.

WAITING.

" Impatient women, as you wait
 In cheerful homes to-night to hear
The sound of steps, that, soon or late,
 Shall come as music to your ear;

" Forget yourselves a little while,
 And think in pity of the pain
Of women who will never smile
 To hear a coming step again."— Phœbe Cary.

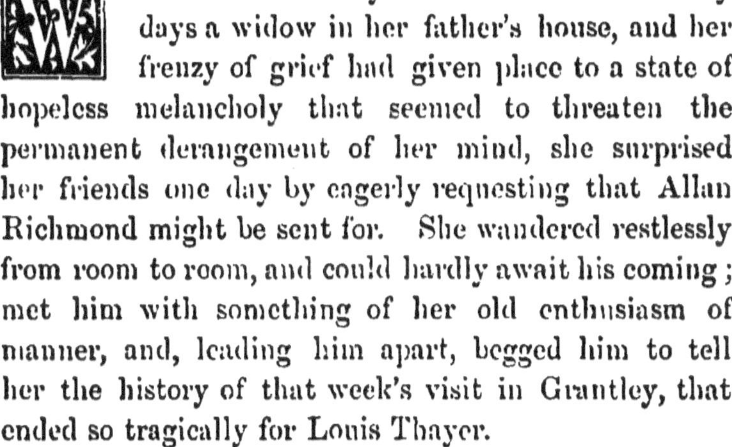

HEN Frances Thayer had remained for many days a widow in her father's house, and her frenzy of grief had given place to a state of hopeless melancholy that seemed to threaten the permanent derangement of her mind, she surprised her friends one day by eagerly requesting that Allan Richmond might be sent for. She wandered restlessly from room to room, and could hardly await his coming; met him with something of her old enthusiasm of manner, and, leading him apart, begged him to tell her the history of that week's visit in Grantley, that ended so tragically for Louis Thayer.

Then, Allan Richmond repeated the sad story. He led her, step by step, along the quiet paths they two trod together in loving fellowship until the hour of parting. He did not spare for her crying. He judged rightly that her tears would do her good. And, as she listened, pleasure mingled with her pain. His intimate association with her dear one, extending far back of her own, his loving appreciation of all that was noble and beautiful in his character, led him to speak so feelingly, that Frances Thayer felt that she had found the one soul who could understand and sympathize with her in her loss. This visit was the introduction to many others, and her watchful parents noticed that they did the mourner good.

It was not until he had been for several months on terms of intimacy with Dr. Willoughby's family that Allan Richmond ventured to declare the love he had long cherished for the younger daughter. So bold in everything else, the young minister was strangely timid in his love. And Frances Thayer, with the first turning away from her selfish sorrow, favoured his suit; "for it was *his* wish," she said, with her arms close about her sister's neck. "O Grace, I think I can bear to live to carry out Louis's plans."

They were married as quietly as possible. The bride wore the gray travelling dress she coveted on a former occasion, and, with as perfect a trust and confidence as ever filled a woman's heart, went with her husband to his country parish among the hills. One request she made before her wedding-day.

"Allan, I want to take Joe with me to Grantley,"

she said, "and care for him as long as he lives. I never can repay him for what he has done for me."

"Do I owe nothing to Crazy Joe?" said Mr. Richmond. "It strikes me that I, too, have a debt of gratitude to pay."

So, back of the Grantley parsonage, they built a snug little cottage, and hither Joe Martin removed his household gods, his beloved melodeon, and his yellow cat. He was made superlatively happy by this arrangement, for he would have followed Grace to the ends of the earth. The affection he cherished for her amounted well-nigh to idolatry, and she possessed great power over him for good, in his darkest moods soothing his fear, and beguiling him of his melancholy. He made the parsonage grounds beautiful with the choice flowers and shrubbery he cultivated, spending every leisure moment during the summer months in this favourite employment.

The care for his comfort their beloved minister manifested, his gentleness and grace of manner, his quiet melancholy, and the mystery in which his early life was infolded, made Crazy Joe an object of interest to the Grantley people. The little children soon learned to love him, stopping on their way to school for a rose, or a bunch of Joe's violets, or to listen to one of the songs or hymns he delighted to sing to them. The older people looked every Sabbath for his serious, attentive face in the gallery; he attended every funeral in the village; and whenever a corpse

was borne along the street in summer or winter, in
rain or sunshine, Crazy Joe followed the procession to
the grave.   And there were not wanting those who,
listening to his mysterious and deeply earnest language
mixed with passages of Scripture, and full of allusions
which they could not understand, mingled their pity
for the lonely man with awe and reverence, and
endowed poor Joe with the name of prophet.

*   *   *   *   *   *

Grace Richmond, the country minister's wife—though
she will probably never again own a *moire antique* or
a *gros grain* dress—calls herself both rich and proud.
She is rich in the wealth of affection her husband
lavishes upon her, and proud with the pride of the
Roman matron whose children were her jewels.   Her
days are full of busy care from morning till night; and
she finds her chief happiness in doing for others; while
Horace Landon, going from place to place in search of
the health he lost by early dissipation, squanders his
immense income upon harpies and quack doctors,
weighs his food, and counts the beatings of his pulse
with painful exactness, and lives his life of selfish
solitude unpitied and unloved.

In the parsonage at West Union there remains only
an old man and his widowed daughter.   The wife and
mother is laid away to rest; and the children whom
Frances Thayer has trained with so much solicitude
and care have gone out into the world to prepare for
their life-work.   They are noble young men.   Everett,

his grandfather's namesake, has chosen the law for his profession, and is pursuing his studies in the neighbouring city; and Louis, a slender, dark-haired boy yet in college, will follow his father's calling. Over this boy the mother's heart yearns in an agony of tenderness and sorrow. He is at once her blessing and her torture. His smile, the glance of his dark eye, and the tones of his voice, keep alive memories that fill her with the keenest anguish. She has been for all these years very sad and silent—" a woman of a sorrowful spirit:" the fire and enthusiasm that characterized her in youth seemingly extinguished in the great calamity of her life.

Once only was she roused to a display of the passion of other days. This boy, this Louis Thayer, a lad of fifteen, was enticed one evening by a companion to enter one of the drinking saloons of the village. His brother reported at home where he had left him; and a few moments later, the young men who were lounging about the bar and the billiard table in the back of the saloon were startled by the entrance of a tall woman, dressed in deep black, who, swiftly crossing the room, caught a lad by the arm and hurried him away. Not a word was spoken. Her black eyes flashed, and a crimson spot burned upon either cheek. From the brilliantly-lighted room, Frances Thayer led her boy to where the moonlight shone cold upon his father's grave. There they knelt together in the snow. The words she said, the anguish he saw in his mother's face as she tore open the bleeding wounds of her heart, caused him to utter vows in that consecrated spot that, God helping him, he will never break.

Dr. Willoughby has been for the last few years a feeble old man; and among his brethren in the ministry, there are those who ascribe this debility to a sudden change in his habits,—for Dr. Willoughby is a total abstinence man. At a ministers' meeting held a few months after the affliction in his family, he rose, and very simply and frankly declared his change of purpose, announcing that he had signed the pledge, and made his covenant with God to drink no more wine. And lamenting his past course, and the evil he has wrought by precept and example, he is striving, in the little time left him, to do for the cause of temperance, with his might, what his hands find to do. When his courage flags, or the infirmities of old age press upon him, and he is loath to leave the quiet of his own fire-side for the crowded hall and the public gathering, his daughter urges him on. "For the day is short, father," she says; "and the night will soon come, when no man can work. Dear father, your rest will be long and very sweet."

He was ill a few weeks since, and his daughter, standing by his bedside, listened to his half-unconscious utterances; and perceiving how near his spirit hovered to the unseen world, she bent over him with eager inquiry.

"Father," she said, "you are looking straight into

heaven; tell me what you see. You are listening **to**
angel voices: oh, tell me what you hear." ·

He lifted his heavy eyes to her face.

"'I have fought the good fight,'" said the old man.
"'I have finished my course. I have kept the faith.
Henceforth'—."

She wrung her hands in her impatience. "Yes,
father! Oh, yes! it is woll with *you*. *Your* reward
is sure; but have you no word of comfort for *me?*
Say, father, shall I see him again? Shall we spend
our immortal life together? In all these years of

sorrow have I made no atonement for my sin? Speak, father!"

The old man shook his head.

"Hush, Frances!" he said, with tremulous solemnity. "I may not draw the veil. Look to your Saviour, my daughter; He only can make atonement for your sin."